C000286098

ABOUT THE AUTHOR

Jennifer Manson is a writer and business woman. She lives in Christchurch, New Zealand, with her husband, two teenage children and two cats. She is the author of "The Moment of Change" and "Tasha Stuart interviews . . ." and also writes for The Press newspaper's "at home" supplement.

The Old Occidental Writers' Hotel

Jennifer Manson

ACKNOWLEDGEMENTS

To my writing buddy, poet Kerrin P. Sharpe;

To my readers: Dianne Whiteside, Lisa Mitchell, Vicki Slade, Stephanie Royds and Caryn Hardy;

To my daughter, Alex, my son, Jono, and my wonderful husband, Paul;

To my excellent accountant, Ann-Maree Ozanne at Sterling Accountants Ltd, New Zealand, for your generous support;

To the Coffee Smiths, corner Durham St and Chester St West, Christchurch, for being passionate about what you do;

To the Café de Paris in Hokitika, a fabulous taste of France in the Wild West;

And to Jay at Red Dot Design for your consistently beautiful cover designs;

Thank you.

All characters in this book are fictitious
and any resemblance to real persons,
living or dead, is purely coincidental.

The owners of

The Goldenall Hotel, Christchurch,

were not involved nor consulted

in the development of this book

1

I sat with my head in my hands, still not awake enough to make this decision. I hadn't slept properly in weeks. Derek waited patiently.

"Say that again?"

"We could wait for a better offer. We might get ten, fifteen thousand more if we found just the right buyer. But that might take a month, or two or three, and it might not happen. I'd hate to see us back at this point in three months' time, with all the extra expense. Or worse, with a lower offer, wishing we had taken this one now."

His words were sinking in. Still I wanted to cling to that elusive $15,000, the difference between breaking even and being able to hold my head up, or admitting I had worked for five months, gone through the huge process of buying a run-down house, putting my creative heart into this renovation, and selling it, just to give $15,000 away.

"We might get more if we wait?"

"And we might not. The Christchurch market's showing signs of recovery, but there's a long way to go yet. I think I can get another $500, maybe $1,000. But that's it for this buyer. There is no more money." He paused, waiting for an answer. I had none. "It could all be tied up tonight, done."

I knew that there was no logic in looking for a price that would satisfy my ego if it just wasn't there in the market, but there was a heavy pebble sitting in the middle of my chest. Another failure. My arms dragged at my sides.

"Okay. I guess it's time to move on. Add a thousand dollars and send it back to them. And tell their agent there were tears in my eyes."

Derek looked at me, a mixture of pity and carefully veiled exasperation. "It's a good price."

I nodded, swallowing taking conscious effort. He passed the contract back to me and I initialled the changes.

"We'll need to get Theo to sign as well."

"Really? We didn't before. This is my project."

"His name is on the title, and if they accept the contract this is the last time we'll have it in our hands. He needs to sign it now."

I pulled myself upstairs to the office where Theo was keeping well out of the way. "I'm going to accept the offer, or as near as. Derek needs you to sign it."

His unspoken question hung in the air.

"I didn't get what I'd hoped. Took a bit of a loss."

"How much?" His voice was quiet.

"$15,000."

His eyes went dull, but he stood up and followed me downstairs, taking the paper, asking where to sign with an unnatural stillness. He left the room without another word.

"I'll see the other agent. We should have an answer tonight. I'll text you."

"I know I'm being ungrateful. Thanks for all your work."

I hugged him at the door and went back to the sofa. I felt relief as I heard him backing down the drive, and the slightest beginning of the return of optimism. This was finished. I could start on something new.

The lift was short lived. I heard Theo moving upstairs, getting ready for bed. I climbed in next to him and Theo turned out the light without speaking. I didn't like the thoughts I found on my pillow and when Derek's text came two hours later I was still awake to read it.

I spoke it out loud. "They've accepted the contract. It's done."

Theo grunted a reply. So he was still awake, too.

2

I woke at 5:30 as usual next morning. The sky was pink. This is always my best time of the day, when I'm fresh and alive, alone with my journal spinning big plans, the first caffeine buzz making everything better and brighter.

It was time to start again, start on something new. I put aside thoughts of money and allowed my creativity to flow. I've never been successful doing things that bore me. My creativity needs to be engaged.

I looked at the blank page in front of me, so full of promise. "What do I want to do next?" And, as always, the answer was there: surprising, harebrained but unmistakable.

Renovate a hotel.

It was perfect. I could take the things I had learned from renovating the house and apply them to something that would make money in the long term. I have great vision for how a place could look, and a way with tradespeople that gets what I want done on time. I'd look for something classic, something with character, maybe something that was already a hotel but run down and shabby, ready for an injection of life. Great marketing, increased occupancy. I'd find a bargain and finally make something work.

I pushed aside the possibility of failure. This idea came straight from my heart. I knew it was the next thing I had to do.

Theo came down later than usual, ate breakfast at the dining table instead of in front of the computer reading the news. His wide shoulders were hunched forwards and the greying hair I used to call distinguished was longer now, grizzled. I took my second cup of coffee and sat down opposite him. I realised I was holding my breath.

"So the house is sold."

"Yes, well, assuming the contract confirms, but there's no reason it shouldn't."

"Have you thought about what you'll do next?"

My gut told me to delay telling him, but honesty's a bit of a thing of mine. "I had the idea of renovating a hotel, getting it up and going, then sell it."

He cleared his throat and leaned back, his arm draped over the back of the chair. Like he was trying to get as far away from me as possible. "You still have the loan from the shop."

"Yes." I used to have a book shop. It didn't work out and I had to close it down. We had two bedrooms stacked to the ceiling with boxes.

"And how much is that now?"

"$150,000." Plus the $6,000 I had borrowed from the family account and intended to pay back straight away but hadn't. I would. I didn't need to include that. I felt a pulse thudding around that heavy pebble; it was bigger than before.

"And now another $15,000 from the house."

"Okay, $165,000."

"And you want to buy a hotel to renovate."

"Not buy! Not buy, get investors. I'd get them to pay me."

The idea curled into a desiccated crisp under his dead stare. He pushed his chair back a few centimetres, placed his feet between the front legs ready to stand, but didn't. The words seemed to come against his volition.

"I can't do it any more, Lisa." He swallowed. "I can't. I can't keep going to work and bringing home my pay cheque and watch you throw it away. How many years is it since you contributed anything to the family?"

Anything? I'd been a mother, I'd kept the house neat, most of the time. I'd organised the bank accounts and bought his mother's birthday presents and loved him and the children unconditionally. But he meant money. And that meant not since I had those part time jobs the first few years the kids were at school. Before I decided I needed to follow my heart, create a business of my own; before I failed.

I looked down at the table. I had no answer.

"I can't do it any more. I love you, but I feel like I'm swimming with weights in my pockets and unless I get rid of them I'm going to drown."

"What do you mean?"

"I mean I have to survive. I can't be married to you any more."

"What if I got a job? What if I paid back the money?"

"How are you going to do that? For ten years we've been going backwards. Maxed out credit cards, final demands on the electricity, not being able to pay the mortgage, living the last six days of every month on baked beans and toast. No. It's too late. I'm too tired. I have to call a halt."

There were tears in his eyes. I put my hand out to him. He stood up and away from the table, out of my reach. "I've got to go now, I'm going to be late. We'll talk again tonight."

I moved around the house mindlessly putting things in their place: loading the dishwasher, wiping down the bench, taking a pile of unopened mail up to my office. There was a terrible ring of justice in Theo's words. Each time I'd borrowed more money I'd known I was betraying my family, and one day they would find me out, a drain, a parasite. Theo was such a good, solid man, so reliable, so understanding. I had pushed him past his limit and known it was happening and denied it to myself. I had nothing to fight back with.

I avoided Brian and Rachel as they left for school and work, leaving Brian's lunch on his school backpack, happening to be in the shower as Rachel left for her gap year job. I sat in one position on the sofa, staring from point to point in the Napoleonic blue and gold room, shifting my view when I couldn't stand myself any more, flinching when the phone rang, when Brian slammed the front door on his way in after school and then again on his way out, when Theo's car pulled in the driveway after work. Another hour later he found me still sitting in the TV room. He stood awkwardly in the doorway.

I raised my eyes from the floor. "Do you want me to leave?"

His hand lifted from his side towards me then fell again. His eyes were black, pupils terrified and huge. "I don't want it. I don't know what else to do."

There was a dead inertia in my body, no will, nothing. "I'll sleep in the guest room. Leave in the morning."

"The kids."

"I'll tell them." My face compressed. I waited 'till the muscles let me go again. I wanted to beg, to plead, but there was such a sense of rightness about the situation; I deserved this. At some level I must have even wanted it to let things get to this point. I nodded, my eyes squeezed tight, and waved Theo to go before I gave way to my tears.

"There's one more thing. I want to separate the bank accounts, take your name off the joint account, the credit cards. We can put some money into an account in your name, to get you started, but after that . . . you're on your own."

I nodded, numb.

"Lisa . . . I hate to see you just take this. I expected you to fight back, to argue."

My mouth opened and I cried like I was laughing, my flat hand touching my lips. Theo took a step towards me but I shook my head. "I know it's my fault. Please just go."

There was so much inside me and so small an outlet for it, my grief crammed up against the dam of my heart, jerking out little by little, choking me, constricting me. It felt bottomless, like it would never end.

I heard Theo's car go again and cried louder. I heard Rachel come in, call for me. I tried to take a deep breath, belched horribly and tried again. My hands wiped my tear-wet face, I stood up, choked my breath again and coughed. She heard me and appeared in the doorway. "Mum? Mum, what's wrong?"

This was the hardest thing, admitting my failure to my daughter. I had thought I was a great role model, strong and independent, following my heart. Hubris.

She swished her long dark hair back over her shoulder. She was wearing too much makeup. "There must be something you can do. You can't split just over money, it's so wrong!"

So wise and so naïve. "Honey, I'm lost at the moment. I don't know which way is up. I've told Theo I'm leaving in the morning. I'll go. Get some perspective. I . . . I'm sorry."

I sat, still and small. She hesitated, came over and hugged me. "I'm not supposed to be the mother." It was an old line of hers, we used to laugh at it. It wasn't funny now.

3

Brian just nodded. Upset but fatalistic. "Who's going, you or Dad?"

"I'll leave, but I'm not leaving you."

He looked up, confused, concerned. "I have to go with you?"

"No, I mean, you can call me whenever you want. Once I've got a place there'll be room for you, whenever you want. I hardly see you anyway, the way you live at Jason's." This attempt at a joke fell flat.

I always prided myself that my children came from a two parent family, so rare in their circle of friends. More hubris.

There was a pause and then he loped around the table to hug me. He was straight out of the shower, smelling strongly of Lynx deodorant. The white school shirt slid under my hands as I clung to him. "You'll be okay, Mum." With a huge effort I let go before he did, images of his childhood flickering past as I did so. I used to be his world.

Brian left for school and the house was empty. I hadn't thought yet where I'd go. I'd do that once I was out. One thing at a time. Focus on the next thing to do. Do it. Then plan the next step. I found my overnight bag, so hopefully packed for a spur of the moment weekend away. I threw in more knickers, a few more t-shirts, my best black trousers, job interviews vaguely in mind. My travel toilet bag was packed, spare toothbrush, cleanser, moisturiser; my makeup lives in my car.

What else? I found a plastic bag and put in my trainers, exercise clothes – you never knew – and a pair of black heels, for interviews again. Downstairs I checked my handbag. Wallet, journal, phone, charger, iPod. Should I take my laptop? Oh, my, what about email? I had no clue how to connect to the Internet away from home. Well, I guessed I'd work it out. I dragged myself back upstairs, found the bag it came with, hardly ever used, packed the laptop, power cord. Done. Time to go.

I stood in the doorway, car keys in my hand. My cat, Fenella, stood by the stairs watching me. I crouched down and held out my hand, taking a few slow minutes to stroke her black fur after she threw herself long onto the carpet. How would I live without her aloof acceptance, the warmth and privilege of her company? I watched longingly as she stood up and walked back down the hall.

I turned to the door again. Should I leave the house key? Probably. But I would also probably need to come back for things I had forgotten, and it would be easier if I still had a key. I was beyond decisions anyway, it was all I could do to pull the door behind me and walk to my car. Something was nagging at me. There was something else I had to do before I left. One more gesture of love for Theo.

I felt the stone fall into my chest again as I realised what it was. I opened my wallet, took out my credit card, got out of the car and let myself back into the house. I cut the card in two with the kitchen scissors and left the pieces on the chopping board. I put my fingers to my lips and back to the severed plastic. "Love you, Theo."

I drove away without knowing where I was going. Pretty soon I had to pull over, tears obscuring my vision. I checked through my list of friends, came up with none I wanted to see right now. I wanted to wallow and I feared either superiority or impatience. Unless . . . maybe Stella. Stella would understand, know what I needed. I cried harder as I thought of her, the first spark of hope and direction.

"Hey, Babe, it's Lisa. Are you free for coffee, for lunch?"

I pulled up outside the Arts Centre an hour early, remembering too late that I was down to my last $35. Who knew how long that would have to last.

"The first thing is, I need a job." I said, brushing through her disbelief. "I need to live."

"You need to grieve. Give yourself time."

"No, that's what I don't need. I want to get busy. And I have no money at all."

"You can go to Work and Income, get an emergency benefit."

"No. I won't do it. I got into this mess because I didn't take responsibility for myself."

When it came to it, I couldn't ask her if I could stay with her. We were already walking in opposite directions after our goodbye hug, self-pitying tears streaming, when she called after me "Wait! Where are you staying?"

I turned to face her. "Hey!" she said, catching up to me and wrapping her strong arms around me. "Come here. I'll take you home."

I put my bags down in her beautiful guest room, Liberty print duvet cover, fresh flowers on the dresser and a view out over the high school grounds where teenagers were streaming back towards their classrooms after the bell. It made me think of Brian, getting through his day with my news in the back of his mind. I escaped downstairs to the living room but the quiet, the space was too much. I needed something do.

The bank. There was a Westpac down at Merivale. Keep moving.

"I'd like to open an account, please, a personal account. I already have a joint account here, and I'd like my name taken off that."

It took a little persuading, but they did it and agreed to send a letter to Theo telling him it was done.

"Would you like to transfer anything to your new account?"

"No, just leave it as it is."

"Well, then we'll need a deposit to open this one."

I sighed, taking out my wallet. "How much? This is all I have."

"$1 will be fine." The teller's curiosity had been replaced by sympathy. She fetched me change from the $5 I handed her, gave me a new Eftpos card and took my old one from me.

"Is there anything else I can do to help?"

"Yes. One last thing. Can you check the monthly payments on one of our joint mortgages? There are three different loans, it's the one for $150,000 – something around that amount."

She clacked away for a minute then turned the screen towards me. "$927.45, due on the 27th." That was only four days away. No chance of me making that payment this month. I sighed. Something to aim for next month. I took a piece of paper and wrote down the amount. I'd think about the extra debt from the house later, once the sale went through and we knew exactly how much it was.

"Thanks. That's all. You've been great."

She handed me her business card. "Any time. You can ask for me by name."

I wandered back along the road to where I was parked. I love my car, a classic British Racing Green Mazda MX5, wooden steering wheel, leather seats, sound system with speakers in the headrests so you can blast the music without bugging other motorists, even with the top down. I ran my hand over the soft top. Better get a job soon or she'll have to go.

I looked into Café Couture, habit drawing me in for a coffee. No. I started the engine, pulled out into the traffic and immediately indicated in and parked ten spaces up the road. Something had caught my eye. What was it? I walked back, looking into the shops as I passed, and there it was, in the café window. "Staff wanted."

The slender twenty-something looked me up and down. "Got a C.V? I'll give it to the boss."

I looked over her shoulder instead of at her face, stung by her disinterest. "I'll bring one in."

I hadn't written a C.V. since before Rachel was born – it must be 20 years ago or more. The things I'd done since then: owning a business, renovating the house, seemed wrong when it was just a waitress job I wanted. Anyway, what did my experience amount to?

I messed around for ages, becoming more and more depressed. In the end I wrote a one page letter. "Full-time mother returning to work. Used to running a busy household. Hard working. Able to work flexible hours." It felt like begging. I just hoped it would do the trick.

Minimum wage is a shock after years of self-delusion. The first month I was on trainee rate of $10 per hour. I looked it up on the tax website. If I worked all the hours they could give me, 30 hours the first week, I would receive $254.79 after tax. It wasn't much but it gave me the confidence to call Theo.

I had woken that morning from dreams of lying in his arms to the nightmare of my lonely bed. I swore I heard his phone alarm go off, and opened my eyes to find my arm stretched out to touch him. The pain was so bad I reached for my phone to call him, scrolled through to his number, then closed it again. He hadn't contacted me, even a text to find out where I was staying. Well, I had no pride left; I opened the phone again.

"Hi, it's me."

"Hi." He sounded worse than I felt. The pebble sunk lower. "Where are you?"

"Staying at Stella's."

"Where's that?"

"You know, St Andrews Square." Only five minutes from home. "How are you?"

"Fine." Not fine, but not telling me.

"I . . . I got a job."

"Oh yeah? That's great."

"Just a café, but better than nothing."

"No, sounds good."

"Theo, can I come home? I want to come home. I've cut up the credit card, taken my name off the joint account. I've got a job - it's not much but I'd be contributing rather than a drain. Please, I miss you so much."

There was a long empty silence. "No. I don't think so."

"But . . ?"

"It took me a long time to get to this point. It's not as simple as just money. I think . . . I think it's too late."

"But, Theo!" My body shook with tears. "I love you so much. I just want to come home."

"I'm sorry. Good bye."

4 a.m.

If I were at home, I would get up now, to feed my insistent cat, ready for breakfast anytime from three. More than anything, she represented home for me; whatever my mood, state or financial position, she was there. I missed the feel of her fur under my hand, the way she was such a familiar presence that I didn't notice when she arrived on my knee, or beside me on the bed. If I was feeling down, like now, she would follow me back from dish to bedroom and curl back up on the bed with me while I wallowed out my mood.

Pushing Theo out of my mind, Fenella settled there as a pain I could focus on and bear.

4

It was a subduing experience working with slim, beautiful, bored young women who shrieked and laughed with each other and spoke a grunting, monosyllabic language to me. But it was money. And it was distraction from the misery that lay in wait behind every activity, looking for a moment's pause. Payday came and there was a small satisfaction holding the cash in my hand. I gave Stella $100, put $100 into Theo's account and kept a glorious $50 to spend on me.

The second week I had 34 hours' work, the third week 38. Each payday the small confidence boost made me pick up the phone to call Theo, and each time I put it back down again. I needed to hear his voice so badly I couldn't stand it, and I had just enough self respect not to make the call.

I'd been back to the house a couple of times, to see Brian, with Theo's texted ok. I noticed little changes, things were neater. The throws I used to artfully drape across the squashy leather sofas were folded, laid evenly over one arm. Magazines were stacked, rectangular, rather than fanned out. The mantelpiece in the family room had been cleared of the clutter of dated birthday cards.

Waiting for Brian one afternoon I took a deep breath and walked into our bedroom. The differences were subtle and devastating. Theo was here and I was not. The ottoman which had always been piled with clothes was clear. My side of the wardrobe was empty, with his jackets and shirts just beginning to spread across the gap. And there were only two pillows, placed squarely in the middle of the bed. I looked around. Where were my clothes, my pillows? I found two suitcases and a plastic shopping bag in the office, ready for me to pick up and take with me. It would have killed me to try to do it. I'd rather live for ever in my weekend's worth of clothes.

I heard the door bang and ran down the stairs guiltily.

"Mum?"

"Here. Hi."

Brian hugged me, brief and awkward.

"Shall we get a drink?" I went to the kitchen and opened the fridge, then realised nothing here belonged to me any more. "Want some juice?"

"Sure. Yeah."

I poured his juice and ran the tap to get myself a glass of water. "How was school?"

"Oh, you know, fine." He looked around the room, took a sip while staring at a spider in its web in the corner of the ceiling.

"I missed you."

His eyes twitched nervously towards me. "Yeah. Me too."

"Are you okay?"

"Yeah." And then he grinned, and it was such a relief to see it. We both know this illusion that he needs me is far more for me than him. But it lets him take what he needs, too, under the radar. "Don't worry, Mum, I haven't taken to drugs or alcohol. No crying myself to sleep at night. You can relax about me."

I laughed, a small strangled out-breath, then nodded, mock serious. "Good. Very good."

He pushed his chair back. "I'm going to Jason's okay."

"Sure. Good to see you."

"Yeah."

"Wait! Just so you know, I'm working at the café on Papanui Road, near the bank. Come in and see me there sometime? And you have Stella's address, right?"

"I'll text if I can't remember."

"Ok. Bye. Love you."

"Love you, too."

Another split second hug.

I washed out my glass and dried it slowly, smiling at the thought of my son. He was just the same; most of our relationship for the last year or two had been by text anyway. I knew he had made a big effort to be here, at a specific time, and sit down with me. It takes so much energy to be a sixteen year old boy, there's not much bandwidth left for getting inside your mother's head. I love that about him. Actually I love everything about him.

Before I left I opened the back door and whistled for Fenella. I would have to give her something to eat to reward her responding, but maybe then she'd sit with me for a while, let me while away my worries in her soothing company. She appeared over the back fence, running for the cat flap then changing direction as she saw the open door and the opportunity for a shorter route. I waited while she gobbled down the few biscuits I had poured into her bowl then called to her from the living room. I'd rather she came on her own, but at this time of day she expected a larger meal, pacing from doorway to fridge and back again, mewing.

I picked her up, holding her away from my body as she twisted to get free. "Come here, sit with me."

She stood tall on my lap, half succumbing as I pushed her into a cushion shape, but then a car drove up the drive next door and she was alert again, up and off my knee and waiting at the door.

I needed to go anyway. I had half an hour before I was meeting Rachel for a drink when she finished work, but I didn't want to still be there when Theo got home. I crouched down and stroked Fenella a few more times. She lay on the floor, stretching her back into an impressive inverted arch, legs long. "Bye, Fen."

I so wanted to take her with me.

Rachel gets me too well, she saw straight through my carefully projected façade to the raw vulnerability. At least I've raised her to let me deal with my own stuff, she doesn't take any of it on personally.

"Mum, you know you keep telling me that everyone makes mistakes, and not to feel bad about it . . ."

"This wasn't a normal level mistake. I have ruined my whole life."

"The same principle applies. And don't be melodramatic. You're alive. You're healthy."

"I so miss Dad."

Her expression softened for the first time. "I know, Mum. He misses you, too."

"Then why won't he let me come home?"

She turned to look out the window.

"Forget I said that. I'm so sorry about everything." I tilted my head one way then the other. "Mostly I'm sorry for myself."

"It's okay, you're getting it together."

"Yeah, I guess I am."

5

Simple though it was, work kept me grounded. It became the best part of my life. As I got more confident the boss started giving me the early and late shifts the other girls didn't want. The barista was training me to make coffee and I was working longer hours, happy to be busy and making more money.

The first week of my second month I worked 50 hours at my new rate of $12.50 and took home $506.01. That felt great until I realised that even working 50 hours a week, nearly half the money would go just covering that $927 loan payment. I set up an automatic transfer of $225 per week to Theo, gave Stella her regular $100 and sat down to think what I could do.

I couldn't stay with Stella forever. I had meant it only to be a week or two. As long as I worked at minimum wage, however, I was never going to be able to meet my commitments and afford a place of my own.

"What are you doing?" Stella came out yawning at 11 a.m., her warm, kind face blurry with sleep, her short dark hair uncharacteristically rumpled. It was Sunday and I was working a split shift, I'd been up at 6 to open the café and would go back at 2 to work until closing.

"Trying to work out how I can live. This minimum wage thing takes a bit of figuring out."

Stella pulled her soft pink dressing gown around her, retying the belt and smoothing out the fabric. She reached for the coffee pot and refilled my mug before pouring her own.

"You know what I thought about that from the start."

"Yeah, but what else is there? I like the job, it's just that once I've paid my loan, there's not enough left to live on."

"What loan?"

I took a deep breath and explained. It felt awful, but it was oddly freeing, too. I've always hidden my failures from my friends and it's exhausting.

"But Theo's got the house, right?" She pulled one foot up under her and leaned forward, elbows on the table.

"Yeah, so? This is a business loan, just guaranteed against the house."

"But what about the equity in the house? It wasn't 100% mortgaged?"

"No."

"So some of that money's yours. Have you talked to a lawyer?"

"I don't want to. I know what's fair."

She leaned further forwards, her eyes intense. "I don't think you do. You're entitled to your share of the equity in the house. Even if you take the loan off it there must be something left."

"No. Theo's supporting the kids. I'm not going after any more of his money."

"Well, have you at least talked to Theo?"

I looked away. "No." My voice was small. The longer it went on the harder it was to call him again. I was afraid I'd just end up begging and rejected once more. I still missed him so badly, found myself reaching across the bed when I woke every morning, my pillow wet, with fresh tears following. "I can't. I'm still so ashamed."

Stella reached over the table and put her hand on mine. "How long is it since you've seen the kids?"

"Brian came into the café on Wednesday. I see him every few days. He knows I'm getting on my feet as fast as I can."

"And Rachel?"

This was harder. "She's busy."

Stella raised an eyebrow.

"I feel like such a failure when I see her. And I can see it in her face, too."

Stella's eyes softened, corners flexing sadly. "You're so hard on yourself."

"About time, don't you think?"

"No, I don't."

"It was a rhetorical question."

Stella's words rang in my head as I worked that afternoon. It was so familiar now it was easy, the rhythm of serving and making coffee and wiping down tables.

Actually I did know that legally I was entitled to a share in the house, that I could ask Theo to buy me out, and even if I took sole responsibility for the $170,000 that represented my business losses there was probably another $160,000 there that was mine. But I didn't want it. I wanted Brian and Rachel to keep their stable home. I wanted to earn back Theo's respect and with it my own. Of course I still hoped he would let me come home once I had proved myself. Of course that was there behind everything. But I pretended it wasn't. It hurt too much to think that there might be more to his rejection of me than he had said. I felt like a teenager trying to prove I was a grownup.

So with all that, I needed to earn more money to get a place of my own. I focused my conscious attention on this dilemma, and tried to suppress the other desire, raising itself again: the idea of the hotel, lurking in the background, still enticing, still exciting, developing like an untended weed.

"I think I should look for a job where I can live in."

"You know you can stay here as long as you like."

"You're so kind. But it was always a temporary arrangement."

"So what kind of job? Matron in a school boarding house, something like that?"

"I was thinking of something in hospitality. Maybe a Bed and Breakfast, or a hotel." I was looking through the job pages in the newspaper. I'd tried the Internet but found I was wading through jobs in other cities and countries. There was nothing here. "Maybe I'll go around and ask. That way I can get a feel for the places as I go."

"So you'll need a new C.V."

I sighed. "Guess so." At least this time I had the café job to put on it.

"And some referees. You can put me down."

"I've never worked for you."

"Yes you have. You did that cleaning the first week before you had the rent to pay."

"Those were the days, huh?"

"Seriously, I've got used to you. It's fine if you want to stay."

But the truth was, I was getting restless. I wanted somewhere I had earned.

It was humbling going door-to-door around the bed and breakfasts in town. I discovered straight away that the hotels didn't offer accommodation and without qualifications I'd still be on minimum pay. I was better off at the café where at least I could walk to work.

Some of the bed and breakfasts did offer a room for the manager, who was generally on call at night, but most of the people I met treated me with suspicion, it took all I had to keep going. I promised myself I'd get rid of 10 C.V.s before I stopped for the day.

"No, I don't think so. It's a quiet time of year, I can handle it by myself at the moment."

The woman was kindly-looking compared with the dragon I had met at the guest house next door. She hesitated as I put my hand out to hold the door open. "Please, won't you take a copy? You never know. Even if you wanted a holiday, I could fill in. Or you might know someone who could use me." This was my last copy, I could already taste the coffee I had promised myself at Coffee Smiths once it was gone. I shoved it into her hand. She looked at me sympathetically and didn't hand it back.

"All right. I'll keep you in mind. You do seem very keen."

"I'm hard working. My marriage . . ." What was I thinking? Was I so desperate for sympathy or did I think it would get me a job? "Well, I'm looking for a new start."

She tilted her head back and gave a few quick nods. "I understand, Dear. I'll put it on the notice board and keep my ear to the ground. I'll call you if I hear of anything."

6

"Mum, I got it, I'm going to Oxford!" Several customers looked around as Rachel came flying across the café waving a pale blue letter, her best friend, Liberty, following behind. It's a long time since I've seen anything break through her controlled veneer; her eyes were bright and her face red. "I really got it."

I came out from behind the counter and she shook the letter in my face and hugged me. I ran my hand over her smooth brown hair. Liberty grinned at me over Rachel's shoulder. "That's great news! Well done!" I pulled her to a table in the window and looked into her shining face. England. So far away.

"I go in August. It's all here, fees and airfares and accommodation, dinner with the High Commissioner." She closed her eyes. She had applied for this scholarship in November but still insisted that her gap year was just a break before starting University locally. "I'm not expecting anything, I just want a year out, to live a little and save some money."

"You'll all have to come and see me! I'll figure out all the places to go, show you everything. You and Dad and Brian. Liberty's coming. She's already got some of her ticket saved." She stood up. "I can't sit still, I have to do something. I'll go home, see if Dad's home from work."

So she had told me first. That was something. "Bye, Liberty, nice to see you." She waved from the door. Rachel spun on the pavement outside and waved the letter at me again through the window. I waited until they were round the corner before letting my tears flow; 30 seconds, then I wiped them again. I returned to the counter more determined than ever to get my life together.

"It's not a competition. This is a sign that you raised her well." Stella's voice was strained thin with exasperation. "Be happy for her."

"Of course I am. Of course I'm happy. It's just the stark contrast. She's eighteen and she's set. She knows what she's doing for the next three years, and after that, look at all the opportunities. And look at me: homeless, broke, barely employed – oh, hell! I know I'm being self-centred. I can't help it!"

I printed out another ten C.V.s to take around the next day. I was running out of inner city options and once I got outside the Four Avenues the quality decreased. I couldn't see myself living in some of these places. Still I asked. The pressure was building.

I walked slowly back to my car after delivering the tenth, with none of the elation I had felt on Tuesday. After Rachel's news this idea suddenly didn't seem enough any more. What was it, after all, except survival? I sat in the driver's seat, had barely enough energy to put the key in the ignition. I had half an hour before I was due back at work.

My head fell back against the headrest and as I closed my eyes tears spilled over, running back towards my ears. I turned my head and looked across Latimer Square, autumn leaves thinning, a wide expanse of green which gave the city room to breathe. There were still some imagination-capturing old buildings here, although the East side of the square was dominated by a bland 1970s hotel. Ahead and to the right, just around the corner in Hereford St, was the old Occidental Hotel. I remembered it from my student days, when it was a less than elegant drinking place. It was worse now with graffiti and boarded up windows, but the cast iron detailing and upstairs verandas retained a sense of grandeur. Now that would be a place to live. For a moment I slipped into delusive fantasy, dreams of renovation and self-importance.

The engine was started and I had pulled out before I knew it. Look where this kind of thinking had got me in the past.

"You must have looked through that five times already."

"There's something here, I know it." Yesterday's job page was open on the dining table again. It gave me a slight sense of control. "There has to be."

Stella was idly flicking through the property section. "Here, what about this. You know I don't want you to go, but you seem determined."

She pushed the page across to me, her finger on a small advertisement. "House sitters required."

Stella stood at the end of the driveway, arms folded across her nightgown, as I put my small suitcase in the boot of my car. "It's only a month, you never know, I might be back." I came around the car again to hug her goodbye. "Have I told you how grateful I am for your taking me in?"

"Only every day. Take care. Tell me when I can bring a bottle over to christen the new place."

I kept the key in my pocket all day, the promise of a temporary place of my own. My work shift was over at four; at ten past I stood outside the beautiful Merivale villa, taking a breath before opening the door. There was a scuffle of paws and a white whiskered face greeted me. I had met Angus a few days earlier, his owners far more concerned about him than about the house. He sniffed me and wagged the back half of his body. "Hey, Darling, how are you?" He made a little noise and all four feet came off the ground at once, clacking on the wooden floor of the hallway as he landed. "Help me find my room?"

I found the little single guest room which I had said would be fine. It had blue floral wallpaper and a tall window looking onto the paling fence close outside. There were lead lights in the top pane. A cloth covered the bedside table and on it stood an ornate lamp, twisted pewter with topaz decoration and a scalloped gold shade. Fresh sheets were folded on the end of the bed.

It felt odd being in a strangers' home, I was reluctant to disturb anything but I needed to get over it. I put my bag on a wooden upright chair in the corner and took four steps into the room to turn on the lamp. Angus pranced around while I stretched the fitted sheet over the mattress, shook the rich linen duvet cover onto the duvet. I smoothed my hand over the crisp pillow case. Maybe it was time I got my own pillows back, time I moved out properly.

Theo and I had met that week at the lawyer's office to sign the papers for the sale of my renovation project. He was awkward and polite; I just managed to keep myself together. Jackie was super-efficient, as ever, and everything went fine until the end, when she got to her usual 45 seconds of social chat. What tripped me was the look on Theo's face when she asked if we'd be doing another project.

"What's the old saying?" he responded, shortly. "Once bitten, twice shy. Well, it's just taken a few more times for us to get the lesson." My face felt like it was set in concrete, but at least I kept from crying until we were in the lift again. I had hoped to get out of the building, away from Theo before losing it.

"I guess we'd better get things moving, legally, too. You have Jackie, if you like. I'll find someone else."

I wanted to pretend to misunderstand him, but I knew I couldn't pull it off. "I don't think she does family law."

"Well, someone in her firm, then. Hey, are you okay?"

Here was the face I tried to banish from my waking thoughts, here were the arms I ached to feel around me. I had dressed for this meeting, been unable to help looking forward to it, and now there was nothing. I was ready to beg him to hug me, kiss my cheek goodbye, anything. The lift ground to a slow halt, there was an agonising pause, click, pause before it opened. My heels skidded on the polished floor; mercifully I recovered without fully falling, but my whole life was in that moment, out of control, inelegant, really nothing of me left in it at all.

Tomorrow I'd go home while Theo was at work and pick up those suitcases. Time for me to consider that my marriage might really be over.

I wandered aimlessly into the lounge of my temporary home. The furniture was soft, saggy, welcoming, with pieces of creamy painted wood interspersed between the sofa and chairs: dresser, coffee table, side table. A shelf was crowded with family photographs, the faces warm and loving, propelling me out into the kitchen. I fed Angus and watched his gourmand's ecstasy without response.

The owners had explained the complex system of remote controls but I couldn't get the television going. In the end, Angus and I curled up on the sofa and both went to sleep. At midnight I dragged myself up and through to the bedroom. Angus was supposed to sleep in his basket in the hallway but after a few seconds looking at each other we agreed he could sleep on the end of the bed. He vibrated with ecstasy as he turned round and round, making himself a spot, his fur blurred. I lay down and my body involuntarily curled into a tiny ball. Only the sound of Angus's snuffling breath reminded me that I was alive.

Stella's a good cook and she's got that "kitchen is the heart of the home" thing going; I'd eaten well with her when I could eat at all. Now, though, I had the compulsion to save as much money as possible. Angus and I walked down to the mall and I stocked up on tinned spaghetti and

Weetbix - that would keep me going for a week or so. At the last moment I threw in a pack of sausages - maybe Brian would come over for dinner.

I put off my trip home yet again and curled up on the sofa with my journal. Today was a rare day off and I felt like doing absolutely nothing. I'd managed to get the stereo working and cool jazz blew in the background. Angus caught my mood and climbed up on the sofa, too, sniffing around my pen; I scratched his head idly and when I returned to writing he moved away slightly, settling on the other cushion. I stretched out and stroked his ears. He tilted his head, then put it down on his paws, closing his eyes and sagging into sleep.

After my night of self-pity I was in optimistic bounce-back. I found myself doodling in my journal. I hadn't drawn anything for weeks and after a while the page was filled with flowers and seagulls and mountains. I turned the page and drew a desert island scene, with beach and palm tree, and me as a smiling mermaid underneath it. The next page: a house with picket fence and balcony, drawing orderly parallel lines in a hypnotic haze.

The next page was a grander building, the balcony this time with cast iron detailing. I drew weeds growing through the flagstones in front but left off the graffiti. This page needed a title. "The Old Occidental Writers' Hotel." That sounded right. I stared at the picture for a while, filling in a few details, adding a little shading. I drew a smiling face at the window, some café chairs out front, a waitress, some flags flying from the roof. My drawing hand felt warm, happy. I pulled my legs out from under me and put my feet on the floor. My shoes were nearby; I put the journal on the coffee table and kept my eyes on it as I tied my laces. Angus' head popped up. Seeing me standing his ears pulled upwards and he hopped down from the sofa, coming back with his lead in his mouth.

"Okay," I told him. I felt different. Significantly different. I looked down at my journal again and realised I had drawn my dream.

7

It was a long walk for Angus; we stood together in front of The Occidental, staring at the battered façade. I wasn't very familiar with this side of town, preferring to stay amongst the busier shops. There was an edgy feeling to the streets here, cafés and nightclubs and night-time noise. The wide cobbled front of the hotel seemed a little vulnerable. I wouldn't be completely comfortable behind these windows in the early hours of the morning. I put my foot on the low steps and ascended. Angus reluctantly left the intriguing smell of the utility box on the footpath and followed.

I turned, for a moment feeling the proximity of the street, but then the traffic sounds receded, becoming a reverberating echo, like I remembered from the glassed in courtyards of the Louvre. What if this were an atrium, visually open to the street but enclosed? The verandas would stay pristine, original, but instead of looking into the street they would look in to a double height glass room. It would be fabulous! I could see it: a café at one end, reception in the middle, comfortable chairs beyond.

My mind circled back to my drawing. What had I written? I took the book out of my bag. The Old Occidental Writers' Hotel. Wow! That was it. And then I could see it, shelves and shelves and shelves of books, the perfect mood and décor. The skin on my arms prickled and goose bumps raised, my pulse beat low in my belly. This was something I knew I had to do.

"Are you crazy? Isn't this precisely the reason your marriage is in the state it's in?"

"Yes. But, Stella, I have to believe in it. It feels so right."

"I thought you wanted to get back with Theo, sort things out. How are you going to do that if you go off on this tangent?"

"Maybe it isn't a tangent. Maybe this will be vindication of everything else."

"So is that why you want to do it? To prove something?"

"No. I want to do it because I want to do it. Because as soon as I get back in touch with myself, start to feel happy again, this is what is there."

"And Theo? Are you going to tell him?"

This was a more complicated question. I was paying my loan. I planned to continue doing that, however I could. Beyond that, was it really his business what else I did?

"I haven't seen him or talked to him, you know that."

"You're avoiding the question. You want to get back with him, right?"

I swallowed. I had almost lost hope. Until I got this idea back and could lose myself in it, my baseline state had been depression and despair. "I do, but there's no point in deluding myself."

"So you think you've tried everything possible to make that happen?"

"Well, I asked to talk to him. He didn't want to."

She raised a sceptical eyebrow.

"Okay! All right. I'll try again."

I had my key but I knocked on the door anyway. Brian answered. "Hi." He doesn't ask many questions, just pretty much accepts life as it presents itself. He turned around and walked back down the long narrow hall towards the kitchen. I hesitated, then followed. I could hear Theo whistling. I didn't want to startle him, and I didn't expect Brian to think to announce me. I took the other route through, turning off the hallway into the family room and approaching the breakfast bar. Theo did a double take, the first glance registering me as a normal part of the household, the second from the new layer of reality.

"Lisa."

"Hi." I'd let him speak next, throw me out if he wanted to, but maybe if I said nothing he'd let me stay.

Brian turned slowly from one of us to the other, finally noticing something unusual was going on. "How are you?" he asked, once it was clear Theo was not going to fill the silence.

I put my hand to my chest then let it drop again. He has such a good heart. "I'm fine. Great."

"You still staying at Stella's?"

"No, I sent you a text. I'm house sitting. 43a Winchester St. You should come by."

"Okay." He turned to Theo again, who had his back to us, sautéing potatoes. Brian held his hand out to him for a second then turned back to me. "Ah . . . did you come for your suitcases? They're in the guest room. Want me to put them in your car?"

"Yeah, thanks. The top's down, see if they will stand in the passenger seat."

He hovered. I handed him the keys, although he wouldn't need them; this got him moving and he headed out the door.

Theo glanced over his shoulder then back to the stove again. It occurred to me he had lost weight, his hair was back to its usual neat shape.

"You look well."

His hand smoothed across his stomach. "Thanks. Yeah."

"And . . . cheerful." That hurt.

"Well, you know. I'm sleeping better. I'm more relaxed."

"Because I'm gone?"

He turned at the sting in my voice. "Because of the money. Because I don't have to worry so much about it."

"Oh!" I put my hand to my mouth. "I didn't realise it was so . . ."

He turned away again. "Anyway, thanks for . . . sorting out your side of it."

You know how sometimes you see a couple where one person is just awful to the other, mean spirited, talking down to them even in public, and you think "How can they do that? That's terrible!" and it's so easy to feel superior, to think "I would never do that." Does it ever occur to you to wonder why the other person puts up with it, why they don't just say "enough, you can't treat me like this!" To wonder whether they have ever said anything about it, told their partner how they feel. Is it possible that the person who is at fault truly has no idea they are doing anything wrong? That their perspective is so skewed that they don't see it? Well, that person was me. That couple was us. I wasn't rude or unreasonable to Theo, but I had lived in a way that made him unhappy and I had had no idea. And he hadn't told me. Did that make me any less at fault?

I blew out a breath. Fault wasn't the issue, but there must be some way back, there must be.

"I'm so sorry. I really had no idea."

He shrugged.

"Can you forgive me?"

"Sure, you're forgiven." His voice was blank and he wasn't looking at me. The food smelled amazing, enticing. I realised how hungry I was, almost forgot what we were talking about.

"Brian, set the table, will you, dinner's nearly ready." Theo took two plates off the top shelf and put them to the side of the stove. I felt Brian return and hover behind me. I looked at the two plates and it was like a slap; I didn't live here any more. Theo glanced at me, uncertain for a moment, then defiant.

I slid off the barstool I was occupying and nodded. "Okay. Bye."

Brian began to follow me out but Theo called him. "Brian, table!"

As I passed the pristine guest room I saw the bag with my pillows, overlooked in Brian's literal translation of 'suitcases.' The plastic crackled as I hugged it to me on the way out the door.

8

I found myself back in Hereford St in front of the Occidental twice more that week. Why shouldn't I be able to do it? My vision was so clear. At least, why shouldn't I try? I let my imagination run and every detail unfolded in my mind. Every direction I looked I saw inspiring, specific visions: the worn, comfortable sofas, the walls covered with shelves, the desks and brass lamps and cardigan-clad clientele. Christchurch is not so much a destination town as somewhere tourists use as a base to fly in or out of, or to tour from. Most spend a night or two here then head off for the majestic South Island attractions: Queenstown, Milford, the National Parks. But writers are a different breed. We could make this a destination hotel, somewhere people come to actually do their writing. A week, a month, in an atmosphere of vibrant creativity. There could be soundproof rooms for people who need silence, space in the café and reception for people who need stimulation, to watch the world go by and energise them as they create. We could publicise it by holding functions: book launches, award dinners, entertain visiting publishers and publicists and writers when they were in town, offer meeting space, hot desks where they could do the work they needed to do.

The art would be themed, and the furniture and the décor. Every detail followed easily, logically. I just needed to inspire others with my vision. That should be easy, I'm very persuasive once I get going.

Let's see. Who would I need?

First, the owners of the building, either to sell it or to buy into the dream. Failing that we could use another building, but I put this contingency aside – this was where the dream was now.

Second, I needed money. I had nothing to put into it myself, financially. And if I was going to manage it, which was my assumption, I'd need a room and a salary at least equivalent to what I was earning now. It was modest, so a profit share on top of that would make sense.

I laughed. Profit! That would be a new thing. So third, I needed a business genius, someone who knew how to make the money work. Yes. That was something I could have faith in. I knew there were people out there whose businesses always made money.

Fourth, I needed someone who knew about running a hotel. A lot of it I could work out, but there was no point reinventing the wheel. And fifth, I needed someone who knew about marketing, Internet marking specifically.

I had finally got a mobile modem for my computer, so I could do some research myself to find out where the world's writers and wannabe writers hung out online.

I lay back on my bed, Angus leaning happily against me, and pictured the finished hotel again in my mind. I could hear the muted clatter of the café echoing off the glass of the atrium. In my imagination I stood behind the reception desk and greeted intelligent-looking guests with their stylish leather luggage, pulling their booking confirmations out of beaten moleskin notebooks.

Then I had another flash, of my failed bookshop being reincarnated in a corner of the atrium, a constantly cycling stream of second hand books finally reaching their destined owner as I whittled away at the static stock which had troubled my dreams for the past 18 months.

I sat bolt upright. Theo had asked me to move the books out of the house. I had forgotten. For a moment my mood dived as I worried where I would put them, then soared again as I saw this as more evidence to show him how I was turning my life around. Who cared where I stored them, as long as Theo saw them go? Maybe that would be enough to get me invited to stay for dinner.

I needed to get my plans down on paper, to tell someone about them, to give them life. Stella wasn't impressed or interested. I had other friends, but no-one who felt right to talk this out with. That night, after closing the café, I spread my papers on the dining table. I made notes, sketches, and an impulse phone call to a friend whose husband knows about property.

"How would I find out who owns a particular building? Does Peter know?"

"Hold on, I'll ask . . . what's the address?"

"Hereford St. I don't know the number."

"He says, get the number and he can find out."

I looked out the window. It was dark. "You stay here, Angus, I'll be back soon."

The building was lit at the front but I couldn't see any number on it. I got out of the car and walked up and down the street. 204 on one side, 212 on the other. So 206, 208 or 210.

It was too late to phone again that night. I sent Peter an email and went to bed.

Peter came back with information about the hotel owners the next day, the company name and the names of the directors, complete with phone number. Now I'd have to do something. I felt hopelessly naïve. I had no understanding of commercial real estate, no knowledge of the hotel business, one small experience in renovating a residential property: financially unsuccessful. I thought there should be grants available for historically significant buildings but no idea if there actually were any. I was woefully unprepared. Perhaps I should go to the council, talk to our architect friend, Roger, talk to Peter about how the numbers work, but all these thoughts left me uninspired. My instinct said to go straight to the owners, sound them out about their intentions, and start from there.

9

During the slow period late in the morning I slipped out of the café and back to the Winchester St house. This wasn't a call to make from a mobile phone on the street.

My heart was beating fast as I picked up the phone. I dialled and hung up without pushing the call button twice and my adrenaline level escalated. Okay. Just do it.

"Hi, I'm Lisa Haynes. I'd like to talk to someone about a building your company owns in Christchurch."

"That would be Mr Black. He's not available at the moment. Shall I get him to call you back?"

I looked at my watch. I needed to get back to the café. "When do you think I might get him."

"Actually he's out of town until Thursday. What was it regarding?"

I didn't know how much it was worth saying to a receptionist, but it would be practice for when I talked about it for real. "It's about a hotel, The Occidental. It's derelict at the moment. I have an idea for it."

"I can email him, ask him to call you. What's your number?"

"I'm tied up all afternoon . . . but if he calls my mobile, yes, I suppose that would be okay." If I could just make contact, I could arrange a time to talk.

I usually put my phone on silent while I worked but I was effectively managing the place now, I could take a call this one time.

I arrived back just as the lunch rush began and spent the next two hours slightly edgy, expecting the call any minute, psyched up to run out, find as quiet a spot as I could and be professional.

"I'm expecting a call I need to take," I told Helen and Janine, who really didn't care. "I might need to slip out again."

By three my edge was fading and when I locked up at five I was very tired and disappointed. Should I call again tomorrow, wait until Thursday? Actually I just wanted to give up.

I heated some of the leftovers I had brought home from the cafe and felt better after eating. There was a text from Brian, too, it always makes me feel good when he initiates communication. It would be great to see him. "Want to come over? Lots of pie." "maybe ill let you no."

A walk with Angus lifted my spirits, too, watching him snuffling enthusiastically at every vertical surface and dent in the pavement.

Brian arrived as I put the key in the door, and at the same time my phone rang. It was him! "Mr Black! Would you hold on one minute please?"

I gestured Brian towards the kitchen and put Angus's lead in his hand, retreating into my bedroom and closing the door. "Thank you for calling me back."

"Fine. Angela said you called about 208 Hereford St. I don't know if you know it's on the market. Were you interested in seeing through?"

"Thank you, yes I would be, but it's just the beginnings of a plan I have at the moment. Had you thought of developing the property rather than selling? I am in a position to oversee the project I have in mind, but would be looking for investment to make it work. If you are wanting to sell, then I would obviously need to find that investment elsewhere."

"What did you have in mind?"

"Well, it's a unique building. Of course, I don't know what sort of state it is in inside. My thought was a themed hotel. A writers' hotel. A destination hotel, where people would come to write."

"We have looked at the economics of a hotel already. We don't feel there's the demand in this part of town."

"I can see that would be true for a standard travellers' hotel. The charm of the building makes it perfect as a destination in itself. The particular theme reduces the cost of renovation. And the idea of people writing here would mean longer stays."

There was a pause. I held my breath. "All right. Let's discuss it. Can you come to Dunedin to meet with me and the other directors?"

I hung up and jumped half a metre off the bed with joy.

Brian caught my mood and we laughed as he wolfed down pie. I gave Angus some sausage roll and he danced around me, paws on my knees.

I told Brian about my idea, too excited to think about whether I wanted Theo to know or not. It occurred to me to ask Brian not to say anything, but I didn't want to put that burden on him, having to be careful with either Theo or me. I carried on through to the idea of being a live-in manager, and saw his face go blank. "Does that mean you aren't coming home?"

This is me. I can run many possible futures at the same time, vividly imagining one then another, and not reconciling them. I had forgotten this opportunity meant closing off my old life.

"Of course I want to come home. It's just, I don't know if that's going to be possible." In a second my alternative life was running: back in my home, with Theo in bed beside me. The thought made my chest ache. "I'd love to come home more than anything." Tears formed in my eyes.

Brian patted my hand. "That's good, Mum. That's good." It was a relief when he left.

The Dunedin meeting was set for the next Monday, my day off. Before then I needed to meet with the commercial real estate agent to take a look through the building, maybe draw up some sketches. At least put some ideas on paper. I knew I was short on numbers, but I could communicate the vision.

10

The building was depressing, faded and smelly with remnants of lurid, badly applied paint from its days as a backpackers' hostel. I looked at the layout of the rooms, figuring out how we could incorporate en-suite bathrooms, essential for the price range I was looking at. As always, though, at the same time as I took in the reality of how it was now, I also saw and felt how it would be. Just as I had experienced the completed atrium, I saw the bedrooms finished: stylishly made beds, antique desks, black and white photographs on tastefully neutral walls. It was going to be beautiful.

Stella loaned me a dress for the meeting, relenting and catching my spirit as she saw how enthusiastic and nervous I was. I wanted to present a confident image with an element of the artist, partly to make up for the lack of practicality of my plan. I had a portfolio under my arm with A3 sketches I had made, filling every spare minute since seeing the building. Of necessity they were rapidly drawn, but actually more convincing for that: there was an impressionistic element to them that implied the details could be easily filled in later.

I left at 4.30 a.m. to get there in time for the 10 o'clock meeting. It is a long time since my student days when I drove this road frequently, visiting friends, unfolding the wings of my freedom. The drive was slower then, partly the road, partly my vintage mini which wouldn't make it all the way there if it was raining and dark at the same time. I still had friends there. Maybe I'd call them this afternoon if things went well. For now I was focused intently on the meeting. Many, many times as I drove I felt my head roll involuntarily, my brain wondering what the hell I thought I was doing and who the hell I thought I was. I knew nothing about running a hotel. And in response was the imperative to keep going.

The initial reaction of the group was the same as George Black's had been on the phone. They had looked at the numbers for a hotel, for a refurbishment, and it wasn't viable. The building needed so much done to it. It was falling apart.

"But the council have offered a rejuvenation grant . . ."

"We're well aware . . ."

"And this isn't just a standard hotel. Most hotels in the city have a night rate of between $100 and $300. As a standard hotel we'd be looking at somewhere in the middle of that range. And most people come through Christchurch for a night or two. As a destination hotel we'd be offering packages for a week or a month at a time."

"A month? Let's be realistic!"

"But I am. There's this thing, very big in the States, called NaNoWriMo . . ."

"What's that?"

"It's the National Novel Writers' Month. November every year. Tens of thousands of people register. It's for people who aspire to be writers to take the challenge of writing a novel, start to finish, in the month of November. We're talking about, what? 20 rooms. I am sure we can fill those rooms completely for the whole month of November just by tapping into the NaNoWriMo market."

"Maybe. But if you're only looking at writers, it's a small niche. And would they really come?"

"That's just it! Professional writers, maybe not. They've got their work methods sorted, their work space working for them. I'm not talking about writers who are already successful, I'm talking about aspiring writers. Very successful, wealthy people aspire to be writers. Doctors and lawyers, professionals. I'm talking about targeting those, for whom a holiday writing in a space that is set up with exactly the creative environment sounds like a dream. The November idea is only the start. The other great beauty about targeting a niche like this is how easy they are to find and market to on the Internet. And it is always easy to sell a dream."

I stood on the pavement outside the building, looking back up at the classic Deco façade, having been politely ushered out with a promise of a call back within a week. I had failed to infect them with my immediate passion and confidence, but they had kept my sketches and showed the occasional flash of insight at my ideas.

I closed my eyes. I was tired and suddenly overwhelmed with disappointment. I had pictured a wild success, instant enthusiasm, grateful thanks and a generous contract to be the life and heart of the concept. Of course, all along I knew that was unlikely, but I'd had to use every delusion I could think of to get myself here at all.

Caffeine. I need caffeine. My addiction levels had raised significantly working in an environment with coffee on tap. The weak filter concoction I'd been given in the meeting had not registered at all in my blood stream. On impulse I took out my phone, dialling directories and asking for the University number. "Frank Frampton, please . . . Frank, it's Lisa. Lisa Haynes. I'm in town, just finished a meeting, so I thought I'd call on the off-chance you were free."

"Of course. Where are you? What a delightful surprise!"

I gave him the address.

"Okay. So just walk up the hill, there's a tea shop, on the corner at the top. I'll be there in fifteen minutes."

I walked along the street, the foggy drizzle chiming with my mood. Just as he said, I found the cosy café, quaint with fogged up antique windows, a wooden framed bay contrasting with the wide flat sheets of glass in the shops on either side. I opened the door, the brass bell tinkling, and stepped back into another time.

I looked for a counter, but there were only carved wooden tables with menus and a door into the kitchen. The wildly swirling carpet was the startling feature of the room. A waitress in a lace apron waved. "Please, sit wherever you like." But the choices were limited. All but two tables were full. A subdued hum of conversation filled the background, quiet and indistinct, like the noise was being sucked out through some invisible vortex.

I took a seat in the bay window and looked out through the fog into the street. Grey umbrellas waded past, like a uniform for the town. I felt out of place and unprepared with my damp hair and clothes. I ordered coffee, relieved to see it come out of a state-of-the-art coffee machine. I was still inhaling the first gust of steam when the bell rang again and my friend walked in, shaking his umbrella and squeezing it into an umbrella stand at the door. He flapped his arms then pulled off a black woollen coat and hung it on the rack above.

Frank's an old friend I had met at university while I was doing my impractical English Literature degree, a flatmate who had become an academic, a scientist, ending up here, where I knew he loved his bachelor's life.

I noticed his hair was still jet black as I half-stood to wave him over. He surveyed the room, then caught my eye. His face lit up. He was just as I remembered.

"Great choice of table. It's the best view in the place." He winked, and I wondered if the ambiguity of his statement was intentional. I waved towards the window, and he echoed my gesture with a wave towards me. A wide smile swelled out of me, from deep inside.

He leaned over to kiss me on the cheek. "I'm so pleased to see you. It's been a very long time."

You know how some people can draw you out of yourself, how a little rapt attention can make you say things you would never have thought to tell to an uninterested audience? Frank is a master of fascination. I felt exciting, interesting, intelligent. Within five minutes I had told him why I was here, the dreams I had for this project. He caught the idea instantly, said there was genius in it, was sure it would work brilliantly. An hour later he said he had to go, implying deep reluctance. Asked for my phone number. Put it in his breast pocket. He stood up. "I foresee success for you, with this. It will be just as you imagined it." His words had a ring of prophesy. I felt my shoulders pull back in response. He smiled, and then he was gone.

I sighed into my cup, tasting the long-cold coffee and putting it down again. I looked at my watch. 2 o'clock. I still had time to catch up with my other friend Karen before she picked up the kids from school, but somehow my hour with Frank had left me dreamy, content. I wanted to hold the mood, so I drifted back to my car and headed North again, letting my mind wander along the current of his encouragement.

I like the road home better than the road South, the concentration of the hills and valleys coming early, with that burst out onto the coast marking the beginning of the ease of the rest of the journey. It can be frustrating to follow the straight and densely occupied Highway 1 after Timaru but today I was in no hurry, driving at 90, easing past the slower vehicles on the regular passing lanes, relaxed and comfortable in my skin. It would work out, I was sure of it. I planned my next blog entry as I drove, debating how much I could say yet in this public arena. I'd be artfully vague. I smiled at the expression. One of Frank's.

I began dreaming in finer and finer detail. I needed an architect. The only one I knew was a friend of Theo's, and that thought threw me into confusion, remembering dinner parties, old times. Well, I'd talk to him, or someone else, soon. It would all work out fine.

I woke early next morning, deciding to pack my bags before work. The owners of this house would be back the next day; this time tomorrow I would have to say good bye to Angus and leave.

Jill at the House Sitters had me a place to move into, not as nice, not as near the café, and only for a week. I felt a trace of apprehension, nothing I could put my finger on, just a shadow of tension in my chest. I've never been great with change. And I had come to love Angus.

I got home after work and threw my keys on the hall stand, greeting Angus and carrying him, wriggling, through to the kitchen. I had cleaned the kitchen and bathroom on Sunday after work, so I didn't want to make a mess. I was just trying to decide about what to do about dinner when my mobile rang.

"Hi. It's me, Theo. I need to talk to you. Can you come over?"

11

I pulled my coat on trying not to project what he might want. Please, please, please, let him be asking me back. But I hadn't heard that in his voice. He had sounded business-like. A little nervous. Bordering on cold.

The front door was open, swinging wide despite the chill in the air. I called through the hallway but got no answer. Closing the door behind me I crept through the house, opening the living room door to find it brightly lit and warm. Theo was loading the firebox. He looked up as I entered.

"Hey." He kissed my cheek and motioned me to one of the leather tub chairs which sat tête-a-tête near the fire. "Thanks for coming. Want a glass of wine?"

I nodded, hope welling inside me. This all looked pre-planned.

I listened as he moved around the kitchen, hearing the small familiar sounds, the fridge opening, the screw cap of the bottle being unwound, the glug of the liquid and the scrape of the bottle as it went back in the fridge door then the door squidging closed again. Theo's usually more of a red wine man. I chose to think the white wine was calculated to please me.

"How is everything? Work still okay?"

"Thanks, yeah, I got a raise, now I'm pretty much managing the place. It's still only $15 per hour, but it makes a difference . . . I'll put more into your account this week."

Theo shook his head, as if to say it wasn't necessary. "I appreciate what you're doing already. By rights we should sell the house, so you can have your share."

"We can't. We promised Brian, remember?"

"When was that?"

"When we moved in here. You remember: he was so devastated about leaving the old place, we promised we wouldn't move again until he moved out." I smiled at the memory, then my mouth turned back down. I'd expected to be here, too, 'till that happened. "Anyway, maybe in a couple of years, when he doesn't need the stability any more. I'm happy to wait until then."

Theo opened his mouth to speak then hesitated.

"What is it? You look like you've got something to say. What did you want to talk about?" I flashed him a hopeful, fake smile.

"Well, it's about the house."

"The house?"

"Yeah. Since you've been gone I've been dusting off some dreams of my own."

"Well, that's great. What are they?"

"I'm thinking of starting a restaurant." His eyes shifted around the room. I sat with my mouth open and finally he looked directly at me. "Well, say something."

"It's just such a surprise."

"Yeah. I know. It's been in the back of my mind for a long time, but it never seemed the right time to take a risk."

I bit my lip. My fault. "So, what has that got to do with the house? Do you want to take a bigger mortgage to finance it?"

"Yes, partly that. I . . . I want to do it here. At home. I think it would be perfect. What do you think?"

"Um . . . I don't know Theo. I have no idea. It's really up to you. . . . How would it work?"

"This living room for tables. You know we had the idea of turning this end of it into a library – well I'm still thinking about that. The TV room would become a lounge area for pre-dinner drinks. I'd extend the kitchen out into the hall. We just need another oven and hob and a few adjustments to make it work as a commercial kitchen. Roger's drawing up plans. Then it's just the parking, we'd have to pave over the front lawn, take out the wall, I'd put another wall up to make the back garden private – we hardly use the front as it is."

He got out of his chair and went to the corner window to point, turning back towards me and holding out his arm for me to come and see. We walked through the spaces and as he talked it all appeared before me. "Once Rachel moves out, Brian and I would move into the back part of the house. I'd thought about doing a couple of guest rooms, too, the en-suite and the upstairs suite we . . . talked about." He looked spooked as my face crumpled and I turned away.

I had dreamed about that suite since we moved in, opening out the warren of rooms upstairs and making a luxurious bathroom of the smaller bedroom, opening out the office and hall, bathroom, toilet and store

63

cupboard into a beautiful living space with balconies facing east and north. We'd even had plans drawn up, but never had the money to do it. My fault. All my fault. I so wanted to come home and do this with him. Tears flowed down my face and my shoulders shook. I felt Theo's tentative hands on the tops of my arms.

"What do you think? I need you to agree. It's still your house too."

I turned in his grip and threw my head on his chest.

"Lisa?"

My fists gripped the fabric of his polo shirt, a primeval reminder of the muslin security cloth I had when I was a little girl.

"Lisa, come on." He tried to pull me away but I pushed harder against his chest, desperate for him to wrap his arms around me.

"Please hold me. Just for a minute. Please?"

His arms moved around me, one hand awkwardly patting my back. It wasn't what I needed. He wasn't there. I pulled away, striding across the room to stand with my back towards him. I bit back begging words. A minute later I had recovered myself.

"Sure," I whispered, then cleared my throat and spoke louder. "I'm really happy for you to do it. I wish I'd known before . . ." I turned to face him. "Do you need anything now?"

"Not yet. We need the plans drawn before we can apply for resource consent. I'll call you when I need your signature."

I nodded, picking up my bag, staring into the fire for a few long seconds. There was so much I wanted to ask him, about how I could have been different, what he wanted now that he thought I couldn't provide. It felt so unfair, that I had fixed all the things he had told me were a problem and he still didn't want me back. Every way I thought to phrase the questions sounded like whining.

"Okay," I said, finally, when the silence got too awkward. "I'll hear from you then."

THE OLD OCCIDENTAL WRITERS' HOTEL

12

If Theo was going to have his dream, I was going to have mine. As soon as I got home I called Stella, got her answer phone and left a message saying I was doing the hotel, come hell or high water. So what if these guys might say no? This wasn't the only building in the city. There might be something that was way better. What did I really need, after all? I wanted a 20 room hotel with a café and public writing spaces. I wanted décor that would easily translate to the book theme. I wanted something with character, but I could add that if necessary. I wanted something that could photograph well, make an inspiring website. Well, I could add whatever was needed for that, as well, I was sure. Give me anything, give me an empty warehouse and I could make something fantastic.

I needed investment? Well, I could get it. Either from someone who knew what they were doing or if I had to, from lots of different people who could see my vision when I described it and were willing to invest a little bit each.

I sat back to contemplate my mood. It was a new one and an old one for me. Anger. Jealousy. Well, why not? I could harness these, translate them into energy and action. There was frustration that there was no immediate action to be taken. The next step would come from the guys in

Dunedin, who would either say yes or no, prompting an appropriate next action from me. Well, in the meantime I could plan some contingencies. Of course, a yes would be great, the next step the renovation. If they said no, I would set two things in train. 1. Look for investors to buy the building. 2. Find other suitable locations.

Damn, I was so wired. Whatever happened I wanted it to happen fast.

Angus was asleep at least an hour before me that night, my mind swirling round and round with ever changing visions, of the hotel, of my home, Theo's restaurant, strangers eating in front of my fire, sleeping in my bedroom. Somewhere in the wild dreams that followed there was another woman in my bed, too, lying next to Theo, naked and sexy and beautiful. My vision closed over with red. What did she have that I didn't? What was he looking for? What would I have to be for him to ask me home?

One of the girls was leaving the café, she had got a job somewhere more trendy on The Strip. Liberty was taking her place, starting tomorrow. It would be almost like having Rachel around again.

Liberty and Rachel have been friends since they were 9, staying close despite years at different schools and different circles of friends. They never fight, not once over ten years, as far as I know.

"I'm really going to miss Rachel."

"Yeah, me too." We sighed together.

"She won't miss us though."

I smiled, bitter-sweet. "You don't think so?"

"Rachel doesn't need anyone, she's fine totally on her own."

"That can't be true, can it?"

"Have you ever seen any sign that she needs anyone?"

I thought back. Over the years she has always seemed totally self-sufficient, spending lots of time alone, making her own choices, her own life. "Maybe you're right. Although . . ."

"What?"

"I remember, when she was three, maybe four, when I used to pick her up from pre-school. And other times, now that I think about it. She used to have tantrums, but never when I wasn't around. She needed me then. To feel safe letting herself go."

"When she was three."

"Yes, or four."

"And since then?"

"Oh, God, you're right! She'll be fine." But as I said it, it didn't quite ring true. I felt I might be missing something.

Brian came in after school, arms swinging, at a loose end. I put a piece of bacon and egg pie in front of him and he smiled wide as he began eating.

"Hey Brian!"

"Hi Liberty."

The girls always wound Brian up when they were together, like they needed someone to fight with, it reminded me of kittens, blowing off excess energy. He took it good naturedly, but even though it continued, over the last couple of years I had seen a different look on his face, a different response when he looked at his sister's friend.

She ruffled his hair and he dropped his head to hide the grin. "Got nothing better to do than hang around with your mum?"

"I'm meeting my friend later. Got half an hour before my bus."

Three customers came in and Liberty moved behind the counter. I'd asked her to serve as much as she could today, while I was there to answer any questions. The till had a couple of idiosyncrasies, but she was working it out. I made the coffees and she put the food on plates, heating a filled croissant and piping cream around a piece of carrot cake. I gestured with my head for her to take the food out. "Then come back for the coffees."

Another two pairs of customers later there was a lull. I watched her look over at Brian again, pulled towards him. "What are you reading?" She looked over his shoulder and he started guiltily.

"Something random. Just picked up the magazine on the top of the pile." He blushed and put it back on the rack. I saw it was the Cosmopolitan with Angelina Jolie on the cover.

Liberty pulled out a chair and sat next to him. The rule was we didn't sit down with customers, but I hadn't told her, so I let it go. I was curious anyway to see them interact without Rachel present. The time for Brian's bus came and went. I opened my mouth to remind him, then closed it. He could text his anonymous friend if it were a problem.

I'd never seen him so shy or so happy. Liberty was cranking up the charm, walking to and from the counter with an exaggerated sway. I had never seen her flirt before, so I didn't know if this was normal, if she was just bored, or if there was really something going on. They certainly had both forgotten about me.

Finally Brian looked at this watch and started, standing up quickly. "Gotta go. See ya."

"Bye," I called, and he turned back towards me.

"Oh, yeah. Bye."

"Come in again tomorrow if you like."

"Sure. . . . Ah, is Liberty working all weekend."

"Sure am! See you, Sweetheart."

He grinned again and tripped on the doorstep.

The new apartment was small and sterile, especially without the beating heart of an Aberdeen terrier to warm it. The best feature was the small balcony, even though the unexpected pots of geraniums turned out to be plastic. It was a fine winter afternoon so I took out a dining chair to watch the sunset, pulling a blanket off the bed to wrap around me. It was strange, this nomad existence. My heart had often pulled against the suburban comfort of my home, beat its wings against the gilded cage. Well, I was paying now. I got what I asked for in my heart.

Once twilight set in I returned inside and considered dinner. I had no appetite. My eyes roamed over the low bookshelf which edged the living room, doubling as built-in seating, thin squab cushions on top. A whole wall of Architectural Digests, a mauled set of science fiction paperbacks and airport thrillers. I thumbed through one of these but could not get interested in the plot so I pulled out a stack of the magazines and began turning pages without thinking.

My mind wandered, into dreams I had long forgotten. I wanted to travel. Not just the brief tour of our early twenties, when the promise was we'd come back and see everything again, but whole years of journeying, through Europe and North America and Africa. Why hadn't I done it? Why even ask the question? I knew why, or at least, I knew the surface reason.

71

Mum got sick and I decided family was more important than pipe dreams. I got pregnant. We had Rachel, then Brian, Theo had a steady job. Life was easy. Except for my aching discontent. I thought I hid it, but it had taken its toll. And when did I stop asking Theo about his dreams? No doubt around the time I stopped acknowledging mine.

I turned another page, to a picture of the Giza Pyramids. What was that doing in an architecture magazine? I had a burst of insight. The years of broken effort flashed in front of me, complete, everything simultaneous. Everything had been a subversion of the dreams I had denied. No wonder none of it had worked. Everything had been to distract myself from the fact that I wasn't following my heart. Oh, what an irony, that in believing my dreams couldn't come true I made it impossible that they should! What would it have taken? A little money. And what did I do with all my perverted efforts? Lose the money that would have allowed those dreams to come true. And I was still stuck in it. My financial responsibilities made it impossible for me to follow them, even now, when every other tie was loosened.

What wouldn't I give to go, even for six months? But it was more out of reach now than ever. I had hardly any savings and I had my loan to pay, month in, month out, for the next twenty five years.

After twenty years of outward acceptance I finally couldn't stand it any more. I had to do something. I had to get away. Something pulled at the edge of my consciousness, the image and feeling of Frank. I heard a voice in my head. "That's where you'll find the answer."

I hadn't taken his home number, so I'd have to wait 'till he was back at work. I got through Sunday, and on Monday I found myself dialling the University again.

13

"Hey Frank. I needed someone to talk to, and it was so good to see you last week. Can I bend your ear for a while?"

The sky was overcast but holding off raining for the moment. I wanted movement, but the best I could do was pace in and out through the balcony door as I talked. I poured out my frustrations, my new insights.

"What is it about you that makes me think you have all the answers?" I asked, as I wound down.

"Because I have."

I laughed. "So tell me then. What should I do?"

"How is your project going?"

"No change. But it's only been a week. There's plenty of time."

"Last time we spoke you didn't sound so philosophical. You thought you'd explode if things didn't get started soon."

"Well, you know me. I get carried away with new ideas. I like things to happen fast."

"And if not, you lose interest. Decide you want to go travelling."

"No! I just . . . that's not fair!"

"So you haven't lost interest?"

I sighed. "When I spoke to you last time, I went away so clear, so sure of the order of the ideas in my head." I paused, staring across the tree tops towards the west.

"And what's in your head now?"

"I know it's crazy, it goes against everything else. I want the hotel, I really do. And I want to go back home, to my darling husband and my charming children. And I want, for the first time in my life, to be independent, to pay my own way. And now there's this new thing, this old dream, to travel."

"So do it."

"Don't tease. Didn't I just tell you I can't afford it."

"Yes you can, in some shape or form. It might not be Europe or Africa, it might not be a year, but at some level you can do it, if it's really what you want. The freedom of travel. A weekend in Nelson would do it . . . or a weekend down here."

"Really?"

"Are you sure you want it?"

"Oh, yes."

"And how do you know."

I looked into the distance, imagining his face, those searching eyes, and felt my soul rising up out of my heart and into my words. "I just know." I tapped my fist between my breasts twice. My brow contracted over my eyes.

Frank's voice was quiet, tight. "Don't argue with it. Have faith. Everything will be fine. I told you, I foresee it."

I let his words hang in the air. The pause lengthened. "You're amazing, you know that?"

"Yes. I know."

I swallowed. "God, and I haven't even asked you anything about yourself, how you are, what life is for you."

"Next time. We'll talk soon."

Curled up under the mohair blanket I alternated between writing out exercises in my journal and staring at the moon in the sky. It was four a.m. I had to be at work in a couple of hours and I hadn't slept at all.

Somehow it must be possible – not Nelson or Dunedin, but somewhere far away. I had scaled back my desire, decided to give myself a month. A month of travel, of thinking, maybe of grieving for my marriage and my home, a month of following this dream. But how was I going to do it? I didn't even know how much money I'd need.

"Well, work it out!" The words were clear like the voice had spoken in the room beside me, but I knew they were inside my head.

"Well . . ." I logged onto the Internet and searched on flights. Where would I go? Not Egypt, that was for another time, when I had myself more together. Where had I always wanted to go, where I would feel confident travelling on my own? England. The States. Australia. Maybe Canada. I looked up the prices. Australia was cheap. The others were all about the same, around $2,500. And a month, staying somewhere. Was there someone I could visit? Yes, but no, I didn't want to do that. I wanted a real adventure. Well, I knew I could get by on very little food. So that left accommodation, maybe a few modest souvenirs. And I wanted to travel light. I've seen people struggling through airports with luggage they couldn't carry. I had lived my whole life for nearly two months with a small overnight bag. And it had been easy, I hadn't even worn everything in that.

I smiled at the challenge, wondered how little I could manage with.

I stared at the ceiling, considering. If I could go anywhere, where would it be? I tried each destination in turn, feeling my way. Australia? Too close, too clichéd. The States? Maybe, but nah. Canada? Too random. England? Yes. I felt back to the one time I had been there, running to keep up with the ten day tour we had booked, rushed from site to site to site with barely time for a cup of tea in between. And despite that, I had felt at home and excited at the same time.

I looked up 'britain rail pass month' on Google to see how much it would cost to travel by train for that long. Okay $1380. So that was $3880 with the air ticket. Next I looked up 'backpackers london' and found a few places for £12 - £15 per night. £450, converted to New Zealand dollars that was $1023.30. So new total $4903.30. Then I'd need spending money, money for food and various other things. Maybe a couple of thousand dollars if I was really careful. $7,000. Well, that was starting to sound like something real. Since my raise I was earning $750 a week, just over $600 after tax. With a place to stay, no bills and usually eating leftovers, I could save between $200 and $250 each week. That was only . . . my heart sank. 26 weeks. Half a year. I had $1700 saved, but I'd need half of that to cover the loan while I was away. Nearly half a year. My bottom lip protruded and I pulled the blanket over my head, dropping my journal on the floor and sliding into the wildest self-pity I'd indulged in since the month Theo sent me away.

14

Through my wails it was a while before I heard my phone. Embarrassed as if I'd been caught in person I wiped my hand over my face and hit the call button. "Hello."

"Lisa? Hi. It's Roger. Listen, I was over at the house talking through some plans with Theo. Brian said you're thinking of doing a hotel."

My first thought was that if Roger knew, Theo knew. Well, he would have found out sooner or later. "Yeah, I was going to talk to you about it."

"He said you're looking for a job in a hotel, to get some experience."

"I was. I've sort of given up, didn't get anywhere."

"There's someone . . . I know someone. I think you should meet her."

I walked through the beautiful building star-struck. There was an antique hush which contrasted with the busy street below. We followed a wide colonial central hall past grand parlours to the rear of the house where a modern commercial kitchen extended across the whole back wall.

"We cater functions here as well as having overnight guests. The house belonged to the McKenzie family and was designed for formal receptions as well as being a family home. Most of the ground floor was used only rarely.

There is a smaller salon on the next floor up which is much more inviting for a small group. We use it as the breakfast room and guest day room."

"How many guest rooms do you have?"

"12, including the attic rooms. There were fifteen, but that was back when it was acceptable to share a bathroom – we did significant remodelling nine years ago, adding en-suites and upgrading the decor. There's also an apartment for the manager on the third floor."

I nodded seriously. I didn't want to appear too eager. "How long have you owned it?"

"I bought the building 30 years ago when my husband died. I wanted something to do – we didn't have children. It's been my life for a very long time."

Sharon was slim and stylish, flexible and quick-moving for her age, which I guessed was around 70. Her strong, white hair was twisted into a smooth chignon. She wore pearls and light makeup, her skirt and twinset in subtly varying shades of pale grey.

"And you have more hotels around town?"

"Yes, but I wouldn't exactly categorise them as hotels. More guest houses. That sets appropriate expectations and allows us to maintain a certain exclusivity. We focus on the quiet and calm in the central location, our guests tend to be discreet, charming, looking for charm in their surroundings to match . . . Here, let me show you the garden."

It was a rectangle of grass surrounded by English trees, bare at this time of year, but enchanting nonetheless. There were two park benches facing across the grass and an iron table setting in one corner next to a stone sundial. I turned to face the rear of the house and my head tipped back to look up at the three-storey-high wall. Above it I could just see the points of the attic dormers. The facing was brick with white stone quoining surrounding the windows and doors. At the front, the façade behind the verandas was plastered, painted the colour of stone. I liked the warmth of the brick better.

"You asked about our other properties. I joined forces with my business partners 20 years ago, after I bought my next three properties. It didn't work well just having paid staff running the other establishments, and I had some like-minded friends with a bit of money to invest. Since then we've bought two more, so six in total. And the next venture is two tourist lodges in the South Canterbury countryside. I am planning to spend most of my time at the newest of these once it opens. New to us, that is, the building itself is 1890s. We hope it will be ready in time for the spring tourist season."

"And so you need someone to manage here?"

"Yes, I do." She appraised me with her shrewd, dark eyes.

"I hope Roger told you I don't have any experience of hotels – or guest houses – other than occasionally staying in one."

"I can teach you what you need to know. It's fairly simple; a lot of our administration, ordering of supplies, accounts etc. are done centrally. It's more important that you have a commitment to customer service, that you are reliable. Roger speaks highly of you. How do you know him?" The question was spoken abruptly, with a hint of accusation.

"He's an old friend of my husband's. They were at school together."

Sharon relaxed, a minute adjustment. Her smile became a touch warmer. Then her forehead flexed. "Husband? I had the impression you were single, willing to live in."

81

"I . . . we . . ." I swallowed and nodded. " I am . . . willing to live in."

She nodded with swift understanding and I saw her smile tighten a notch again. "Well, as I said, Roger gave you a glowing recommendation . . . so more details: we have staff in daily to clean and serve breakfast, to help at checkout time and be available when the manager is out; but at night the manager is on call for emergencies, it needs to be someone with good common sense and a cool head under pressure. Do you think that's you?"

"Yes, I do."

"And then there's your idea for the Writers' Hotel." My head jerked up. Roger hadn't said he'd told her this. "Once the new lodges are up and running we'll be looking for something new. It's always good to diversify, and I liked your ideas about the niche market, the longer stays. But that would be a little way down the track. All my energy at the moment is going into the country."

She turned and I followed her back into the house, my mouth hanging open. Could it work out so simply? I wanted to kiss Roger. I'd find him as soon as we finished here.

We walked up a back staircase to the next level. There were four doors on the narrow landing. One of them was open, a maid in the process of making the bed. I caught a glimpse of small leaf-print wallpaper and an antique dressing table. It reminded me of my bedroom in Angus' house. Sharon stepped over the vacuum cleaner in the doorway. I followed her across the room to a window overlooking the garden we had just left. Two large sash windows let in lots of light, bouncing off the high ceiling and sparkling on the bevel of the dressing table mirror.

Sharon opened the bathroom and gestured me to look inside. It was tiled and clean, with the same leaf motif as a frieze at eye height. The shampoo bottles were elegant; a stack of white towels balanced on the edge of the sink ready to be lifted onto the rack above the end of the bath.

We followed the hall to the grand staircase landing, and peeped into the breakfast room where two tables were still occupied. Croissants, cold meats and cheeses, cereal and fruit made the buffet enticing. A few murmured "Good mornings" and we continued our tour.

We saw into three more rooms, smaller and smaller as we progressed up the house, each with its individual charm. I loved the attic room with ingenious built in storage and bed set into the eaves. The bathroom was tiny, sink almost on top of the bath and no shower. "The water pressure doesn't make it up here, and height is an issue. But the bath works fine."

The staircase split three ways at this part of the house, each room having it's own short private flight of stairs. For a moment I fantasised about coming home to a room like this, so self contained, self-sufficient and private.

"Now let me show you the manager's suite."

She opened the door with a flourish. The main room mirrored the breakfast room below, the bedroom corresponding to the lounge area. A door opened onto a balcony above the full veranda a floor below. I stepped out, immediately engulfed in rising traffic sounds. A balcony. One of my long term dreams. Having one for a week had renewed my taste for them.

"Do you think you could live here?" Sharon smiled smugly, confident in my approval.

"Oh yes!"

"And you wouldn't mind pitching in with whatever needed doing? Cleaning, serving breakfast, dealing with the ever-surprising requests of visiting tourists."

"I like variety, and I like to be busy."

"Very well. Excellent. When can you start? I'd like to get you in training as soon as possible."

My contract at the café said one week's notice, but the owner relied on me now, so I offered to work two. Still, she was disappointed I was going, offered me more money to stay. I was sure this was the right move, however – a way forward for the moment, and possibly a step towards my dream.

15

The magazine with the picture of Egypt was still open on the coffee table as I packed up to leave the apartment. I turned away from it, closing my eyes, then turned again to put it back on the shelf. I had to give up on the travel to follow my bigger goal.

"No you don't." It was that voice inside my head again.

"Yes. I do. I can't give up on this opportunity. I told Sharon I'd start in a week and once I'm trained and the lodge is ready I need to be there full time."

"Well, start in a week. Learn what you need to learn . . ."

"And?"

"And tell her you need a month off before she leaves."

"Can't do it. It'll be months before I have saved the money, even with the salary."

"There are other ways to get the money."

"Like what?"

"Like sell your car."

My eyes widened and I sat down on the magazine shelf. If I'd had that idea inside me why had it only come out now? Of course, I loved my car, never wanted to sell it, but if it were a choice between the car and the trip, it was easy. I wanted this experience.

"Okay. I'll talk to Sharon. See what she says."

"Sharon, it's Lisa. Listen, I didn't mention this before, because I wasn't sure if you would be willing to hire me without experience, but I've been planning a trip overseas for a while now, and I was wondering about bringing it forward so that I can take it before you leave for the lodge. I know it will be much more difficult to take a month after that, but it occurred to me it might be possible before." I held my breath.

"Well, let me think. I certainly would prefer it were before if you can change your plans. We have about three months, and we'll know how things are going after a couple of weeks. About six weeks from when you start would be ideal. How soon do you need to know?"

"Sharon, I'm so grateful. I had all but given up on it. I'll talk to the travel agent, and let you know."

The day I left the café I also paid for my flights. I didn't know about the 8% holiday pay I was due, and it came to nearly $600. It was a good week. I had finally got together all the bills from the renovation and taken them to my accountant. On Friday she called and she told me I was due a refund for all the tax I had paid before 31st March.

"You have tax credits of over $80,000, you won't be paying tax for a good while, even at the rate you're earning. And Theo can claim back half the losses on the house, too. Make sure he knows to include that on his return. Depending on his tax rate that will be $2,500 or more."

I could have cried with relief. Somehow this was even better than getting the refund myself.

Working at McKenzie House felt like home from the first day. I loved the hush and the peace. I loved the way the guests spoke in whispers even at breakfast. I loved how easy it was to clean rooms that were cleaned daily, removing just the merest trace of occupation to bring them quickly back to perfect. I loved the way Sharon taught me to see detail at a level I had never seen before, ironing duvets, straightening pens on the reception desk so they all lined up in the same direction; I have never arranged flowers, not properly. Sharon showed me how easy it was to create a beautifully balanced composition simply by putting in each stem one at a time and pausing to think before placing the next one. The line of least resistance, threading the stems into the easiest gap, meant the creation of a balanced arrangement was automatic.

Sharon had a hearty laugh, not very frequent, but with a wonderful, surprising texture when it rang out. She smiled her approval as I learned quickly. Once the final checkout was done on my fourth morning, she took me into the breakfast room and offered me coffee.

"Lisa, you're doing so well. You learn fast, did you know that?"

"I'm starting to realise it. It feels like I was born to do this, it's so much fun."

"I was wondering how to manage it – I need to get down to Fairlie later in the week to look at colours and carpets. There's a certain amount I can do from here but I need to see the samples I have on site. I was going to go down for the day, but I wonder, would you be willing to be here for a night if I stay down there? You could use my apartment."

"Sure, I'd love to - you'd have your mobile in case I have questions?"

"No, the lodge is out of coverage. But there's a phone. That's no problem."

"And . . ."

"Yes?"

"If it's not being used, could I stay in the pink attic room? I wouldn't have to disturb your things then, and it's my favourite."

"If you prefer. We're unlikely to be full for the next few weeks anyway, I'm happy if we can get to 60% occupancy at this time of year."

I wondered if it was time for me to float the idea I had, for when I was full time manager. But no, not yet. There was plenty of time.

It had occurred to me that rather than me staying in the apartment, I could have the little pink room. It brought in much less than the larger rooms, and the hotel didn't have a suite.

We relatively often lost bookings to families and people with larger requirements than the standard rooms. I thought we could do more weddings if we had a really special accommodation option, for the bride to dress and for the couple to stay in afterwards. I wondered if Sharon would consider sharing the extra income this would generate with me as a profit share bonus.

But the idea could wait. One thing at a time.

"Mum, I'll be okay." Rachel stared at me across the café table, increasingly nervous as my tears became increasingly obvious.

I would miss her so, her cool self-sufficiency, her rudeness under pressure, her talent and beauty and piercing sense of humour.

"I know you will. I'm just sad." I had got lower and lower as I witnessed the effervescence of her preparations. She rarely shows pleasure so her shining face was something to remember and treasure as she brought her final schedule to show me, then a day or two later the dress she had bought for the formal events.

She'd been less pleased when I told her my plans. "You always do this. Anything I do, you copy."

"I do not!"

"What about when I started learning the trumpet? You couldn't leave it alone. And when I had my hair cut, and two days later you had yours done the same. And I hate it when you borrow my clothes."

"That isn't copying. And you never said . . ."

"But this is in another league of creepiness. I get a scholarship to England and suddenly you're going there on holiday! Can't you let me have anything of my own?"

"I've always wanted to travel, and I've never had the chance."

"Well, don't come and see me. I am starting University on my own."

Truthfully this hadn't occurred to me. She was leaving and I was taking a trip. I hadn't thought about the two overlapping. "Okay. Okay. Listen, before you go, can you give me a day? I'd like to go somewhere, just the two of us."

Rachel's reaction put me off-balance, and it was in this state that I got the call from the owners of the Occidental. "Sorry, it's not a goer for us.

The building's still for sale, maybe you can find some other investors. Get back to us."

I was disappointed, but tried to let it go as I prepared to leave. I had the trip to look forward to. I would think about this later. I met Brian to tell him I was going. His reaction was automatic acceptance, as it was to anything I said I was doing. I wasn't worried about him, he had Theo at home and his friends, and it was only four weeks, but for my own sake I would have liked a little enthusiasm, or concern for my safety, or a sign that he'd miss me – just something!

16

"Hi, Lisa, it's Theo."

"Hi. What's up. Brian okay?"

"Yeah. I just need you to sign the resource consent forms for the change of use of the house. You're . . . you're still okay about it?"

"Sure. Yeah. Do you want me to come over?"

"I don't want to put you out. It will only take a minute. I'll come to you."

"I can take a break in about an hour."

My stomach was in knots waiting for him. I showed him into one of the large parlours on the ground floor where I knew we wouldn't be interrupted.

"This place is great."

"Thanks. I mean . . . yeah. What do you need me to look at?"

He rummaged in his bag. I watched the top of his head, ash brown curls still profuse, that mist of grey still at bay at the edges. I so wanted to reach out and touch him.

"I brought the plans, too, if you want to look at them."

"Sure."

He laid out the pages on one of the long tables while I read through the form in front of me. I signed it, put it on top of his bag and went to stand next to him. He pointed out the changes to the kitchen, talked about where the tables would go. Our shoulders were nearly touching, glanced off each other more than once. He took another sheet from underneath and put it on top.

"Here's the upstairs, pretty much as we planned it. Your storeroom becomes the bathroom, see here, we've managed to fit in a separate bath and shower. At the top of the stairs there's a tiny kitchen, sink and cupboard and room for a little fridge. Microwave above. The window will give it great light. That was Roger's idea. It adds another dimension. Then the current bathroom comes out and everything opens out. There are balconies here and here. Great, huh?"

"Where are the stairs?"

"Just where they were. I know we talked about moving them to bring back the wide hall, but I've had another idea, I saw it in a magazine. We're going to panel the left side of the hall with mirrors, to give the illusion of width and a double stair case. We'll take out the solid banister and put in something more elegant. It will cost a fraction of moving the stairs."

"Sounds great." I walked away.

"Lisa?"

"It all looks fantastic. I just feel a little left out."

Theo's enthusiastic face closed over.

"Don't worry, I'll get over it." I gave a fake little laugh. "By the way, I'm taking a trip, I'll be away a few weeks. Is there anything else you'll need from me in the next while?"

"Not until we get the consent; the loan application is next, but I expect it will be at least a couple of months. Where are you going?"

After Rachel's reaction I didn't want to be accused of copying. "Europe. You know I've always wanted to go back . . . What's that look for?"

"I always wanted to go back, too. We could never afford it."

A week ago his expression would have made me feel guilty. Now it was just annoying. "It seems I can't please anyone."

I stood at the airport check-in counter alone, no-one here to see me off. Well, it had been a solitary adventure I was after, so this was fitting. The week before I had stood in the same spot while Rachel checked in, Theo and Brian waiting in the background after Rachel had snarled that she didn't need an entourage.

"I have a window seat in row 47 or an aisle seat in row 36."

"Window, please."

"And your luggage?"

"Just this." I held up the small leather backpack I was so proud of. Two light t-shirts, two pairs of knickers, socks, a pair of black cotton trousers. I had tried washing them out by hand, they dried easily overnight. Small bag of toiletries, phone, iPod, tiny digital camera. Notebook and pen. Rough Guide to Britain. A folding umbrella. A pair of light leather flats. I was wearing jeans, trainers, a warm jumper and a beautiful silk scarf I had inherited in Rachel's big throw out.

The woman checked the return date on my ticket. "That's for a month! Amazing."

I grinned. "I know."

She handed me my boarding pass and passport. "Have a great trip!"

I walked to the passport control desk, had a memory-flash of watching Rachel walk through it. This time it was me. I handed my papers to the woman behind the desk. A small giggle escaped me. This was the start of the adventure.

The big, open space of the departure lounge was refreshing after the crush at the check-in counter. First I found my departure gate so I would know where to be when the time came. That wasn't for over an hour, however, and I strolled through bookshops, souvenir shops, duty free shops, determined to save my limited spending money for when the real holiday began. Even the café didn't tempt me, although I'd been too excited to eat much breakfast. I'd wait and eat on the plane.

I found a seat at the gate and watched, enthralled as planes took off and landed. Soon, a large Air New Zealand aircraft pulled up and the flexible tunnel moved out to meet it. I saw passengers flowing out and away, behind glass, heading immediately down a long ramp to the arrivals hall. I reflected on the various possible scenarios: tourists, locals returning home, business people. My mind flipped forward to my own return. Would I be different? What was I coming home to? I used to be the centre of a family, and now I was alone. I continued staring towards the glass, unseeing now.

The flight was called and I queued nervously, watching the people around me to see what to do. A man in uniform took my boarding pass and slid it into a machine, returning a small portion to me. He gestured down the long tunnel. "Enjoy your flight."

"Thanks."

It was dark and strange, I could feel the concertina walls surrounding me. There was a queue again at the aircraft door, a friendly smile directing me to my seat, and I was there. I squeezed past the man in the aisle seat and slid my backpack under the chair in front of mine. I sat down and disentangled the seatbelt from the cushion. Everything felt so unreal. I flipped through the magazine in the seat pocket, pressed a couple of buttons on the individual movie screen – nothing. Then I leaned back in my seat and looked out the window. Wow.

Takeoff. Announcements. Drinks and peanuts. I was attentive to every detail but my sense of loneliness was getting harder to ignore. Finally I decided to give in to it. I tore the thin blanket out of the plastic bag. Luckily the seat right beside me was empty. I had introduced myself to the guy on the aisle but he didn't seem keen on talking and was now deep in a book with his mp3 player on. I turned my face against the window plastic and let the tears flow. Time to feel sorry for myself and get over it.

I was supposed to catch the train into London but I couldn't resist stepping outside at Heathrow to get my first whiff of English air. There was an unreality about arriving, being in a totally different country, an old world. The diesel fumes and humidity seemed miraculous.

I caught the Paddington Express and once there bought a one week tube pass. I had booked a week at the Piccadilly Backpackers, to take some of the uncertainty out of getting started. After 28 hours flying, I really wanted to sleep now but I knew I wouldn't be able to check in until later. Still, finding it gave me an objective, I'd scout the surrounding area, buy

95

something to eat, find out the cheap places. My cheeks bulged with a held-back smile.

Rachel had phoned when she arrived in Oxford. "It's just like in the movies, old stone buildings, cute little tea shops. My room is so tiny and gorgeous, looking over a courtyard. I just want to sit in the window and watch the students."

I sent her a text now, unsure of her response. It was strange she was only an hour away. Maybe she would come in for a day. I'd leave it up to her.

I found a bakery and bought an iced bun. There was a Tesco Metro a couple of blocks from the backpackers – that would be great for eating inexpensively. I looked in the windows of some trendy cafés, reading the menus. The food was expensive but if I was careful I could afford a coffee or hot chocolate every day.

A little further afield I found a huge bookshop. Waterstones. I went inside and lost myself reading for nearly two hours.

I went everywhere: Hampton Court, Harrods, the famous museums – the museums were free, which meant I could eat those days; the palaces were so expensive to get into.

I walked around Westminster, saw Parliament, Westminster Abbey and stood on Westminster Bridge, looking up and down the river. There was Covent Garden, the London Eye, the National Gallery, the Tate Modern.

I loved everything, but my favourite was Eltham Palace, not really a palace at all, but a wonderful Art Deco masterpiece. I could have stayed there forever.

Rachel ignored my invitation. "Maybe come to see me at Oxford."

Well, fine. I didn't feel like being the grownup just yet anyway, I was still finding my way around.

The week done, I started my rail pass, I'd got a three week one in the end. I was so brave, just turned up at Waterloo with a vague intention of heading south west. I looked at the destinations, my one page fold out map of England, and got on a train.

Oxford was the last stop before I was back to Heathrow for my plane. Rachel's voice had been uncharacteristically quiet. "I thought you might come earlier. Aren't you heading back soon?"

"I've been in Cornwall, and then up North, in Scotland. I wasn't sure you wanted me to come."

"Yeah, come. I'll get a camp bed for my room, okay?"

"Brilliant!"

She was waiting on the platform, already looking different, more studenty, more English. It was drizzling and she was wearing a long woollen coat.

"Aren't you cold?"

I held out my arms, surveying my foldable shower proof jacket. "A bit. But this is all I brought with me."

"You could have bought something."

"I was saving my money. No need now, though, and I've got a bit left. Let me take you out for dinner."

"Oh, no! I want you to come to college. You need to see it."

"Okay, fine."

"Are you too cold? Do you want to take the bus? We can walk, but . . ."

"I'm fine. I'd like to walk, I've been sitting all day on the train. Can we get a coffee, though? I'm starving."

She watched me closely while I drank my coffee and ate my buttered tea cake. "I love these, have you ever tasted anything so good?"

She raised her supercilious eyebrow, but didn't answer the question. "You're different."

"So are you."

"Yeah, but . . . I'm supposed to grow up."

I laughed. "So was I. Maybe it's just taken me a bit longer."

"What did you see? What did you like best?"

"I loved London, seeing all those places for real. But I was glad to get away from the crush of people. In Scotland everything was quieter, I stayed away from the cities except to change trains, found some great country towns. I liked how friendly everyone is in the backpackers, the guests anyway . . ."

"You didn't find the owners so friendly?"

"Sometimes yes, sometimes no . . . Rachel . . ?"

She swallowed. "It's the same here. I thought at first that no-one liked me, that I'd done something wrong. But maybe it's . . ."

"Culture shock." I nodded. "It took me a while to work out, too. Of course, most of the people in the backpackers are foreign. But shop keepers, café staff . . . it takes a bit of getting used to."

Her expression lifted a bit. "I thought it was just me."

"But you've made friends?"

"A few. There's an American girl in my court, Amy, and I share my rooms with a girl from Bristol, Caroline. She's okay, a bit reserved, but okay."

I'd never heard Rachel describe someone as reserved before. She was more likely to criticise someone (me) for being the opposite. I stood up and slipped my arm through hers, pulling her out of her chair. "Come on, show me where you live."

17

Stepping off the plane in Christchurch was like waking up from a dream. Even flying in, seeing the Port Hills, felt like dropping back into the nest of reality, in the best possible way.

It was a huge surprise to find Brian and Theo waiting for me. Brian gave me one of his rebounding hugs. Theo put a hand on the top of my arm and kissed my cheek which was soon wet with tears of exhaustion and wildly confusing emotions.

"Where's your luggage?"

"This is it."

"Wow, really?" He took the bag from me. It felt weird not having charge of it for the first time in a month.

"I saw Rachel."

"I know. She phoned. She sounded so pleased to have seen you. I'd like to go over myself, but . . ."

I looked at his wistful face. "You should go. Even if it's just for a few days to see her. Oxford is really something."

"Well, maybe. It's not that easy."

"I think it precisely is that easy."

He looked over at me, half sad, half curious. "Where shall we take you?"

"To the Guest House, I guess. Although I don't start work until tomorrow."

Theo started the engine and looked fixedly out the front windscreen. "Then why don't you come home for tonight?"

My body froze. There was profound silence; I was pretty sure Brian was not even breathing in the back seat. "That would be really nice. Thanks."

There were more changes since I was here last. The usually perfect guest room, that lovely view the first step inside the door, was now Theo's bedroom, bed rumpled, books piled on the bedside table. I liked the fact that he had moved out of our bedroom, hoping it meant he wasn't happy there without me.

"It's closer to the shower," he said defensively.

I shrugged; I was just so happy to be home, invited home.

We walked through to the living room. Brian hovered. "Ah, I guess I'll go see Jason, can I?"

Theo and I looked at each other, each waiting for the other to speak. "Yeah, sure, thanks for coming to meet me."

Another micro-hug, and a moment later the front door banged, shaking the house. I smiled. I had missed that noise.

"You must be hungry. Want some lunch?"

I sat on the barstool at the breakfast bar while Theo put gourmet sandwiches together, cream cheese and smoked salmon on ciabatta. He even garnished the plates with dill – I would never get to that level of detail for a sandwich.

It was a still spring day with the sun shining. "Want to eat outside?"

Anything to please him. I thought, with regret, of the number of times he had eaten on his own in the garden while I sat inside protecting myself from an insignificant breeze. I smiled a new wide smile. "Sure, I'd love to."

He brought the plates out then went back for wine glasses. My favourite Sauvignon Blanc. Was that just coincidence? I dusted off a couple of chairs and sat down, turning my face to the sun.

"You look relaxed. Happy."

All at once my face crumpled. My eyes squeezed shut. I put my hand to my mouth, spreading the fingers slightly to cover as much of my face as possible.

"Lisa?"

"I'm just so happy to be home."

Theo reached a hand out to me and ducked his forehead down to touch my shoulder. "I know." He straightened up, emotional moment over, and pushed my plate closer to me. "Here, eat. You'll feel better."

A muffled laugh escaped me. As if I could feel better at this moment than I already did.

I had a shower, borrowing one of Theo's shirts to put on afterwards. "I never want to see those three t-shirts again!" It felt gorgeous to be fresh and clean and have Theo's crisp cotton, infused with his perfume, flowing around me. We sat down on facing sofas and the awkward silence made me terrified he'd change his mind and send me away.

"Tell me about Oxford. What did you do?"

Filling the silences with news of the children. At least it was familiar, easing us into comfort with each other again. Then it was my turn to ask news of Brian, but so little had happened out of the ordinary in a month, my two days with Rachel filled much more time. Brian had sat a couple of tests, stayed out with friends. "And I've seen him a couple of times with Liberty. Did you know about that?"

"Oh!" I hadn't seen this coming. I knew he liked her, but she was so sophisticated, a woman, and he was still a boy. "Yes, I guess, he hung around a bit at the café, but she's . . ."

"Out of his league?"

"So much more mature."

"Well, I don't know if it's serious. He goes around with a moon face, but that's nothing new. She's just as breezy as always."

"So why do you think it is anything? She could just be missing Rachel, hoping he'd fill the friend gap."

"It's something, trust me. I'm not sure about it, but I guess we just have to let it play out."

"I guess so."

"Lisa . . ." He leaned across the coffee table and took my hand. "I wondered . . ."

Was he going to ask me back? I held my breath again.

His lip twitched. He bit the corner of his mouth. He was looking into my eyes and I was dissolving. He leaned further forward and brushed his lips against mine. I stood up without knowing I was moving. He was around the table, arms around me, kissing me like he used to so long ago; it felt almost the same, except for the heaviness in my cheeks, residual sadness. After a very long time he pulled away. "Would you . . ?"

I nodded; he lead me through to the guest room, his room. "Or maybe . . ?" and we headed upstairs. The room felt cold, somehow lifeless, but the sheets were fresh and the room tidy. "Make yourself at home, I'll just take a quick shower."

This was always my ideal, to anticipate the act of love, prepare myself mentally. With the warm-up we'd had, the months of dying in my sleep for lack of this, the light-headedness of jetlag, I could barely wait for him to come back. Which made it all the better when he did.

I woke in the deep dark of night, disoriented. My arm flung outwards and touched him. Wow! I was home. Just like that. I stifled a laugh, not wanting to wake him. I would never take him for granted again, carry my financial weight. If he still wanted to do the restaurant, that would be great, the perfect family business. I spared a thought for Sharon, then closed her out again. That situation didn't fit into my future now. Maybe I could find her someone to take my place. I knew a lot of talented women.

My eyes grew accustomed to the moonlight and I watched Theo's shoulder rise and fall, attempting to lull myself back to sleep. It was no good. I was wide awake. I got up and crept downstairs, closing the kitchen door behind me so the coffee machine wouldn't wake him. I wondered if Brian had come home last night, if he had wondered where I was. I hoped he had slept at Jason's, I always felt weird about him suspecting Theo and I of having sex at any specific time.

I was still wearing Theo's shirt and felt sexy as I roamed the house in that and nothing else. I was thinner than when I lived here; I often forget to eat when I'm on my own. I glowed remembering Theo's appreciative comments, catching my side view reflected in the black windows. I leaned over towards the bookshelf, taking another peek at my reflection, the thin line of my thigh. I felt pretty hot. That was new.

I pulled a book off the shelf and opened it but read barely half a page over the next couple of hours; the play of my hopeful thoughts was so much more appealing.

At five thirty I crept into the bedroom to find the rest of my clothes. I'd walk down to the French bakery, surprise Theo with breakfast. The old familiar walk, something I'd not thought to miss, made the miracle of homecoming so real.

My favourite tray, plates of croissants and pain au chocolat and escargot, apricot jam, orange juice, coffee, cream. It was early to wake him, but he'd gone to sleep when I did, nearly 12 hours before.

"Hey, Babe, breakfast."

"Lisa?"

"Yeah, Honey, it's me."

I pulled apart a croissant, happier watching him eat than tasting the food myself.

He smiled at me with a mouth full of pastry, swallowing the over-large bite with effort. "What time you need to be back? I'll give you a ride."

I stared at him for one long, uncomprehending second and then my pretty little bubble burst.

18

I dragged my feet up the steps for my anticlimactic homecoming, not turning to watch Theo drive away. This should have been a triumphant moment, returning to my new life with the wisdom of my odyssey.

Sharon's welcoming smile cheered me, however, and I got straight to work reading through the list of new arrivals expected, then helped the maids with the ten rooms which needed to be prepared for tonight.

"Lisa, I have some things I need to do in town. Would you pick up the Andersons from the airport? The arrive on Air New Zealand from Auckland at 12.30. Their rooms are ready, room 14, and 34 for the teenage girls." She handed me the keys to the Galaxy. "Take the trailer, too, I'm not sure how much luggage they'll have."

Airport pickups were one of my favourite parts of the job, I loved the expanded sense of the guests' experience, and the chance to get to know them a little on the ride in.

"Oh, and when you get back, I have some good news for you."

"You can't tell me now?"

Sharon smiled mischievously. "No. But see if you can guess."

What could I guess? What could be better in the job than I already had? A raise, a bonus, the weekend off?

I waited in the arrivals hall with my laminated sign, watching for a couple with two teenage girls. That must be them: tanned, glowing with health, quintessentially Californian. Then I did a double take. There was something familiar about the younger girl. It took a minute to place, but I was sure I had seen her, several years younger, in a movie.

The girls took the third row of the Galaxy, Mrs Anderson sitting up with me and Mr Anderson in the row between. They were friendly and chatty, full of their Auckland experiences, raving about the warmth of New Zealanders. I found myself smiling with pride.

"It's so good for Laura and Peach to be among such real people. They get a little rarefied with the group they hang out with."

"Yeah, and it's good for them to have less around them than they do at home. You should have heard the complaints about the limited wardrobe when we first left home, but now they're fine, hardly seem to notice."

I thought about the dozen or so large suitcases which had almost filled the covered trailer. "You've been travelling a while?"

"Yeah, first Hawaii, then Tahiti, three weeks in Australia, and we'll be twelve weeks here in New Zealand. Laura is going to be in the new Peter Jackson movie. The girls' tutor is joining us at the end of the week, when we go on set."

"I thought I recognised her, from 'Hell on Earth'?"

"No, that was Peach. We have two actors in the family now."

"That must be fun."

"Fun? You have no idea, the drama, the tantrums, and that's only us! Actually, really, the girls are fine. And we all love the travel."

I parked in the five minute space out front, and carried three of the smaller bags up the steps.

"Let me show you your rooms so you can get settled. Then if you want any local information, we have everything you might need here."

Sharon arrived as I was bringing in the last of the cases, dragging it with the wheels bumping up each step. "This must weigh 30kg. I hope it belongs to the senior Andersons, I don't think I could get it up the attic stairs."

"Shall I ask them to unpack it? I don't want you to hurt yourself."

"I'll be fine." I paused four steps from the top. "I'll just take my time."

"Well, when you're done, come and find me. I want to give you the news."

We sat in the bay window of Sharon's apartment, the door open to the veranda. I noticed the room looked different, barer; there were bags packed at the door. With the lull in activity, a dull ache of disappointment settled on my face and chest. I longed for Theo. I hoped Sharon would get to the point quickly, distract me.

"Did the Anderson's tell you? They're coming out to Fairlie Lodge at the end of the week."

"They said they were filming in New Zealand, but not that."

"It's so wonderful! The film is all on location ten kilometres from us. They were going to set up a caravan village but when they heard we were opening, they booked the whole place out. They'll still have some of the caravans, with a marquee for catering, but we can put those in the grounds. I'm taking Pierre with me - can you help Cathy in the kitchen for breakfasts? Pierre will come back to cook for the two functions we have booked in the time."

I could see why she was excited, but why did she think I would guess this? She made it sound like it was good news for me. "Sure, I'll help. She'll need to teach me, though, you know I'm no chef."

Sharon waved away this touch of negative. "I'm leaving tonight to get things set up. I know it's sooner than we planned, but you'll manage, won't you?" It wasn't really a question. She was over the moon, there's no way anything I said would keep her here. "But before I go, there's something else. Charmaine and I have been discussing your Writers' Hotel. We want to do it. We want you to do it. There are things to work out but we've talked to the bank and we've talked to the owners, and we can do it. I have my pet architect looking at it tomorrow - of course, you know Roger - " Her smile was wolfish. "You'll go with him. Talk through some plans, he'll work out a budget. Assuming he can work it within the price we've discussed, we're all set." She clasped her hands together. "Wait. I need to take a moment. I'm so excited about the film! But I need to focus on this for a minute so we are clear."

My head was spinning with questions, but Sharon held up her hand as I opened my mouth to speak.

"The plan is that you manage here as we discussed, for the salary we discussed. But we hire some more day help so that you can oversee the renovation of the Writers' Hotel. There will be a bonus if that comes in on budget. I thought $10,000 was a nice round figure - you agree?"

I nodded, not sure what I was agreeing to.

"It will mean extra work for you, but I think you'll enjoy it."

I nodded again.

"By the time it is ready to open, Fairlie Lodge will be ticking along, and we can work out how to juggle managing the three. My thought is that you will move into your hotel full time, be the heart of it, as you said. An increased salary, and profit share, to keep you focused on making it work. Oh! It's too much to think about now! That part we can work out nearer opening time. For now, will you do the renovation and be here, for the salary and bonus? It will mean lots of work, lots of work." She looked doubtful for a moment.

"Sharon. Thank you. It's a dream come true." I stood up, walking out onto the balcony, staring over the rooftops along the street, and to the Arts Centre across the road. "Is it really true?"

Sharon leaned on the railing next to me. "We've both got dreams coming true. Listen, if you're okay, I'd like to go. Time to get this adventure started. Cathy has packed your things, you can move in here from tonight."

"No, really, I'm just as happy where I am, and maybe we could let the apartment." We walked back inside. I gestured around us.

"No, the phone is here, and people know where to find you. Besides, didn't you say you'd like your son to stay sometimes. He can't do that in that tiny room."

Brian. Yes, it would be great to have him with me here if I couldn't be with him at home. I closed my eyes. This was exactly what I had wanted . . . and I would have given it up in a second to have my old life back.

She kissed me on the cheek, pulled back, then pulled me into a hug. I felt like a ragdoll in her thin arms. Her voice jarred my body. "I'm just so excited, and so nervous, I could scream!"

The room seemed very empty once she had gone, as if she had sucked some of the air out with her. It was quiet, just the hum of cars passing below. I pulled the balcony door closed and the silence rang. I turned in the space, taking in the proportions of the room. After six months I was in a semi-permanent home. I let the air empty out of my body, willing myself to relax. A project and a home. What more did a girl need? I burst into bitter, helpless tears.

19

Once I had cried myself empty I waited a little longer, eyes closed, for the familiar lift of optimism. It was feeble, but I could feel it growing. I would have my hotel, just like that, and a bonus! But first things first.

I fetched my bag from upstairs, placing it on the large bed, and went down to the ground floor to get my bearings. After a month away and only a few weeks' experience before that, did I really know enough to make this place run? Sharon was available on the phone, at least once she got there. Had she left the number? Yes, there were brochures for Fairlie Lodge on the counter. Cathy was rummaging in the supply cupboard under the stairs.

I looked through the bookings. Still two lots of guests to arrive before tonight. Two rooms available, three now that mine was vacant. And only two lots of guests who were staying over from last night. Room 11 and room 25. The phone rang and I reached out to pick it up before I realised it was the fax ring. Cathy appeared.

"Hey, hi Lisa. How was your trip?"

I like Cathy, cheerful, energetic, gets on with things. She's younger that Sharon, maybe 55, dumpy but with an economy of movement that keeps her grey, permed hair perfectly arranged at all times.

"It was great. But there's been plenty of excitement here, it seems."

"Yeah. Sharon's been like a schoolgirl. It's nice to see."

"Think we can make this work without her?"

"I think so." She stepped aside and I looked up to see a couple approaching through the outside door.

"We have a booking. Name is Costner."

"Hello, pleased to meet you. You have room 14. If you would just fill this out. Cathy . . ." But she was one step ahead of me, already taking the bags up the stairs.

We had talked to Roger when we were planning the renovations for the family house, but that was years ago now, a dim memory. It was a long time since I'd seen him socially, and thinking of him necessarily brought Theo to mind.

We met on the steps of the hotel. He kissed me on the cheek, then pulled back and looked into my eyes. I turned away from his pity. "I'm so sorry about you and Theo. You seemed so . . ." I swallowed, nodded. He was trying to take my hand, but if I had any more sympathy I would lose it. I turned gratefully as the real estate agent bustled up with the key.

We stood back as she fumbled with the lock, swearing.

"Isn't this great?" His eyes caressed the front of the building.

"Yeah."

We stood shoulder to shoulder, neither of us seeing the decay.

"Sharon has told you the budget?"

"Yes. I think we can make it work."

"And did she tell you my idea for the atrium?"

"Briefly, but I'm not sure I've got it right. Explain it to me again."

We stepped back down onto the cobbles. The agent swung the door open and looked expectantly at us. When we didn't move she turned her wrist over and looked pointedly at her watch.

"Perhaps you don't need to stay, if you're pressed for time." The last thing I wanted was to feel under pressure to rush.

"My instructions are that I need to be on-site while you are."

Did she want to sell it or not? Her commission on this must be huge. I flexed my shoulders back to shake off my annoyance.

"We are going to be a while. There is a lot we need to discuss and Roger will need to take measurements. Maybe you have some phone calls you could make."

She nodded and moved away to perch on the garden wall, taking out a notebook and balancing her mobile between chin and ear. I relaxed and turned back to Roger, drawing my idea for the space in the air between us. It was glorious to see the spark light in his face.

"Yes, I see it, it will be fantastic! Expensive, but so worth it for the extra space."

We wandered through the warren of neglected rooms, seeing and creating possibilities. "Do all the rooms need en-suites?"

"Yes. Except the staff quarters. They'll be able to share."

"Staff quarters?"

"The little rooms at the top – they won't be large enough for guest rooms, and I like the idea of being able to offer staff space, it's a great draw for better quality people. But it can be pretty simple. I'd like to build in furniture, too. I saw a little place in a travel magazine once where the bed and a chair were movable and everything else was built in: wardrobes around the bed head with recessed shelves, desk. It was very efficient. If we do that, I think we can get the bathrooms into the shape of the rooms themselves in a lot of cases. They'll be small, but we can use mirrors and light to make them feel bigger. The downstairs rooms can be more luxurious, with space and bigger bathrooms, a couple of suites.

"The other thing I want to talk about is soundproofing a couple of small studies, just room for a desk and a chair looking out over the courtyard. For people who need silence to write."

Roger was taking notes, nodding, brow furrowed.

"Is that a problem?"

"No, just taking it in, just taking it in. Let's look once more, then I think we need to go somewhere else and talk. Some of your ideas are new, surprising. I need to listen to you talk more before I get too attached to a particular way of thinking about the building."

The agent's head appeared around the corner. "You're finished?"

"No." Roger beat me to an answer. "We're not."

After the door finally closed behind us with a petulant bang, we walked along Latimer Square to the Bicycle Thief, taking a table in a dark corner. There were a few patrons scattered around, but no-one within distinguishable earshot.

"So. Tell me what you have in mind already. It's a hotel for writers. This much I knew, but there's obviously more to it than I realised. Studies, writing spaces, desks, bookshelves. Put it all together for me."

It seemed I had been dreaming these spaces for months, they were so clear in my mind. I knew the colours on the walls and the carpet and the shapes and the light; everything. I was nervous I wouldn't communicate it well enough, that we'd head off on divergent paths and the end result wouldn't match my vision.

Roger put a reassuring hand on mine. "It will. We just need to work together closely. I'll do some sketches, very fast, and you can check them. We won't do proper drawings until I'm sure we're on the same track . . . you still look worried." He turned my hand over and held it in his.

I closed my eyes and bit my lip. Now it was so close to being real I was scared to hope. This wasn't just a pipe dream any more. Then what if it were another failure? Like everything else I had ever done. I didn't know if I could stand it. I had a flash forward to telling Theo. "The hotel is closing. I couldn't make it work." The expression on his face was so familiar I wanted to vomit.

"What if it doesn't work?" My voice was a hoarse whisper.

Roger's eyebrows pulled together. "What do you mean? I don't understand."

I looked into his eyes. He really didn't know what I was asking. "You think it can?"

"I know it will. Now, let's look at some details . . ."

20

I loved how easy it was to be usefully busy. Even when I woke at three a.m., then four, then five the next three nights, there was something to do. I'd creep down to the laundry to fold towels out of the drier or iron duvets in the wide press that ran along the back wall. If my mind wandered into less than happy thoughts I could bring it back with images of perfectly presented rooms, full of the life of past and future guests. I was supposed to take a day off each week but apart from catching up with Brian or having coffee with Stella there was nothing I wanted to do. Saving had become reflexive now; shops held no appeal. The time I spent talking over plans with Roger was break enough from McKenzie House. I had perfect balance, as close to happy as it was possible to be. Except for one thing: I didn't know how to face Theo again.

I had managed to get through the journey back here and out of the car without him seeing my disappointment. I gagged at the idea he might realise what I thought was going to happen, that he would take me back home and things would be even better than they were before.

"Maybe I never understood him at all. How could I be so wrong?"

Stella's eyes were kind. "This is really common after a break up – the body's needs take over. You and I talked about this, right back at the start. You didn't expect it?"

I looked down at my hands. "I did, early on. Those first few weeks I even hoped for it." My voice was small. I wouldn't admit this to anyone but Stella. "But he wouldn't even look at me. This time it was so different. We talked. It was lovely." My voice trailed off. "He said he loved me."

Stella's face filled with pity. "It's not exactly original."

"Oh, God! I know. I just want to run away and hide." I picked up a cushion and held it over my face. Stella said nothing. I looked up at her again. "I miss him so much. If it's just convenience sex, I'll take it if I can't get any better."

I've never seen Stella angry before. Her voice was uncharacteristically sharp. "Pull yourself together! Go find someone who respects you if you want a relationship."

"But I only want Theo!" We stared at each other. "And I really think there's some hope."

I thought she would berate me for being a fool, but instead, after a long moment, her mouth twisted into a rueful smile. She sighed and nodded. "All right, then take what you can get. Ask him out for dinner."

I felt like a school girl as I picked up the phone and put it back down again 20 times in half an hour. For minutes at a time I stood totally paralysed. If I didn't do it soon he would have left for work. That gave me an idea. I'd wait, leave a message on the answer phone. At least that way there could be no instant rejection.

"Hi Theo, it's Lisa. Listen, I have my evening off tomorrow, I wondered if you'd like to . . . get dinner or something. Let me know . . . Send a text if you want. No big deal." What a lie.

I lost myself in the busyness of breakfast and early checkouts. Cathy had me on hash browns and waffles as I'd proved myself incapable of frying an egg and having it look decent once it got onto the plate. We'd thrown out at least half a dozen before she gave up. When there were no orders for me to do I restocked the croissants and breads, tidied the cereal boxes, checked everyone had everything they needed. It was a wonderfully soothing atmosphere, muted, yet full of the hopes of the day.

I stepped out of the breakfast room to answer the phone. It was Sharon, excited, chattering about the film crew, the stars, spilling out her excess energy to me now that they had all left for the day's filming. "There's so much for me to do, getting everything tidy and ready for lunch, but I wanted to catch up with you, make sure everything was okay. You wouldn't believe how nice they all are, how they gush over everything, love everything. I thought they might be hard to please but they love New Zealand, love the scenery, love each other and love the lodge. It's so easy. And they're right, it really is so beautiful here, so different from the city, so quiet, so peaceful. Except when everyone's here, of course, then it's controlled chaos. I don't know why I can't stop talking. How are things there, anyway?"

"Everything running like clockwork. Blossoms still out, new leaves starting. Happy guests, happy staff. All good."

"And the Occidental?"

"Roger and I will finalise plans for the council soon. I guess you'll want to see them before we send them in?"

"I don't have the focus for it. Did you get as many en-suite rooms as you thought?"

"24."

"Great! Much better than 20."

"And we can make 6 little staff bedrooms with two bathrooms."

"Fantastic! I didn't know you were thinking about that."

"I knew that space wouldn't be any use for guests; it just seemed like a good idea."

"Sure. Listen . . ."

I was distracted by movement in the doorway. I looked up to see Brian and Liberty walking in. Why wasn't he at school? There was something about the way he had his arm around her, too; he was usually more guarded with me around. I put my hand over the phone. "Go up to my apartment. I'll be there soon . . . Sorry, Sharon, I didn't catch that."

"I said, as soon as Roger has an estimate of costs, let me know. I think that's all I need to know for now. With more rooms things will be easier. The layout I trust Roger for, and you, of course. I have to go, I'll call again at the weekend."

Liberty and Brian were on the sofa, his arm still around her and now he was holding her other hand, too.

"What is it? Has something happened?" Liberty's face was so stricken. "Is Rachel okay?"

"We're pregnant." The words sounded so ridiculous on Brian's lips I almost laughed. As it was I couldn't suppress a smile. "What?" he frowned.

"I'm sorry. I don't know how to react."

"Oh."

"You're not angry?" Liberty's normally confident voice was quiet.

"Why should she be angry? I told you she'd help us."

I felt a glow in my chest.

"We've been a bit stupid," Rachel whispered. "I thought you'd tell us off."

"Oh, like I've never made a mistake." I felt a moment's relief that it was Brian, Liberty, not Rachel. This possibility flashed in front of me, constricting. "Let me get us something to drink, take a minute. When did you find out?"

"Last night . . . I'd . . ." Liberty began to cry. Brian tightened his grip.

I knelt in front of her. "It'll be okay. You're okay. What would you like to drink? Coffee?" She shook her head hard. "Glass of water?" She looked up, a tear hanging off the end of her nose. She wiped it away with the back of her hand. "Yes?" She nodded. "Okay, you just cry if you want to. I'll be back in a minute."

Walking downstairs to the kitchen I tried to imagine what she was feeling. I know when I was 19 being pregnant would have seemed like the end of the world . . . or would it? My friends used to talk about it like that, but it was like when people said how terrible it would be to be blind, I couldn't agree, I thought it would be an interesting challenge, to learn how to live. Of course, I was perennially bored back then. I remember thinking having a baby would be an interesting adventure. But Liberty wasn't me. If I wanted to know how she felt, I'd have to ask her.

Watching her take gulping sips from her glass I saw a parade of emotions cross her face. Confusion, fear, softness. Brian wasn't drinking, he was focused entirely on her, protective, alert.

"Do you know what you want to do?"

"No. I don't want to get rid of it."

I saw Brian stiffen at the idea. "I think we should get married. I can get a job."

Liberty pushed him away, shrinking back along the sofa. "I don't know yet." She turned her eyes to his for the first time. "Don't rush me. I need to decide for myself."

Brian looked up at me, pleading.

I held out a hand to pacify him. "Liberty needs time, Honey."

"Yes!" She pulled at a tissue she was holding, twisting it hand over hand. She also looked up at me. "I don't know if I want to keep it myself. But I don't want an . . ."

Someone needed to say the word: "Abortion." They both shuddered. "Why, Sweetie? Are you scared?"

A goddess shone out as she looked at me now. "No. I'm not scared. I just won't do it."

"Okay."

"What's okay?" Brian's face was suspicious now.

"Everything. You have time. So take your time. Stay here for the day if you want, take some time to think. You can sit, talk, go for a walk in the park if you want. If you want some time on your own, Liberty, send Brian downstairs, I'll give him something to do . . . don't be annoyed, Darling, you need to give her time alone if she needs it."

"I want to look after her."

"She'll tell you if she needs anything, right?"

Liberty straightened up. I saw her begin to return to herself. She patted his hand like he was a little boy. "Give me half an hour? Then we'll take a walk."

I showed Brian how to strip the beds of the rooms we were changing over and gave him the vacuum cleaner. It was unexpectedly nice working with him, close but separate. He seemed to forget the situation for a while, humming to himself, but then I felt a change of mood. "She's not going to dump me, is she? It's my baby, too."

I looked over at him. He had stopped the vacuum cleaner and was staring at me. My instinct was to lie, protect him, but I knew it was better to be honest. "I don't know. We'll have to wait and see. Whatever happens, you'll make it work."

He shook his head, denying acceptance. He pressed the vacuum button again and turned away.

21

I walked Brian and Liberty out and followed them along the road with my eyes, instinctively taking out my phone as I did whenever he left, checking it was on in case he needed me. And there it was. I must have missed it in the noise of the vacuum cleaner. A text from Theo; yes to dinner!

I grinned then started to panic. What would I wear, what would I say, where should we go? Well, at least Brian had given us something to talk about if we ran short of more intimate conversation. Was I pleased or annoyed about that?

My emotions tumbled from subject to subject. I realised I was excited about becoming a grandmother. Grandmother! At 42! I could still have children of my own. Did I want another one? It was a question which arose occasionally, if I admit it, whenever I was bored. I'm so shallow. I followed the fantasy idly through, of Theo and me back together, with a baby, bringing up our baby and Liberty's as if they were twins.

Get a grip! It's just a date. A date! Wow. Was that what it was? I did a little dance, duster in my hand. Oops, better get moving, Roger would be here in fifteen minutes, to talk through the plans. I arranged the soaps and shampoos on the bathroom shelf, took a final look around the room and closed the door.

Okay. Take a breath. Brush my hair. Get hold of myself.

"These are great!" The final drawings were laid out before me, coloured with indoor trees drawn in, bookshelves and statues. "I hadn't thought of statues!"

Roger smiled. "They just seemed to fit."

"Yeah."

"So do we go ahead with these as they are?"

"Yes, they're perfect. Have you done the costings? That was the only thing I couldn't tell Sharon."

"I'll get a quantity surveyor out in the next couple of days, if we can prise the agent from her lair again. But I'm confident enough to submit these for consent now. Especially with the extra rooms, it gives us a little more flexibility. We want to get the ball rolling in case the council wants any changes."

"But we don't own the building yet. Isn't it a bit risky investing time and money when we might not even get it?"

"Whatever happens the purchase will be dependent on us getting consent. Relax. There's no reason it won't work."

I frowned. Something in that wording wasn't perfectly reassuring. I stared at the coffee table while Roger rolled up the plans and prepared to leave. I stood up as he pushed on the plastic end of the poster roll.

"Lisa . . ."

I brought my attention back to him. "Yes?"

"I was wondering, if you'd . . ."

"You need to know something else?" I looked closer at his face. He was blushing.

"No, I . . . would you have coffee with me? Or drinks. I mean, go out with me?"

The guffaw escaped me before I knew it was coming. "I'm sorry. Really. I didn't mean to laugh. It's just a bit of a surprise."

He turned away. Several thoughts flashed across my mind. I was flattered. Was I interested? Maybe this would get back at Theo. I didn't want to hurt Roger's feelings. "Wait. Yes. I'd like that."

He turned back, a grin on his face. "I know tomorrow's your night off. How 'bout then?" Should I say I was seeing Theo? He wouldn't have asked me out if he knew.

"I already have plans, for tomorrow. Could we have lunch instead, maybe Friday?"

He looked disappointed. "Okay. Lunch."

"Or I could make you dinner here, some other night. I need to be around, but it's usually pretty quiet in the evening."

His beam caught me by surprise. "Just name the day."

It was like a guilty secret, having dinner with Theo knowing I was seeing another man the next day. It gave me a flirtatious confidence I enjoyed very much. Even the waiter noticed, winking at me as he complimented my order.

"You seem happy." Was there an edge of disapproval in Theo's voice?

"Yeah." I knew I should tell him about Brian and Liberty, Brian had asked me to, but I wanted to keep the attention on me for a little while. "What have you been up to?"

"I've started the renovations."

"Already? I thought you needed to increase the mortgage for that."

"We will eventually. But you remember part of it was on revolving credit, there's $20,000 there I can use to start. I hope that will take us half way. You don't mind?"

I shook my head. "It's just a surprise. You do whatever you want." That wording didn't come out quite as I intended. "Tell me about it."

I watched his face as it lit up talking about the mirrored hallway. It was like he was standing right in it as he described how it would be. He looked younger, his eyes and cheeks shining.

"You look great."

"Thanks. It's doing me good to do something for me for a change."

I felt a sense of accusation. My head pulled back, away from him. "I never stopped you from doing what you wanted."

"Yeah, right." He looked away.

"Well, blame me if you want. Be my guest. Then you won't have to face your own cowardice." Where did that come from?

"What?"

I shrugged, fighting the impulse to take back my words. "Are we done? Oh, no. Brian asked me to tell you his news."

His face grew long as I described the scene with Brian and Liberty the day before. "What are we going to do?"

"I don't think there's anything to do, precisely. Not yet. It's a baby, not the end of the world. It's a blessing."

He actually snorted, not some minor little sound, but one that had people at other tables turning to look. He shook his head. "You are so irresponsible. Blessing! They're teenagers."

"Well, good luck controlling this situation, Granddad."

He recoiled from me, face suddenly pale. "Granddad."

"Relax, they didn't do it just to make you feel old. It's not personal. There's going to be a baby. We can either enjoy it or curl up and die."

22

I kept telling myself this was no different than the house renovation, just bigger. It was even easier, in a way: I had responsibility for part of the budget but the money wasn't actually mine. The purchase of the building came together without me – I wasn't even in the room when Sharon signed the agreement. In the end she had decided to do it alone, without her partners. Well, that was her business; for me there was a wonderful freedom to the fact that this was my concept, my project, but the financial responsibility lay elsewhere.

The building work came first. Roger was overseeing that part, and I was on call for detail decisions.

"Roger tells me he's having the time of his life, working on this building." Sharon had called from the country to ask how it was going. Her voice was warm and happy.

"Yeah, he loves it! So do I."

I called a moving truck to pick up the boxes of books that Stella had kindly been storing in her garage since I moved them out of home. We would tuck them away in a corner of the building somewhere, so that as each room was finished I could load the book shelves which were to be the signature of the décor.

I wanted black and white photographs for art, some of those 1950s Paris pictures of couples in cafés, famous philosophers, the occasional shot with a typewriter and someone hazily visible through a cloud of cigarette smoke.

I searched the second-hand shops for antique luggage, carrying through the theme of the writer's journey. We would play up the few remaining period features of the building. Roger had the idea of using relics of architectural cast iron wherever we could, on the short flight of steps up from the atrium, for example. He had some salvage sources and every few days turned up with something new.

Brian was staying with me more than Theo now. He didn't say much but reading into the occasional casual comment, Theo was still freaking out about the baby. I put Brian to work, to keep him from moping, mainly, although it was nice to have the cupboards sorted and the cars clean. Liberty turned up about once a week, ignoring Brian to follow me around. He was always down after she left.

"I don't know what she wants from me. She won't even talk about getting married, living together. She says she doesn't know what she's going to do."

Poor kid. Whatever their relationship had been before, there was no joy in it for either of them now. "I know it's hard, but you have to give her time to decide what she wants."

"Do you think she'll say yes? Shall I keep asking?"

"No. I'm sorry. Maybe let her know, one last time, that you're willing . . ."

"Not just willing, I want to!"

"Just tell her that one last time, and then let go, if you can."

"But what if she decides to have it adopted?"

"I don't want that either, but it's her choice."

"Why? Why is it?"

"Because she's the one who would be looking after it. Unless you want to."

There was a slow dawning in his face at my throwaway comment; his eyes glowed. "Maybe I do."

My head gave a surprised little jerk backwards, my eyes widening. "Well, that changes things."

23

Filming finished just before Christmas and Sharon came back for a week. I moved into my old room and Brian alternated between using whatever room was free and staying with friends when we were fully booked.

I took Sharon through the building site, nervous because it was such a mess. She wasn't daunted, however, nodding as I described my plans and seeming to see it all around her as I did.

"What's the schedule?"

"Three months of building work once they get back from the holidays, and then the painters can start. We'll begin at the bottom, with the public areas, and work our way upwards. It's possible we can open once the ground floor is done, start with a book launch, open the café, and fill the rooms as each area is complete. What do you think? Or should we wait 'till it's all done?'

"No, open, by all means. It will take a while to build up business, may as well start as soon as possible, as long as there's not too much disruption, noise or smell."

"Okay. So around the middle of May. I'll phone around the publishing companies, see if I can get a good event booked for the opening. It would be great if we could have a major New Zealand writer doing a launch, to start things off, an excuse to make a bit of a splash."

"You're okay doing that?"

"Sure."

We stepped back out into the courtyard. The atrium was assembled but not sealed yet. There was a weird half-way feeling to it, a dull echo, like a muffled whisper. Outside there was construction fencing securing the site.

"It's going to be great."

"Yes, it is."

We walked outside. I padlocked the fence behind us and we got into Sharon's new little BMW Z4. "An unforgivable indulgence with so much going on, but it's a tiny drop in the ocean compared with the new hotel, and I'm driving so much now it's important to enjoy it."

I turned to put on my seatbelt and heard the key go into the ignition, then felt an unnatural stillness beside me. I looked at Sharon who was staring straight out of the windscreen, hands on the wheel. "I hear you've been seeing Roger. Socially."

"Yes."

"And how's that going?"

"It's not, really." Some instinct told me to play it down, although we were a semi-regular item now. "We're old friends, a few casual dates."

"Well, I'd advise against it getting any more serious. I'd advise against it very strongly. All right."

Whoa! "All right." I kept my voice light, then held my breath.

"Very good."

I exhaled as the car started, and the moment was over.

No chance of sneaking Roger into my bedroom while she was here, then. I had sort of been hoping it might get to that point some time soon, but until I was really sure, I didn't want Brian to have to deal with it.

Anyway, it was too weird. I would ask Roger about it when we met for lunch tomorrow. Instead of him picking me up as he normally did we were meeting at a café. Suspicious.

When it came to it, I realised how odd my question sounded. "Roger, is there any reason it's not a good idea for me to be going out with you?"

"What do you mean?"

"I'm just checking, before I let things get too far." I flashed him my best smile and he grinned back, interested now. "Anything dangerous about you? Anything I should know? Are you on the run from the police?"

"No, no and no."

"Anything else that you can think of?"

"No." He was still grinning, enjoying the game.

"Any reason at all why my boss would warn me off seeing you?"

His expression fell and closed over. He pulled his lips together.

"Well?"

His eyes flicked over mine and found a safe spot up to his left. "There is some history there. I didn't know she knew we had been dating."

"And I didn't know it was a secret." I had dismissed the idea they had been lovers; she was 25 years older than him. "What sort of history?" He looked into my eyes and away again. "Oh." So that was it, and she was jealous. "When was this?"

139

"When I first started out in my own practice. We had a lot of similar ideas about architecture, art, life. She gave me my first big project on my own. We got on well."

"You were together? How long?"

"Five years."

Wow! "And then what?"

"It got a bit intense. I wanted to have a family, a lighter relationship."

"So you broke it off? Was she upset?"

I didn't like the shifty look on his face, or the way he continued to avoid my eye.

"I didn't break it off, exactly, just kind of scaled it back. It's been years since it was anything regular. It just became an occasional affair."

"So when did it stop completely?"

His eyebrows raised and he blew out a slow breath.

"You're not still sleeping with her?"

"Umm . . . She gives me a lot of business." His expression was apologetic.

"Did you hear what you just said?"

"I know. I know. But you know how sometimes it's just easier . . ."

"What?"

"To go along with things. Not make a scene. Leave well enough alone."

God. Another coward. Men give off this aura of being so in charge of their destiny, and then you find out something like this. I'd been better off with Theo. I stood up.

"Lisa . . ."

"It's okay, Roger. I wouldn't want to come between you and business. Or let you come between me and my job, for that matter."

"Lisa, please, I'll break it off. I really like you. I've always liked you."

"Oh, please." I think I even rolled my eyes. I dropped my napkin on the table and left him to pay for my half eaten lunch.

I passed Sharon as I stalked back into the guest house. I could hardly look at her either. "I've broken things off with Roger. He's all yours."

She had the grace to look embarrassed. Maybe I should have waited until Cathy was out of the hearing, but I didn't care. I was so pissed off I was almost looking for her to fire me. Instead she became creepily obsequious. "Lisa, I didn't mean . . . I'm so grateful you've taken such good care of this place . . . I want us to be on good terms."

I nodded as I walked away from her upstairs. "Yeah, whatever," I muttered under my breath, like a teenager.

I had a bath when I got back to my room. There were things I should be doing, but let Sharon handle them. I needed to wash off the sense of sleaze. Thank goodness I hadn't slept with him, somehow the thought of touching the same skin that she had was too gruesome for words. I got out of the water feeling marginally better and looked at myself in the mirrored wall opposite, appreciating my slim new shape. Running up and down stairs, carrying bags and vacuuming, making beds and ironing had toned my muscles. My hair was healthy, loosely tied to keep it out of the water, and my skin was glowing from the heat. I felt primeval satisfaction that I was the better specimen, still fertile, fresh and pretty. Not like that old prune.

"Okay. Get over it. She hasn't changed. She's been kind and generous." But I knew I would never be able to see her the same again, even though I was already over Roger. And was I really any different, ready to ignore this whole situation to keep hold of my dream?

There was an email from Rachel, chatty and full of news. I took my time replying: I had been waiting to hear that Liberty had told her about the baby, but she hadn't, and it was time Rachel knew. I chose my words carefully; this would come as a bit of a shock.

Brian came in just as I got back to reception. "Mind if I take a walk?" I asked Sharon, already taking Brian's arm and steering him back out the door. I slid his bag off his back and dropped it behind the foyer sofa.

"No, no, we're fine here." Still trying to pacify me. Well, good.

We strolled along Worcester Boulevard, keeping step but saying nothing. On a whim I turned my steps towards the museum, Brian following. "Did you want to talk to me?"

"No, Honey. I just needed some time with someone uncomplicated. Let's not talk at all."

He pulled his shoulders back slightly, stood a bit straighter. "Okay."

I used to bring him and Rachel here when they were little, when Brian was in the pushchair and I wanted some shade after the heat of the gardens, then later when they had school projects, or when it was raining in the holidays. After a few minutes Brian stopped in front of one of the displays. "I remember this."

I had a flash of memory, a little boy running to lean against the rail. I hadn't taken to motherhood naturally but looking back those were such blissful times.

"I loved the big globe best."

"Yeah, I remember. Shall we go up there now?"

He nodded, finding his way by age-old memory. I followed him, marvelling at his innate sense of direction. I had forgotten that about him.

We stood staring at the globe for five minutes or more. I soaked up the peace that was seeping through me. It wasn't so complicated after all. Maybe I could just forget it. In three months Roger would be done with the hotel. On Sunday Sharon would return to the country, and when I saw her again this could be all in the dim past.

"You okay, Mum?"

"Yeah. Give me a hug?"

He looked reflexively round to make sure no-one was looking.

"Thanks," I said as he stepped close while I wrapped my arms around him, patting me quickly on the back with his forearms. "I'm fine now. Thanks." And just for the moment, it was true.

24

"Do you ever wonder, 'what's the point'?"

Stella's coffee spoon halted mid-stir. "Point to what?"

"Life."

"It's pretty simple. To love and be loved. That's me, anyway. I don't know if other people are actually different or if they just pretend they are." Stella pointed to the picture of her grown-up boys. "Nothing means as much to me as they do."

"Oh! And I know it's the same for me, with Brian and Rachel, but it's just not enough on its own. There has to be something more."

"Well, sure. But you're enjoying the renovation. You sounded so excited when you told me about the hotel, and then when you knew it was going ahead. You love that."

"In my head I know it. But just at the moment I can't generate any enthusiasm. It could all disappear and I just wouldn't care. What is the point, after all?"

"You're numb. You're grieving. You've got to let it out. Let it go and move on."

"I've let it out. I've cried until there's nothing left. I don't want to admit it, but I just don't care any more. About anything. Don't look at me like that. I'm telling the truth. It's like my heart is gone."

"It hasn't gone. And you do care."

I shook my head. "Something's changed. I don't know when or why. Lately I just put one step in front of the other, out of habit. I know all this is what I wanted to do. But I really can't remember why."

Stella gave me the number of a psychotherapist. I think she really thought I was going nuts. But I was coping. I was functioning. I was doing my job. I took Liberty to the doctor, made sure she was eating well. Made sure Brian got to school on time. Just every day it got harder and harder to keep going. I noticed Brian looking at me strangely. Even Liberty finally came out of her inward focus for long enough to ask what was wrong.

"Nothing. Why does everybody keep bugging me? I'm fine! I keep showing up, don't I? You don't see me taking to my bed or haunting the staircases at night or exhibiting bizarre behaviour."

I felt guilt shoot through me as her face fell, and a sense of slipping logic, reality distorting.

"Lisa, maybe you need to see a doctor."

If she wasn't 32 weeks pregnant I think I would have slapped her. It was a flash of feeling, like a hot spear through ice. In a moment it was gone again. I turned away from her deliberately. "No."

That night the phone rang. It was Theo. "I don't care what Brian said." I told him, pre-emptively. "I'm fine. He shouldn't have asked you to call."

"He didn't. What do you mean?"

"Nothing. But why . . ?" Belatedly the catch in his first hello hit my senses. "What is it? Rachel?"

"No, Honey. It's Fenella. She was hit by a car. She's dead."

I thought I couldn't feel anything. I was wrong. I hung up the phone blindly, reaching to place it on the table and hearing it drop onto the floor. I crept with arms outstretched to the door and locked it, then found my way back to the bed. I pulled empty space towards me and felt my frozen heart break; the pain was excruciating. I thought I was going to scream out loud. Everyone else needed something from me, usually something which cost me dearly from my deficit of love. My darling cat was the only one who gave as she took from me, gave more than she took from me, tuned into my mood and accepted me. How could I stand that she was gone? How could I stand that I hadn't seen her, had her with me, all these months. I thought I was dying but I found as my fresh heart tore out of me that I was terrifyingly alive. I had no-one to nurture me, no-one to help me and I was completely incapable of even knowing what I needed, let alone supplying it for myself. I knew I had people who loved me but I hadn't really felt it for a very long time.

My chest shook as I inhaled and exhaled, inhaled and exhaled, it hurt so much I wanted the breathing to stop. My heart ached from the pressure of my sobs, caged in my unyielding chest.

"It's a cat, it's only a cat." But I felt she was my only link to the unreachable soft bliss of life and I missed her more than I had the capacity to stand.

I dozed and woke, dozed and cried, woke again and felt the cold of night upon me. I dreamed I was waking and woke from the dream. I had been banished from my home, and from Theo, one more unbearable time.

25

"I need help. I don't want drugs."

My doctor looked at me, broken and trembling. Her eyes flexed warily open. "What happened?"

"My cat . . . my cat . . ." My voice faltered. I had a weird bird's eye perspective of how I looked but I couldn't change it, I couldn't behave any differently.

"Did you come on your own? How did you get here?"

I glanced towards the door and looked back into the doctor's face again.

"Wait here."

She came back with Liberty, fingering the car keys, eyes wide.

"What happened?"

Liberty looked at me. I knew she wanted me to speak.

"She . . . she's been depressed." I resented the word, but nothing came to my mouth to contradict it. "She just . . . shut down. She and Theo separated" – another word I resisted, a frown contracting my face – "a few months ago. She seemed fine, but then she wasn't. I don't know how to describe it, just sort of not there the same. And then a few days ago, her cat died . . ." I swayed on my chair, needing movement "and then . . ." I felt her arm wave near me. I wanted to push it away, but I didn't want them to think I was crazy.

"Her cat," the doctor repeated, blankly.

"It just seemed to knock her over an edge. She was functioning, and then she wasn't." I felt Liberty's arm across my back, her head on my shoulder. A jerking movement told me she was crying. I didn't move.

There was a very long silence. "Lisa. What would you like me to do?"

I closed my eyes, feeling tremendous relief in the thought of saying nothing. It was like floating, like being in an isolation tank.

"Lisa?" another long pause. "Lisa?"

"I think we need to arrange emergency psychiatric care." Liberty's head jerked away. The sudden briskness of the doctor's voice cracked through the delicious stillness.

"No." Two voices, mine and Liberty's together.

"Is there somewhere else she can go, somewhere she'll be looked after?"

"I'll find somewhere. I'll look after her. Brian will help. But can't you give her something . . ."

"She said she didn't want drugs . . . but yes, it's either that or . . . I'll give you a prescription, see if you can persuade her to take it, and I want you to call me every day."

Poor Liberty, I thought, she's got enough to handle, I should help her; but the thought was distant, as distant as the hand that lead me back to the car.

"Brian, what are you doing here? Why aren't you at school?" It felt like I was pulling together wisps of fog to create myself, taking little elusive pieces to make a barely viable whole.

"I called in sick, and it's the end of term tomorrow." He sat on a folding chair near the head of my bed, leaning forward as I strained to speak. "You rest some more."

"But why? I don't need to rest." Why did I need to rest? I hadn't done anything. My arms felt as if they were welded to the sheet, as if to lift them I would have to lift the world.

"Take a drink of water. The doctor said you need to drink, and to eat if you can."

The thought of food was exhausting. I raised my head an impossible few centimetres to drink through the straw which appeared in front of my eyes. Like an invalid. I closed my eyes and listened to my heart beating. My head fell heavy onto the pillow. Sleep.

Next thing I woke shaking. "Open your mouth." Brian's voice was scared. I felt a pill on my tongue, water washing it through, uncomfortable as it spilled down my neck. A hand held mine as I slipped back again.

"Is she asleep?" Liberty.

"Yeah, she's been quiet today." Today. Were days passing?

"You go take a walk. Cathy's here on the desk now, and there are only six rooms to do. I can sit with her for a while."

I felt a pull in my chest as Brian withdrew. Liberty took my hand. She felt warm, calm, with a double centre. This presence was soothing. "Thank you, Liberty." There was something else I needed to say. What was it? "Sorry?"

"I didn't say anything. Are you awake?"

"I'm sorry." I tried to activate the muscles around my eyes but they were disobedient, the lids stayed down. I felt through the room with my other senses. "Can we have the window open?" The hand left mine, there was movement and then air stirring, life-giving. I let go the effort to open my eyes and sank into sleep again.

"Brian, what?"

"I just want to try it. I have to try something."

"I don't know . . . but she spoke, while you were gone."

"What did she say?"

"Thank you. And sorry."

"Well that's good."

"Brian, it's been five days now. I think we need to call your father."

"No. No. Let's try this. She just needs something. She needed a rest, and now she needs something else."

"Bri . . ."

"If it doesn't work I'll take it back. It won't hurt to try."

I became aware of a soft, high sound. A small weight pressed on my chest. More movement. A light thrumming. If I could just open my eyes.

"Mum?"

"Lisa?"

A hand took mine and placed it on a warm ball of fur. My muscles moved to shape around it. A round body. Two tiny front legs. The rasp of a tiny tongue on the base of my thumb. The flat weight became four tiny pressure points, shifting and turning. Then it was like a tiny wisp of God's breath blew through me and I opened my eyes.

He was a ginger blur with flat blue eyes, a serious expression. My hand moved to stroke his tiny back and he walked further up my chest to sniff at my nose. "Hey." My voice creaked.

"Mum?" I turned my eyes and found Brian, Liberty, scared, with the beginnings of hope and relief.

"His name's Herman. I got him from Jason's cousin. We don't have to keep him. Only if you like."

I felt a small pull at each corner of my mouth. "He's beautiful." They looked at each other. Liberty let out her breath. "Would you take him for a moment?" Brian picked him up and cradled him against his chest. I put my elbows behind me and pushed up against the pillow. "I feel so tired. Weak." I sat still for a moment, then held out my hands. Brian put Herman into them. He felt so much smaller than he looked with all the fur. I held him to my cheek. The life of him caught at something inside me. "I'm so sorry."

"It's okay, Mum. You just needed a rest."

"I didn't mean to frighten you."

"It's okay." His voice was firm now. It was kinder not to argue. "You should have something to eat."

"All right."

"What do you want? Eggs? Toast?"

"Tomato sandwich?" Where had that come from. It felt like I had never had a specific desire in my life before.

"Okay!" He headed straight for the door.

"Lots of butter. And salt." I nuzzled my head against Herman's back again. Liberty pulled the chair nearer and stroked his chin. "I really am sorry."

"I know. I know you are. And it really is time you stopped saying it."

I drank some more water and handed Herman to Liberty so I could pull myself out of bed and across to the sofa. I wanted to feel the breeze from the window on my face, hear the traffic and the birds. Herman clawed his way out of my arms and across my shoulders, tugging his way through my hair and balancing on the sofa back. He was sniffing the air, too. Liberty pulled the window almost closed. "You don't want to go out there."

Brian returned. The sandwich was the best thing I had ever tasted, fresh and sharp, salt bringing out the flavour.

I pointed to the camp bed. "Have you been sleeping here?" I looked from Brian to Liberty and back again.

"Me."

Liberty indicated her round belly. "I would have, but it's just not possible. I've been managing the guests."

I inhaled through my nose and let out a whoosh of air through my mouth. "I'm surprised I haven't been fired. What does Sharon say?"

"We didn't tell her. Just that you have a cold and laryngitis."

"But how . . ?"

"Cathy's helped. It's been okay."

I sat up quickly. "But what about the renovation? There must have been heaps of decisions to make."

"It's okay." Liberty put out a cautioning hand. "I went myself. Roger had most of the ideas, and I pretended to check things with you. He gave me swatches and I brought them back here and phoned with answers. You'll just have to live with what I chose." She grinned. "It was sort of fun, actually, if it weren't . . ." The grin faded. "But you're better now?"

I nodded with more conviction than I felt. If it could happen once, couldn't it happen again? Where did I go? "And Theo? You didn't tell Theo?"

Brian shook his head. "Everything's okay. Just . . . will you get better now?"

"Yeah, I think so." I took another bite of the sandwich to reassure him. Actually I did feel better. Through the fatigue of muscles which had been still for too long I felt awakening strength. My mind was beginning to clear. Herman was wobbling on the arm of the sofa and Brian lifted him onto the floor. We all laughed as he toppled over, crossing his front legs trying to turn too fast.

26

The decoration of the public areas was almost finished and it was time to arrange the rest of the books and hang pictures in time for the opening tomorrow. Electrical wires still hung out of the walls in the foyer, but I'd been promised it would be finished today. We worked around the tradesmen, making real the vision in my head. The writing area would also be a bookshop, Sharon happy for me to take the proceeds because of the ambience the activity provided. I would cycle through books from the other rooms as the first set sold, and we would thin out the bedroom shelves as necessary. I would decide later whether to continue buying to restock the second hand books. I had the beginnings of an idea to sell books whose writers had stayed with us.

Looking at Liberty, four weeks away from due, the nine month gestation of my dream seemed perfect. The opening was a book launch, as planned. I was nervous – what if it didn't go well?

Sharon had had the idea to offer free rooms to the author and publisher in return for them offering a reduced-price opening promotion to the book launch guest list. We had filled 10 rooms for the first night, with four couples staying on for a night or two afterwards. I was disappointed it wasn't more but Sharon was phlegmatic. "Do a great job and business will grow, word-of-mouth. We have the web promotions, and you're still phoning publishers, right? It will happen."

We'd also had local publicity as the renovation progressed, people were delighted we were saving the building from further deterioration and decay. If we could make the café a hangout for local writers they would help spread word.

Brian and I moved in at the same time, taking two of the three small bedrooms on the front corridor of the attic floor. It was a double celebration, with my completion-on-budget bonus coming in and being paid straight off my loan.

I still tired easily but Brian ran up and down the stairs with suitcases and boxes, a joyful bound in his step, grinning at me each time he came back for more.

Herman was in his cat carrier. I stuck my fingers through the cage door and he bit and sucked on them, purring and mewing alternately. He nudged up against them for a while, then finally gave up and went back to sleep on the blanket against the back wall.

"I'm not sure, Brian. There will be so many people about, and if he got outside . . . Maybe we should ask Theo if he'll take him."

"He'll be fine, Mum. Don't worry. Cats have great instincts. Anyway, he's yours, not Dad's." His jaw jutted stubbornly.

"But . . ." But I just couldn't bear it if anything happened to him. If he got lost, or hurt or . . . It scared me so much I couldn't say it out loud.

"Mum, you have to trust him. For now we'll keep him upstairs, I'll put his litter tray in the bathroom and there's the fire-stop door, he won't be able to get out until we let him."

"But . . ."

"Trust, Mum, that's what you always say to me."

I sighed. Would the 'me' who used to say that, ever come back?

"Bring him up, we'll let him out, show him around."

I smiled as I watched him tentatively poke his nose out of the open cage door. One paw came out, and then another. He sniffed around the corner, then retreated back into the box again. I sat on the floor and leaned my back against the bed to watch him. We'd both take our time.

There was still a lot to do before tomorrow. Thank goodness Igor, the chef, was stocking the kitchen and taking care of the menus. I felt out of my depth and energised at the same time. Getting these books out of their boxes felt great as well, the possibility of retrieving some of my previous failure. I loved the familiar feel of the books as I arranged them alphabetically, enjoyed the long-forgotten skill of estimating positions as they came out in random order (how had that happened – surely I packed them from ordered shelves?) They felt solid as I stood most of them up straight, using others stacked flat as bookends.

In amongst it all I was revolving my conversation with Brian in my head. When had he got so sure of himself? He sounded so certain as he told me his plans, to leave school, take one of the attic rooms and be a full time father. My first reaction was to say he couldn't leave school, what about his future, he was only seventeen. I opened my mouth to ask how he was going to look after a baby and realised that by leaving him to look after me over the past weeks I had both forfeited that right, and given him some of the training he needed. Babies were more demanding, it was true, but their demands made sense, they were positive, forward-moving, unlike a catatonic mother who might have lost her mind forever.

"I knew you hadn't. I knew you'd be back to yourself when you were ready."

I noticed he looked me in the eyes more steadily than he used to. Like we were equals.

"I don't know about having a baby in a hotel, Honey. What if the crying disturbs the guests?"

"If he cries I'll walk him in one of the soundproof writing rooms."

My mouth fell open. He had really thought this through.

"If you don't want us here, I'll go home with him, but I'd rather we were here with you."

"And Liberty? Is she sure she doesn't want to . . ?" He had it all planned out so well. What if it didn't turn out the way he expected?

"Mum, chill. I'm resilient. If Liberty decides to keep him, I'll cope. But she says she wants to keep studying and I . . ."

"That's what worries me. What about your study?"

"You didn't complain about Rachel's gap year."

My eyes widened. I hadn't thought of it the same way. "But Rachel was . . ."

"Working in a dead end job. Whereas I'll be bringing up my son, giving him a great first year. What exactly about that seems worse to you?"

I held my hands up, laughing with shock. "Okay. You win. You're right." I reached up and ruffled his hair. "I love you."

"Mum!"

27

Brian was handing around food, easing in and out of the crowd gracefully, smiling as people accepted what he offered. Liberty was behind the bar, waving away my concern about her being on her feet for two hours at a time. "I'll take a break when I need to. Do you think I'd miss this?"

I took a moment to stand back and watch. The author whose book was being launched was surrounded by a knot of avid guests, backed into a corner, looking like his introvert's brain was overloading. I stepped in and put a glass into his hand, dispersing the fans somewhat and earning a grateful glance. The publicist was cheerfully selling books from a table near the door which swung back and forth as more guests arrived. People were picking up the brochures I had placed on every available surface, promoting the writers' retreats we offered, aimed at local writers wanting a focused space and time, as well as national and international guests.

We were also offering creative writing lessons from one of the city's best creative writing teachers, poet Sarah Benson, as part of the plan to become a venue for literati events on a frequent and regular basis. We had priced the lessons high, $40 per person per lesson, but I knew they were worth it, people would love them and leave inspired. I wanted to build up to at least 40 people per lesson, and Sarah was sharing the proceeds, half the income with a base rate twice what she usually asked. They ran twice a week, on Saturday mornings and Wednesday nights. We would start in the shop/lounge area and spread into the café as required.

I had slept in my room for the first time last night, loving the tiny space as I had anticipated. Sharon suggested I consider a suite as I had at McKenzie House but I was happier as I was, now Brian had a regular space of his own. And I wanted to be near my grandson, too.

Grandson – a scan had shown the baby was a boy. I had a conceptual idea of what having a grandchild meant, but it wasn't like when I had my own children, when they seemed such real people even before they were born. In this case I would have to meet him before I could love him fully.

I stepped up onto the low stage at the end of the room, looking across the heads of the crowd. The thing that struck me most was the familiarity of the echo, exactly as I had heard it that first day of standing in this space, back then open and dominated by the road.

I had invited Frank to the opening. He caught my eye and I waved him over.

"So now you see it, exactly as I saw and heard it, all that time ago. And it was exactly like this. It's like I stepped forward in time in order to bring it back with me. I have no sense of having created, or even invented it myself. I want to thank you, for giving me the confidence."

He bowed. "You had it all, all the time. I only mirrored what I saw in you." He pointed to a far corner. "Who's that? An intimate little scene."

Sharon and Roger were toasting each other. I grunted. This was the first time I had seen them together since knowing what I knew about them.

"That's my boss, and my friend Roger."

"The architect? Well, he's certainly besotted."

I looked again. "You're right. He loves her. Funny, I assumed it was the other way around."

So what was he doing with me? Why had he asked me out? Did I have it so wrong, thinking he preferred me but was too much of a coward to say so? Perhaps I was the rebound when she left him for the glamour of the movies and the out-of-town hotel. And was he the real reason she was back now, at McKenzie House again, when I thought she loved the country so much she would stay there forever?

"You seem lost in thought."

"It's nothing. Nothing . . ." I turned my attention back to Frank. "Come, let me show you around."

People started to fade out, waving cheerfully. I came and stood near the publicist and waited while she bade farewell to the Mayor. "A good night?"

"Lisa! It was fantastic! This place is fantastic, so inspired."

"So you'll come again?"

"If it's okay I don't think I'll ever leave."

I smiled. This was fun. I forgot to imagine this bit, the gratitude. I had seen happy guests, but in the distance, not relating to me.

"And your room?"

"It's GORGEOUS! Tomorrow I want to see around the whole hotel."

"You're on. What time do you want breakfast?"

"I won't sleep, I'm so buzzed. So how 'bout ten."

She walked over and pulled the arm of her author. He was reading in a corner, half turned from the thinning crowd. "Is it over?"

"It's over. You can go now."

I saw the relief on his face. "Can I get you anything? Tea, a nightcap?"

Amelia patted his arm. "You didn't eat anything before the party, and you probably didn't get a chance during. Do you want something now?"

He nodded.

"Omelette?" I offered. "French toast?"

"Omelette would be wonderful, and that tea - Earl Grey, if you have it."

I turned towards the kitchen but Brian was ahead of me. "That's okay, Mum. I'll get it."

He makes a better omelette than me, anyway. "We'll bring it up to your room."

"Actually, I would love to hear some silence. Can I use one of those quiet rooms, just for an hour or so?"

I glanced up towards the ceiling and pointed at one of the sash windows on the 2nd floor. "The Mahy room is the best. You know how to find it?"

He nodded.

"Then we'll bring your food up there. Enjoy the silence."

He walked quickly away. Amelia put a hand on my shoulder. "Thanks. Just what he needs before the book signing tomorrow. You're a doll."

"Can I get you anything? Would you like the other quiet room?"

"No. But are you free? Would you indulge me by listening to me talk for a while? Debrief? My mind is buzzing."

"Sure, I'd like that. Just let me tidy a few things first."

"Great. I'll meet you in the upstairs lounge."

28

Sometimes life hands you lots of change at once. The hotel was open, the baby was due in a few weeks and Theo had asked me to come and see the completed renovations on the house. It had taken nearly as long as the hotel, but now he, too, was nearly ready to open.

"Lisa, I know it's . . . I'd just really like you to see what I've done. Would you come over?"

Would I? I felt tears on my face at just being asked. "I need to do the breakfast service, make sure everything's running right and then see our author off, but maybe early afternoon?"

"Just if you have time."

"Theo, I have time." I wouldn't miss it. "I'll see you at 2." And I literally jumped in the air after I hung up.

The first thing I saw as I approached the house was the new balcony in the centre of the second storey, French windows opening onto a small, simply-railed space, just like the pictures I used to draw as a child. As often as I had imagined the balcony from the inside, in the dreaming space of my marriage, I had never visualised it from the outside, never overlaid my childhood imaginings onto my adult life to realise how identical they were. I took a deep breath and knocked.

Theo was shy as he opened the door. I don't remember ever having seen him uncertain before. Or maybe just once, the day Rachel was born, and he reached out to hold her for the first time. Now, as then, his movements were measured, planned.

He helped me off with my coat and hung it on a new rack just inside the front door. "What do you want to see first?"

"You lead the way." But I was already looking into the guest room, something was different – the linen, I realised, luxurious and textured, and new cushions cascading off the pillows. I stepped towards the bed. The bookshelves had been tidied and the stacks of old magazines removed from the bottom shelves. I could see deep purple towels hanging in the en-suite bathroom.

We walked through the lounge, re-painted, new curtains and extra seating added so that two or three groups could sit here at the same time. Through the window I saw the hedge had been manicured, the gravel raked. There were travel books, art books, on the coffee tables.

"Just makes you want to sit down and relax for a couple of hours."

"That's the idea."

How long was it since I had done that? I hadn't been okay just being me, being quiet, for a long time. Maybe if I could have done just that, sat and read for a couple of hours, at peace with myself, it would have prevented my disappearance. Brian was always telling me to chill, not to worry so much.

The door was open into what used to be our family room. I saw tables and chairs and stepped out into a full restaurant. It was so weird, the way the space was the same and yet totally different. It was like being in two places at once, my family life echoed here, but faintly; the new reality, Theo's new life, was stronger now.

Through the kitchen hatch I could see the new commercial fridge, filling the space which had been light shelves and cookbooks. "Come and see." Theo's face was shining with pride as he showed me the changes to the facilities: second oven, double gas hob, the array of chopping boards and the new sets of knives and pans.

"Here's the menu, I'm starting simple." He took the paper out from under a magnet on the fridge. I smiled as I saw some of my old favourites. "Simple flavours, nothing complicated. And the desserts pre-made, you know that's not my passion."

I nodded at the short list, chocolate mousse, lemon meringue pie, home made ice-cream. "And the cheese board, of course." That was always Theo's choice.

He opened one of the fridges. "I went mad, look." One whole shelf was full of rounds and wedges of ten different sorts of cheeses. The smell was vivid.

"You'll have to watch what else you keep in here."

"I know." He nodded seriously. "The desserts are in the other fridge . . . Come and see upstairs."

This was the change I was nervous about. How would I feel to see my vision realised for others?

It was exciting the way the space opened out into the light-filled room. What used to be a labyrinth of hallway, office, bathroom, toilet and store room was now completely open, windows on three sides. The floor was covered in luminescent sisal and light cane furniture invited me to sit, relax, dream here, too. The north balcony I had seen from outside; now I saw there was a matching one facing east. Previously that wall had only high windows from the toilet and bathroom. Dawn is my favourite time of day, and I had often gone to those windows and stretched up to see the first rays of the morning sun. Outside there were two small chairs, a table. There was a coffee cup, too, as if someone had sat there recently.

"Had breakfast here this morning?"

"I bring my coffee up every day. Won't be able to when there are guests here, but it's beautiful."

I turned away, stepping too suddenly into the bedroom. This was different, too, the bed, our bed, turned against a different wall. A small table and chairs sat next to the window, so someone could be there and look out. The wooden bench which had been Theo's last Christmas present to me was at the foot of the bed. He saw me looking at it, my mouth hanging open. "You don't mind? Of course, it's yours if you want it."

"I don't have space. But thanks. Maybe sometime."

"Sure. I can easily get another one."

I turned from this sentiment, too, feeling it somehow applied just as much to me. Had I forgotten to wonder if Theo had had other women since I left? No, not forgotten, just done as much as I could to preserve my sanity by distracting myself from the speculation whenever it arose. Again I moved into the next room to get away from myself. This time it was the bathroom, large and bright. This used to be the children's bedroom when they were small, close so I could be sure they were safe in the night, check on them, hear them if they got up. Now a raised bath with tile surround lay against one wall, a huge glass shower filling half of the rest of the room, with toilet and basin in between. The large window facing the street had louvered bi-fold shutters two thirds of the way up. They were open now, but would work well for privacy when closed. The high window with the view to the Port Hills was clear; it was at head height, and unless you got close to it you couldn't see any other houses. The floor was tiled and warm, and the same deep purple towels as downstairs added texture and strength to the otherwise monochrome space.

I realised Theo was watching me. "Well, what do you think?"

I felt awful, but that was because it was so perfect, so true to my dream. "It's beautiful, really, you've done a great job."

"And?"

"And nothing. What do you mean?"

"You look like you're thinking something else."

"No." I stepped back into the sitting room and opened the balcony door. Any excuse to turn my back on that curious gaze. I had imagined this so many times, stepping out onto this balcony, it was like returning to a past life, familiar yet unreal. "You need chairs here, too."

"Wait, I'll get them." The legs of the folding chairs clanged against the rail of the outside door. I sat. Theo went back for the table. I sighed into the breeze and closed my eyes. There was a slight chill in the May air. The leaves of my favourite Liquid Amber tree were changing colour. I had forgotten this tree, the view from my office whenever I looked up from filing, writing reports, struggling with my tax. I loved it so much I couldn't look at it.

"Shall I get some wine?"

"It's a little cold."

"Do you want to go in? Or I could bring coffee."

"Hot chocolate?" Theo's great at hot chocolate, makes it just as I like, rich and dark and sweet."

He grinned. "Wait here."

Why was he so pleased? Hope and confusion; this was my dream but it wasn't made for me. Even Theo wouldn't live here, it was guest space, to be let for money. Why did that seem sordid when I was doing exactly the same myself? The difference was that my vision, the Writers' Hotel, had always been planned for that purpose. Theo and I had talked about this space for us. Immediately I thought this I felt a warm glow deep in my belly. Last time I was up here we had had that wild night. There was no-one here. While I'd been seeing the house I was internally focused, but now I had seen it, got used to it . . . Theo was in a good mood, cheered by my compliments and positive reaction. It wouldn't take much to turn his thoughts to intimacy. I imagined being in bed with him and closed my eyes as a rush of static rolled over my skin. Yes, I'd like that.

I heard Theo's step behind me and felt him pause as he stepped through the door. He could always feel this mood in me. He handed me my cup, a secret smile on his face. We both drank, pretending we didn't know what was about to happen. It was bliss, drinking chocolate and anticipating sex. I felt so in control of the moment, trusting it enough to delay. I put my cup back on the saucer, took a moment, then allowed myself to shiver.

Theo took the cue. "You're cold. Let me warm you up." He took both our cups and put them on the table inside, returning to put an arm around me. "I think you should come inside. It really is getting chilly." It was only three thirty but the sky had clouded over giving the impression of night closing. I pulled the door behind us and felt Theo's arms around me, hesitating for a moment, giving me space to object, before moving his hands up to my breast and pulling me against him. My eyes closed and I pressed my shoulders back into his chest. There was a separation in this physical hunger. I wanted my life with him, emotionally, but in the moment I would take this pleasure in a Faustian bargain, selling my soul and emotional happiness for a stolen hour of pleasure. I told myself it wasn't a choice, that this took me nearer to what I wanted in the long term, but actually, I didn't know or care, really. All I felt was his hands moving, his body full against my back, the movement and shape of him. "Where do you want to go?"

"Nowhere."

He took the blanket from the back of the cane sofa and laid it on the floor. We made love with the view of amber leaves flashing whenever I opened my eyes.

This time I left quickly, not giving away any expectation. I had a sense of power, of being able to command a repeat of this afternoon, and of wanting to wield that power with caution, to strengthen it by using it sparingly. I made sure I left before Theo wanted me to go. I told him lightly that he had done a great job with the house, made sure I sounded uninvolved, like it had nothing to do with me. I didn't say what was in my heart, that I wished we were doing it together. I didn't say I wanted to see him again, just said a casual goodbye and floated home, buzzing with post-coital intoxication, and a sense of a rich, promising future.

29

Cathy looked up from the desk as I walked in. Her eyebrows raised. "Good afternoon?"

"Yup. What do you need me to do?"

"There are a couple of things I need to take care of. Take the desk?"

"Sure." I loved the way Cathy kept things ordered. Every piece of paper was lined up, stands of brochures were all square and straight, I looked out into the space. There were two occupied tables in the café, a couple of older women having coffee and one of our male guests hunched over a laptop, staring out through the glass to the tree-lined square. As I watched his eyes narrowed and he returned to his keyboard and screen, typing furiously. I recognised a moment of inspiration and smiled. That was what I had imagined.

My blood was flowing creatively. What was the next thing for me to do? The physical hotel was now reality; to make it work we needed a steady flow of guests – this was less tangible and less easy, and it was the most important part of my job now.

Where would I find writers? And not only professional writers – those would already have the structure of their writing in place, an office, or a place they go, and a routine which might not involve travel and novelty.

What I needed were the people who loved to write, or even just loved the idea of writing, but had never been able to indulge it fully. A week at The Writers' Hotel would be total self indulgence. And from that perspective, I wanted to provide activities for partners as well.

But first things first. Where would I find these people? Where did they hang out, what did they read? The idea of a writers' hotel had an intellectual glamour. I was sure if there were an article in the right magazine it would attract just the right people. Well, then I needed to write an article, offer it free to the magazines. And make it sound objective, like I was not involved. Write in the third person. Okay. In the gaps between desk enquiries – and one exciting off-the-street check-in – I made some notes. Tonight I'd type it up into something formal, and tomorrow email it off to some magazines. Which ones? House and Garden; the airline magazines, Condé Nast Traveler – why not aim high? I'd do a web search, too, to see where writers congregate online. I'd heard about the Society of Authors. Maybe I could go to a meeting or two. I had a feeling if I could tap into the local authors and aspiring authors some of them could become regular guests.

My plans were interrupted, however, by a text from Liberty.

I called Cathy back to the desk. "Where's Brian?"

"He's been helping in the café. He's not far away."

"Liberty's in labour. Can you do without us for . . . I don't know how long we'll be."

"Sure. I'll hang around 'till you get back. My chance to try out one of those swanky new rooms."

It turned out to be a false alarm, but plenty of opportunity to see what Liberty meant about her mother. I've known Diane for years, of course, but only casually – once the girls became independent, walking or biking to each other's house, my interaction with Diane faded back to almost nothing.

"She always seemed fine."

"That was when I was 12, when she still thought she was controlling everything I did. She totally flipped when she found out I'd tried smoking. Imagine if she'd known about the other experimentation! And this pregnancy thing has her freaking out."

"I don't get it. Doesn't she want a grandchild?"

"It's not that, she's got three already, my brother has everything the way she likes it, marriage, good job, everything planned. She can't stand me being 'out of control.' "

"Does she know the plan? That Brian will be full-time father, that I'll be helping, that you'll keep studying?"

"Well . . ."

"You haven't told her?"

"I just . . ."

"Why not?"

"I'd have to explain it to her. She'd expect me to justify it. She'd drive me crazy with questions."

"So what does she think? That you're dropping out?"

Liberty's voice was quiet. "I told her I'm having him adopted."

"But why?"

"Because it's simple. I don't have to explain it."

179

"But isn't it breaking her heart? To think she won't know her grandchild?"

Liberty looked at me as if I were mad. "No. She's not breaking her heart. She told me it was a responsible decision. Given I'd 'missed my chance to get rid of it.' I told you. She likes things tidy."

I hadn't believed her, assumed she was exaggerating, hard on her mother the way teenagers sometimes are. Well, this short trip to the hospital convinced me. I didn't know how Liberty bore it with such elegant self-control.

I wrote my article, sent it off, jumped for joy when the Air New Zealand magazine sent a photographer to take pictures and got over my disappointment that it would be at least a couple of months before it was published there. I would have to think of something else. But that would have to wait, too. This time wasn't a false alarm, and 12 hours later I had a grandson. Matt.

We sat around Liberty's bed, Brian and me and Theo, and cooed over the baby and laughed. I felt like singing. It was almost like being our old family again, with the adult Brian and his baby boy a weird implausible anomaly, like a time-warp, life looping back on itself. I remembered lying in a hospital very similar to this one when Brian was born.

Liberty wanted to be out but her mother expected to take her home without the baby. It was easier for her to stay in a couple of days rather than face the explanations just yet.

She was besotted with Matt, that was clear. But she was willing to hand him over to Brian, too, and watch with maternal care and approval as he handled him reverently, confidently. Liberty's eyes met mine with mutual surprise. He was wise, loving, grown-up. The feeling he had for his son filled the room.

I wondered if Liberty was going to break his heart, say she was going to bring Matt up herself, without him. Seeing the overwhelming love on his face made my heart churn, with love for both of them, and fear for both of them, for all of them. She had such huge power, and so little certainty. I was sure she didn't know herself what she wanted.

30

I monitored Liberty closely as the time came to leave the hospital; I saw her tunnel-like focus as she watched Matt feed from her breast.

"You can't do it, can you?"

She looked up at me with a startled expression. I think she had forgotten I was there. "What am I going to do?"

"What do you want?"

"I want everything. I want my baby and I want University and I want my old life. But I can't have it. I can't have it all. I just have to let him go."

"Do you think you can?"

A long pause. A sigh. "No."

"Well."

"What?"

I had had a lot of time to think, to make plans. "Brian has it all worked out, a cot at the end of his bed, living at the hotel, working at the hotel part time with me helping out with Matt. There's an extra room."

"But how can I afford it? I won't have time to work, and be with Matt and go to lectures."

I shrugged. "I'll work it out. There may be something you can do – not right away, but in a few months. In the meantime, you can have your room for free . . . I don't know the details yet. Do you want it?"

She looked back down at Matt and nodded, sighing deeply with relief, her mouth curving in a glorious smile.

It felt like Christmas bringing them home. Theo came with Brian, helping carry Liberty's bags up to the top floor, Brian bringing Matt in his car seat, Liberty slow on the narrow upper staircase. Brian had moved the cot into Liberty's room without comment. I didn't know what he thought about the change – he seemed fine, accepting as always.

Most of his interaction with his son happened without words, and I couldn't take my eyes off him as he moved in orbit around the child. He was tuned to Liberty, too, stepping forward to take Matt at the end of a feed before she had even shifted her weight to hold him up. He paced calmly, rubbing Matt's back in a slow circle, lifting him away from his chest once the air had come to stare piercingly into his eyes. Their mutual gaze was exclusive, intimidating, complete.

He piled the pillows on Liberty's bed so she could sit up, helped her into bed, made her comfortable. He left the room and returned with a glass of water. I remembered the raging thirst that came at the start of a feed, wondered how he knew what she needed before she did. Matt was gurgling in his car seat, happy.

Theo had stood back at the doorway, but now Liberty waved him in. He nodded, went straight to the baby, held his finger.

"Dad, he's ready for a feed. Want to pick him up?"

I re-ran the change of sounds in my mind. Brian was right, he was working up to a cry, though still some distance from it.

"Once he's fed shall we give him a bath?" Brian was calm but Liberty looked scared.

"I don't know. Do you know how?"

"Sure. The nurses showed us."

"Okay then."

Brian had asked me to take him shopping several weeks before, taking me by surprise with his questions about what we would need. I had suppressed a superstitious dread spending money on a child I wasn't certain would be his. If he felt it, he ignored it. Now he brought through the simple plastic bath, a set of clothes, baby wash and a soft cloth. The central heating was on; Brian turned the tap of the radiator to maximum, laid out a towel on the end of the bed, moved Liberty's bag off the luggage stand. He left the room and returned with the bath steaming full. We all watched as he placed it on the stand and swirled in some of the wash fluid.

Liberty moved to disengage Matt. "No, let him finish. It will stay hot for a while."

I slipped behind Brian to check the temperature; he caught me, rolling his eyes at my lack of confidence. "I just wanted to be sure."

"It's okay, Mum." He grinned. I hadn't seen the cheeky expression since Liberty went into labour – or for a long time before that, come to think of it. I grinned back. He'd grown up so suddenly, but he was still my boy.

Once Matt was finished feeding, Brian burped him and laid him on the towel, carefully undressed him, and carried him to the bath.

I stepped up to help him, taking the cloth from the bed. Brian put out a hand to take it, then turned his head over his shoulder. "Do you want to help?"

Liberty nodded shyly and eased herself out of bed.

I sat back with Theo on the window seat out of the way, watching the miracle of this new family. Theo took my hand. He had tears in his eyes; which meant that in a few seconds, I did, too.

A minute later, Herman poked his head around the door, curious. I went and picked him up, holding him on my knee. Theo scratched his head and he started to purr.

I called Rachel that night, as soon as I thought she'd be up.

"I can't believe I'm an aunt! And Liberty's a mum!"

"And Liberty and Brian, I've never asked you how you feel about that."

"Weird! Totally weird! But cool with it, too, you know. Especially now. I wish I could meet him – the baby. Maybe I could get back for Christmas?"

I knew what she was asking. Could we pay for her ticket? "Sure, I'll talk to Dad, see what we can do . . . Listen, do you know anything, about how Liberty feels, what she plans with Brian?"

"Mum, I can't answer that question. You'll have to ask her yourself if you want to know."

"I guess it's not my business."

"Finally, she catches on! It's a miracle!"

We settled quickly into a routine. Brian helped Liberty mornings and evenings, and much of the night, too, I suspected. Late morning I took a four hour break to look after Matt so Brian could work with the cleaners, earning his room and board and pocket money. It so took me back, spending time with a newborn. I wished I'd been as confident with my own children, not so nervous about getting it right, not so guilty that I wasn't working. This time I revelled in every detailed minute.

Liberty took the week off lectures, then there was the two week semester break. She went back when term started, but just for minimum time; bringing her assignments and reading back here rather than working in the library. Brian drove her the first few weeks, while she was still recovering. He didn't have his full licence, so I looked after Matt for the half hours he was gone, sometimes taking him out in his stroller, thickly wrapped up against the winter.

Sharon had been sceptical about the arrangement, concerned about possible disruption to the guests. I was pleased to be able to report how well things were going. Brian had hardly had to use the soundproof rooms at all – with his miraculous, instinctive premonitions of Matt's every need, he would hardly begin to whimper before he was satisfied and quiet again.

When Matt was four weeks old I turned my attention back to marketing. With my lack of focus on increasing occupancy we were barely ticking over. It wasn't a major concern yet, but I needed to get things moving soon or we would be in trouble. I felt out of my depth and reluctant to admit it to Sharon: this had been my vision after all, and I recalled sounding extremely confident about how easy it would be when I sold her on the idea of this writers theme. As I mulled over the possibilities, short of inspiration, my thoughts turned to my fount of wisdom. Time for another trip to Dunedin, and Frank.

"I think you've got your priorities wrong. You're chasing money, but you need to be a person money comes to."

"You've lost me. A person money comes to?"

"By which I don't mean money, I mean, someone people want to be around. You want money. Well, money comes from guests, and guests need to want to come. Get into the mind of the guest and provide what they need. If they sense you need money, they won't come within a mile."

"But I do need money! We need 50% occupancy across the board to make it work. I wish I'd never said I could do it. It seems impossible."

"Tant pis! Time to give up, then."

"Bastard. You know I don't mean that."

"What happened to your vision? You were inspiring when you told me about it."

"I don't have time for vision – that makes it sound so far off. I need things to happen now."

"So you're desperate."

"Yes."

"Really desperate."

"Yes!" I wanted to kick him under the table.

"Then I can't help you."

My foot flexed. I pulled it back in time. My lower jaw came out and I bit my upper lip with my bottom teeth. A beat. Two. "Right."

"You won't be able to do anything until you aren't desperate any more."

"But you see, that's the thing about desperate. It doesn't go away. It just turns into more desperate."

"Exactly. So you can't work with it. You've got to get past it."

I braced my feet ready to push back my chair and leave. "You don't get it."

He held me with his eyes. I let my feet relax again. "Yes. I do."

I thought we had reached a stale-mate, that we would sit here forever, him being obtuse, me not being able to explain any other way. I wanted to break his stare, but didn't. Half a minute passed. I had the feeling he was trying to tell me something, was waiting for me to understand something. Gradually my stubbornness relaxed, morphing into curiosity. Was there something there in his eyes I wasn't seeing. Get past the desperation. But how?

"You just do it. Decide to do it. Trust yourself. And see. There is always something more than you see. Look for it."

I shook my head, wanting to get it, beyond confused.

Then it was he who stood.

"Wait."

He smiled. It was infuriating. "It's okay. The answer is there. Go home. You'll have it before you get to Ashburton."

"Really?"

"Really. Trust me. I foresee it."

I did trust him. So I nodded, accepting the kiss on the cheek he offered, and watched him go.

I drove up the hill, out of town, then down the long straight slope of the Kilmog. I hope he's right. I hope the answer's coming. Otherwise I'm in really deep trouble. I tried to relax, breathe through the panic. The hills flicked by, then the sea, then the town of Oamaru. I stopped for a coffee, staring into nothing.

The Waimate turn-off. Still nothing. Timaru. Still nothing. Temuka. Still nothing. And then the flash. One word, echoing out of the distance. NaNoWriMo. I had said it at the start. The month of novels. If I could do it this year, we would be set forever.

Brian and Liberty were walking along Hereford St with the stroller, covered over against the light rain. I greeted them cheerfully as I drove up the alley to the garage, wound down the window to say hello. "Mum, did you forget? You were supposed to have lunch with Dad today. He called four times. I found your mobile at reception."

My reactive laugh turned into tears. I had been so excited when Theo invited me to lunch. I was losing my grip totally. "Oh, God. Was he angry? I've had other things on my mind."

"I'm really sorry. I did want to see you."

"No problem, Lisa, but I can't talk now. We're a waitress short and there's a big party."

"Oh. Okay. Fine." And then, like the dawning of a new country, a new idea blossomed. Theo might need me. I might be able to help. "Um . . ."

"Yes?" His voice was less than patient.

"Do you want me to help out. Cathy's on tonight, and there aren't many guests in. They can do without me here. Would you like me to waitress?"

"Would you?" His relieved acceptance felt like a watershed.

"Sure. I'll be there in ten."

I brushed my hair, changed my t-shirt and was out the door.

Theo handed me a notepad, tied a long apron around my waist. I held the brush of his hand across my buttock as a memory to savour later, scanned the menu as I passed the entrance desk and walked purposefully to the table he pointed out.

"Are you ready to order?" I'd never served in a fancy restaurant before, but I'd eaten in a few. I was sure I'd get it in no time. Theo went back to the kitchen, and through the evening, whenever I caught his eye, he gave me a smile. Something had definitely changed.

We sat in the kitchen together after the other waiter had gone, keeping an eye on the last couple in the corner every few minutes. "I want them to feel like they've got all night, not that we're waiting for them to leave."

He pulled up a couple of bar stools and poured us each a glass of wine. "Thanks for saving my life tonight."

"Sure. It was nothing."

But the look in his eye told me it was not nothing. Was this what was missing for us all along? For me to realise he wasn't an island, that he had needs as well as me? All those early years when I was complaining to my girlfriends that he didn't meet my needs, before I figured out an aggregate of relationships which met me in different ways, was he just as dissatisfied as me? And had he continued that way?

I was pretty sure he was less demanding than me – in fact, I knew it. Was he waiting for this all along, for me to help him, with something, anything, and not asking? Oh, God, no wonder he left me . . . well, asked me to leave him . . . you know what I mean.

I looked at my watch. "It's after eleven. I better get back."

"You don't want to stay?"

I looked deep into his eyes. Yes. I want to stay. "I need to get back."

He walked me to the door, kissed me. "Thanks."

"Any time."

31

Sharon called early next morning. Sunday morning. "I dropped in last night. You weren't there."

"I had a family matter to attend to. Cathy was here."

"Another family matter."

"Yes."

"I see. Anyway, I wanted to hear where you're up to with the marketing. Things aren't going as well as I'd hoped."

I felt the familiar plunge of impending failure, panic fluttering in my chest. "I'm going to send an email today to the organisers of the American National Novel Writers' Month. It's coming up in November. If we can get them to say something on their web-site we could be full for the whole month."

"This is the idea you told me about when you first raised the idea of the hotel."

"That's right." I was eager, relieved to have something to say.

"And you're no further with it? This is the first contact you're making?"

"Well, it's still four months away." There was silence. I desperately needed to fill it with something. I was out of my depth, had no clue what I was doing. What if she found out? "I have lots of other ideas, but I want to see how they go, I'd like to have a success to report before I tell you." Lies, lies, panicked lies. Just like with Theo.

"I can leave it with you, then?"

"Yes, leave it with me."

"And you still think we can reach 50% on target?"

"Yes."

"All right. I'll check in again in a few days for that success report."

It was such a relief to get her off the phone. Until the voice in my head started screaming, that is. "You're never going to do it, you're going to fail again. Who do you think you are?"

Panic.

I shied away from what would happen if things didn't improve. I wouldn't follow the logic through, closed my eyes and refused to see it. It took a lot of energy, keeping my mind off this dangerous course. I felt irritable, angry. It was a relief to return from the phone to reception, smiling at the guests. Later I went to the little office. Ignoring the marketing would not make the problem go away.

My thoughts were scattered. I went to the NaNoWriMo site and looked for someone to contact. Great, an email address. I opened my email and was distracted by incoming messages for a few minutes. Then I created a new message and typed in the address. What was I going to say? It had to be punchy, appealing, or it would just be ignored. Oh, how did I get myself into this? It was never going to work. I slumped onto the desk and stayed there until I heard a movement behind me.

"Liberty, hi."

"You okay?" She had Matt in his stroller, asleep. She saw me glance his way. "I just needed a change of scene. He wasn't settling in his cot, but three turns of the hallway and he's fast asleep. I thought I'd go for a walk. I saw you as I came past. What's up?"

I opened my mouth to say I was fine but the words came out different. "I don't know what the hell I'm doing." And I realised tears were streaming down my face.

"Lisa! Calm down! Tell me what's going on."

A laugh came through the hiccoughing sobs. "It's okay, I'm not disappearing again. At least, I don't think I am. It's just . . ." I waved at the computer, at my barely begun email.

"Okay, start at the beginning. Maybe I can help."

She pushed the stroller back and forth as I talked, resuming the movement each time Matt stirred. Her intent frown and intelligent questions encouraged me, and soon I forgot myself in the practicalities of the problem.

"We need 50% occupancy, soon, to keep things going. That's weekdays, weekends, everything. I've never marketed a hotel before, and this one is not a standard hotel. Add to that we have very little marketing budget and I'm lost."

"But you've done marketing before. Your bookshop, your other businesses."

"But never successfully."

"Well, what about Sharon? She's run several hotels. She must know."

"I don't want to ask her. I said I'd do it myself."

Liberty's eyes narrowed. "I thought you two got on well. Why stand on pride now?"

I shrugged and she let it go. "Well, think laterally. Who would want to stay here and where do you find them?"

I told her my NaNoWriMo idea, the themed month of November. "But I'm stuck. I sit down to write the idea in a way which will appeal to the organisers, and I go blank. It's so important. What if I screw it up?"

"Then talk it out first, tell me."

"Well . . ." It took a couple of goes, but then I was fluent, waxing rhapsodic about the creative environment, the camaraderie, the freedom from distractions.

"Here." Liberty pushed the stroller handles towards me and edged me out of my chair. "Say that again." And she started typing, translating what I said onto the screen.

"There, that's done. Have a read." We swapped positions again and I scanned the text.

"This is brilliant! Perfect."

"Well, hit Send."

It took a few seconds for it to sink in and then my heart lifted. Something was done. A step was taken.

"Now, where else?"

"I don't know . . . the Society of Authors? Local writers?"

"Okay. Dictate!"

Brian poked his head into the office, hair tousled. He had done the night waking shift with Matt and slept in. "I wondered where you were. Shall I take him?"

"I was going to take him for a walk."

"I'll do it."

Another half hour and Liberty had sent off three more emails. "People will get it, you just have to describe it in their terms. Inspire them. Do you want me to do some web research, find some more organisations we can target?"

"Would you?"

"Sure, easy. Let me earn my keep."

"I can pay you. There isn't much budget, but what you're doing doesn't cost us anything for advertising. Even a few hours a week could make a big difference. What do you think? Would you?"

Liberty laughed. "Lisa, it was my idea. Now let's go celebrate!"

I asked Igor for two coffees and Liberty sat in one of the armchairs at reception while I stood behind the desk. Policy was to have it manned at all times, although it was often quiet, as now. Liberty took a notepad and pen and scribbled some more ideas.

"You know lots of the famous hotels sell souvenirs."

"What sort of thing?"

"Coffee cups, towels, bathrobes, whatever – with branding. You could have journals, too, writers love journals. And their friends would see them, ask about the hotel."

I had already thought about selling notebooks, but not of branding them. "Great idea"

She doodled for a while, chewing her lip.

"What is it?"

She looked up.

"You look like you've got something to say."

"Well . . . Listen, you don't have to listen to me. But whatever it is with Sharon, I think you should work it out. Be honest with her. Ask for help. The longer you leave it, the worse it will get. And this is your home now. You used to like her. Get to like her again. And another thing . . ."

"I'm still thinking about the first thing . . . well, okay, what?"

"Maybe you could just . . . relax a little. You've done a great job here, it's beautiful. Wouldn't it be so much more fun to believe it will work? It is already working, and it will only get better."

32

Believe it will work. The words took hold and worked magic. I heard the echo of them as I stood at reception, answered my emails, helped with the cleaning and watched over Matt. Images flashed in my mind, brightened versions of the first inspiration: writers working in the bookshop, laughing together in the café, filling the guests' shelf with works of their own. I found myself singing as I went through my day, confidence bursting. And then I took that scary step and called Sharon.

"Can we talk? I'd like to fill you in, get some advice."

Her voice was different when she replied. We'd got frosty with each other ever since the Roger incident. Now the friendliness returned.

"Of course. Advice on what?"

"Well, I know I had ideas about the writers theme, innovative marketing. But you have years of experience in hotels. I think some of the standard advertising, promotions, would help us, too. Everything we can do will make a difference. Can you come over some time so we can talk?"

I could hear her smile. "I'd enjoy that. And I have some other news for you, also."

She wouldn't tell me on the phone, but as soon as she walked in I saw the golf ball diamond on her finger. She laughed like a schoolgirl. "Roger and I are engaged."

Another happy couple. And Sharon would never have to worry about her financial contribution, like I had. I envied her. "Congratulations."

"I'm so giddy I could scream. And I never thought I would marry again. 30 years!"

I felt that hot pebble again, appearing in my throat and dropping in slow motion through my chest, down to the pit of my belly. "I hope you'll be happy."

"We thought we'd have the reception here at the hotel. What do you think?"

"Sounds great. Have you got a date in mind?"

"November 27th – there's nothing to wait for, but at the same time I want to have everything just right, just lovely. I need to find something to wear, something pretty but not ridiculous on a woman of my age."

"If you look like you do today, you needn't worry. You're radiant."

She laughed again. "Thank you. Now, you. What did you want to talk about?"

I explained the steps Liberty and I had taken with the marketing, and the other ideas Liberty had which she was following up. "I thought it would make sense to send out a mailing to your email list, also. I know we said the market was different, but your clientele are wealthy, educated. They could be a connection to the people we want to reach. I was thinking a 'Calling all writers, aspiring and developed' – something like that. Make it sound like an adventure, the whole package, and ask them to send it on to people they know."

Sharon nodded.

I went on. "I'm also thinking about the book clubs - a lot of would-be writers are great readers - how can we tap into those?"

Sharon took out a notepad and pen. "Leave that one with me - I have an idea, at least for the local ones. Any other ideas?"

"I've been thinking about where writers, particularly aspiring writers, might be. I know there are areas of the big cities where literary, arty types live. I've been toying with the idea of convincing some of the independent bookshops to hand out bookmarks - but maybe that's a way down the track. I don't even know how to find out what those shops might be. And then there's the chance of becoming too successful, creating demand we can't satisfy."

"Let go of that hesitation. If we're full, we're full. As a destination hotel, people will be willing to book dates around us, not just vice versa."

"Okay. Maybe you're right. Oh, and there's one other thing I wanted to ask you, make sure you're okay with. You know my husband, Theo, has opened a restaurant."

"Yes."

"It's in our old home, 1890s character, quite in keeping with the hotel's historic theme. I've been putting together a package, staying with us, and breakfast, a few activities - the tram and gondola, trip to Akaroa, picnics that can be taken out into Latimer Square or to the Gardens. I was thinking of including a couple of dinners, well marked up, of course. I'd like one of the restaurants to be Theo's. If you don't mind."

"Good idea."

"You might want to try it first?"

"Actually, Roger and I have eaten there a couple of times."

"Oh." I frowned. "You didn't say."

She raised her eyebrows, as if to say it was none of my business. I guess she was right. But it still felt weird.

Theo was overwhelmed at the idea of my providing him with patrons. There were tears in his eyes as we came to the end of the discussion over how it would work, what he could offer and how to price it.

"I expected my friends to help, to tell their friends, to recommend people eat here, but whenever I ask people, there's a coolness, like I've made a faux pas, like I've asked them for money. Getting started hasn't been easy. So . . . I'm grateful. Thank you, Lisa." He leaned forward like he was going to kiss me. I so wanted him to but something made me clear my throat, turn away. I didn't want him to think I was buying his love, although perhaps that's exactly what I was trying to do.

"It's nothing, really. It will work for both of us. And we don't know how it will work out, yet, either. It may not fly."

He looked at the floor, mumbling this time. "Well, I'm still grateful."

I had had lunch with Stella and her words of advice were still ringing in my ears. She had accused me of still hankering after him, of refusing to enjoy the fabulous life I have because I didn't have him. "You have to let him go. You won't be happy until you do."

I knew she was right, but there he was, so adorable. Especially when he admitted his insecurity, his lack of confidence that his restaurant would work. Wow, wouldn't that be something, if he failed at something, and I could be the understanding one? He was risking our house. I almost hoped he lost it so he might forgive me, or so I could rescue him. This perverse thought made me remember.

"Hey, big news! I paid off another $10,000 of my loan this week."

He looked up, his eye glinting. Another tear? "You did? That's great!"

"Yeah, I've been saving, I wanted to do it in one hit. And then I sold some books from the hotel. There's enough to send to Rachel, for her ticket home at Christmas."

"Really? That's brilliant. I was wondering how we were going to do that. Thanks."

I grinned. "No problem. Well, I'll run this past Sharon, but I know she was impressed when she came, it'll be cool. So now we just have to wait to sell some of the package holidays. In the meantime, we'll keep your brochures at reception." I turned to the door. Something felt different. It was like we were two kids on a see-saw and the balance had tipped. If I was on my way up, did that mean Theo was on his way down? Maybe we could reach equilibrium. That would be good.

33

If I looked back through the bookings I could tell you exactly when everything changed. One day we were quiet and I was worried about my job; the next we were so busy I didn't have a moment for myself. It was weeks since I had taken any time out, between reception and training staff and giving Brian a little time out from Matt. I had talked to Theo a couple of times on the phone and he had come in most weeks for an hour with his son and grandson, but I hadn't talked to him properly, face to face, since July; now it was October and in three days the first of the NaNoWriMo guests were arriving. We were booked out, and more, for the whole month. The overflow were filling McKenzie House and Sharon's other places – she was delighted, November was usually pretty quiet – and being transported here for the various activities as they wished.

I wasn't unhappy, this was my dream come true. But I wished I had a chance to clear my head.

When I snapped at one of the new maids for the third time that day, Cathy stepped in.

"It's okay, leave it to me. Lisa, I'll take that. Why don't you go out for a while, take a break."

"Are you crazy? You know how much there is to do."

Cathy looked me straight in the eye. "Take a break. Come back in a good mood. It will make everything easier."

For a moment I was angry, a cold retort came to my lips. That's when I knew I was at breaking point – no-one ever gets angry at Cathy. "Can you manage?"

She raised her eyebrows and gave a slow, exaggerated nod.

"Well, maybe I'll take Matt out for a while, get some air."

"Then take him somewhere he'll be entertained, so you don't have to do it."

I found Brian reading in his room, Matt gurgling under the play frame. "Hey, Hon."

"Hey, Mum. Anything up? I'm not working 'till this afternoon, right?"

"No, that's right. I'm going out for a while. Mind if I take him?"

"Sure, no. When will you be back?"

"A few hours. Why don't you go see Jason?" I worried about how little Brian saw his friends, even though he didn't complain.

"Okay, thanks."

"I'm ready. You've got everything you need?"

Cathy looked up from behind the reception desk.

"Sure. Have a good time."

Matt's car seat was heavy on one arm. I steered the folding stroller in a weaving line towards the exit. How often had I wished for automatic doors, but with the foot traffic outside they would be hyperactive. I pulled my shoulders together and backed out with the stroller and car seat knocking together. A male guest jumped up, too late to help. He waved apologetically. It was an effort of conscious will to stretch my mouth into a reluctant pseudo-smile of thanks.

I looked into Matt's eyes as I buckled him into the front seat. I felt my pulse slow and a real smile spread across my face. He'd soon be out of the rear facing seat, and have to go in the back. I'd miss the feel of his calm eyes watching me as I swirled through the city traffic.

"Let's go to the zoo."

Some of my best days when Rachel and Brian were small were at Orana Park, the slow stroll along the broad central avenue, leaning on the pram as the endless antics of the Meerkats provided a mesmeric focus for toddler and child alike. Brian never sat so still anywhere else, for anything else, but the animals kept him enthralled for twenty minutes together. Usually it was Rachel, projecting forward to the next exhibit, who asked to move on.

Even driving with Matt was relaxing, I forgot my worries and moved into a twilight state of content, a quiet, meditative experience. I had the sense of waking up as I stopped the car. I sat with the engine off in the Orana Park car park until Matt squeaked, attracting my attention. "Just a minute, Honey."

I pushed my sunglasses to the top of my head then removed them altogether. The day was glary but I had realised Matt didn't recognise me the same, didn't relate to me the same, if he couldn't see my eyes.

On a whim I bought a season pass, glanced into the shop, ghostly images of 4 year old Brian and 6 year old Rachel running from stand to stand in frenzied indecision over what one thing they would buy. Always just one thing. The choosing was a delicious ordeal.

The Safari Shuttle was getting ready to leave; I preferred our own pace, stopping to free a twig from one of the swivelling front wheels of the stroller and letting the vehicle go first. Matt twisted around to see me, pulling himself forward. He was getting so strong. Brian used to complain about being tied in, throwing himself against the restraints. Matt just used them to pull himself forward, gripping them near the seat and leaning out to look around the side. I talked as we walked, pointing forward and describing what we could see to allow him to relax back and enjoy the ride.

We stopped at the Meerkats and I squatted down beside and slightly in front of him, arm stretched out towards them. He grabbed my hair as it swung near his face and laughed as I tugged against him. I pushed my face near his and he let go of my hair, grabbing my cheeks and pushing his nose up to mine. My smile reached down into my chest. "I love you too, Sweetheart. You are the best company."

34

Most of the rooms had emptied to make way for our Novel Writers' Month guests. Everyone had pitched in to clean and prepare the rooms and now it was almost eerie, waiting, knowing the rush was coming, but hearing nothing. Logically it didn't feel so different – there were locals eating in the café, but they, too, kept glancing over their shoulders as if they felt something in the air. A month was a long time. What if something went wrong? The fact that I had no idea what that something might be just made things worse, scarier. I've never been good with uncertainty.

It was almost an anti-climax. The first couple seemed perfectly normal: charming, in fact, pleasant and conservative and easy. Cathy took them up to their room; we had arranged early check-in so they could come straight from their flight. She returned. I raised an eyebrow.

"They're lovely," she said, and we turned to watch the door once more.

The first formal event was welcoming drinks. Once everyone was gathered, glasses in hand, I realised I was expected to say something. Relax. I told myself. Remember everyone's here to have a good time.

"Good evening, writers and partners. Welcome to the Old Occidental Writers' Hotel. We are delighted you are here for the first annual

NaNoWriMo experience; thank you for coming all this way to be with us. For those of you who don't know, the hotel opened in its current form just five months ago. It has been a hotel on and off since 1861 but the concept of the Writers' Hotel is new. We think it suits the building exactly. We hope you will benefit from the creative atmosphere just as we have. Tomorrow is the 1st of November, the time for the creative flow to begin. For tonight, relax, get to know each other, wish each other luck for the journey of a lifetime. I am Lisa Haynes, manager of the hotel. Please come to me for anything you might need."

I enjoyed the polite applause enormously, and the small crowd which immediately gathered around as if I were someone famous. This was unexpected. I had imagined being the heart of the hotel, but anonymous, not a focus in my own right.

The Writers' Month package included tickets to several local attractions, a dinner each week at Theo's and a day with a tour guide. Optional extras were classic car hire for a trip to Akaroa or Hanmer. Brian had worked out a "Standard Tour" and an "Alternative Tour" and in the first few days he went from group to group finding out their special interests so these could be incorporated into the tours as well – Christchurch has a lot of independent specialty shops: Radar for records, Scorpio for books, and a quaint little café in Brighton, The Jungle Patrol, for antique New Zealand china. He had his full driver's licence now but it would be a couple of years before he could take paying passengers, so we had hired a driver – Brian would take care of the commentary and navigation.

Liberty's exams were over; she and I would look after Matt between us, and she was working on the various events of the month and new marketing ideas whenever she had time.

I was helping Igor in the kitchen preparing breakfast trays when I heard the shouting. Igor and I looked at each other and I put down the individual portion jars of jam I was holding. Igor jerked his head and I nodded, turning towards the door.

"I knew this would happen as soon as my wife told me she wanted to come to this Third World, backwater country. Do something about it!"

"Can I help?"

He turned to me with a stare that made my hair blow backwards.

"Who are you?"

"I'm the manager."

He looked me up and down, his thunderous expression turning into a sneer, then turned away, muttering. "For God's sake, I should have known, a woman."

Igor had followed me out and stepped up close behind me. "It's okay, thanks, Igor." He didn't move. "Really. I'll call if I need you."

It takes a lot to break through Cathy's friendly calm, but this guy had done it. There was a tear in the corner of her eye and her face was tense.

I put a hand on her shoulder. "It's okay, I'll deal with this." She hesitated. "You go." My voice was quiet, just for her. I could feel the bluster brewing and deliberately shielded her as she walked towards the hall door.

"Hey, where's she going? I want you to fix this, missy!"

"I'm sure I can help you."

"Oh, so I'm going to have to go through the whole damn thing again!"

He was a big guy and his voice boomed through the atrium. Everyone in the café and at the reading tables was listening, fascinated. It was like a child having a tantrum in a supermarket. As long as it was only the child screaming, as long as the adult stayed calm, it was fine. If the adult lost it as well, then it became nasty, leaving a bitter taste in the mouth of the witnesses.

"Please, tell me what the problem is."

"That room is the size of a mouse's dick, there's no shower, it looks out into some crappy alley. God, you people should be ashamed to even offer a room like that, but it's all in line, crappy airline, backward airport, taxi with no air conditioning, drove here with the goddamn windows open for Christ's sake. And I can't even get a proper goddamn cup of coffee. Haven't you people heard of Americano? I can even get one of those in Italy, for crying out loud."

I waited. He seemed to have run down. Poor guy. Was he always like this? The whole world must hate him. I wondered where his wife was. "Mr Hollis, is it?"

"Yes!"

"I know you were due to arrive yesterday, were you delayed in your travel?"

"Yes we fucking were! Goddamn incompetence! A little bit of ice on the runway and our flight doesn't take off from Portland and then they tell me in Los Angeles that the plane left without us. We were a lousy thirty minutes late and it couldn't wait. And then they tell me there's no other flight until the next day! One flight a day! Little tin-pot country . . ."

I let him run on for a bit. He would let me know when it was my turn to talk again. I felt Brian come up behind me, a protective presence.

". . . so what are you going to do about this fucking room?"

"There are a couple of options. I spoke to your wife myself when she made the booking. She's a keen writer, very enthusiastic."

"I don't know what the hell it is! Can't seem to keep her happy but she's got to be prancing around with her 'literary' friends."

"I explained to her the hotel was full, that we were putting the extra bookings into nearby historic guesthouses. She was very disappointed, said she wanted to be here."

"She thinks it's some sort of shrine! She was so excited." His face softened for a moment, then the volume of his voice picked up again. "And then we finally get here and this!"

"She asked me if there wasn't anything, the smallest cupboard, and I said the only possible room was on the staff floor . . . she seemed quite excited, but perhaps she didn't pass on that conversation to you. Is she also unhappy with the room?"

"No, she called it a goddamned 'garret' – she's always on about a 'garret.' But I told her, you're taking advantage."

"Well, if you would like to come with me, I'll take you to the other hotel, show you what we have there."

"Well, all right."

Brian stepped forward. "I'll take him." His voice was low, his face concerned.

"Where's Matt?"

"With Cathy."

"Would you like me to telephone up to your wife, ask her to come down so she can go with you?"

"I guess I'll go get her myself."

As he disappeared through the door the whole room relaxed. I realised how unnaturally quiet it had been. Someone laughed and the complex echo of the atrium resonated again.

Brian turned from watching the doors swing behind him back to me. "You okay?"

I grinned. "I'm fine. He was way easier than Rachel at her four year old worst!"

Brian picked up the car keys. "Where am I taking him?"

"McKenzie House, room 14. But I think he'll be back."

"Yay." I love Brian's deadpan humour.

35

Mr Hollis and his wife, Celia, walked through reception and out front to where Brian was waiting. Celia looked low and embarrassed, eyes on the floor with the merest glance at me as she passed. I hoped she'd stand up for what she wanted. Cathy appeared from the hall.

"What did you say to him? He actually apologised!"

"I didn't say anything. I just listened."

"I hate scary guys like that."

"Scary? Nah, he's a pussycat. Sheep in wolf's clothing. You watch, we'll be best friends from now on."

In twenty minutes they were back, Celia smiling, her husband sheepish. "Well, if she wants a garret, she can have a fucking garret."

I smiled, nodding. "Let me show you where you can sit when you want a bit more space." I put a hand on his arm. It was a finely judged thing.

"Are you patronising me?"

I tipped my head on one side. "What do you think?" I flashed him a big smile, surprised at how I was warming to him.

Now Matt was able to sit up unaided and amuse himself with hand held toys, Brian chose to do more reception work. There was a space just off to the side where Matt could sit and watch the world go by, Brian with one practised eye on him at all times. No-one was checking in or out but there was a constant stream of questions about local attractions, activities, calls for taxis and restaurant recommendations. Brian loved to help and the guests loved him. The looks of shock as they realised Matt was his son changed to admiration as they saw how he was with him. I came upon more than one serious conversation offering him advice.

"Don't you mind?" I asked him, not sure how I could protect him from it if he did.

"No. They mean well. I just nod and smile."

The atmosphere was of nervous excitement in the first few days, descending into a mixture of quiet panic and settled satisfaction, depending how the ideas and words were flowing for the writers. Some wrote longhand and others used laptops; some worked in their rooms, some in the café, the bookshop, the lounge. We had created a booking system for the soundproof rooms and ran a shuttle service to the public library.

One of the older women looked up from her notebook on a café table and caught my eye. I walked over. "Hi Lillian, how is it going?" Lillian intrigued me: she contrasted with her group, frowsy, unconcerned with her appearance. Whereas the others all wore makeup and coordinated clothes, Lillian was just as likely to appear in sweat pants with hair un-brushed, as now.

"It's not going as I expected."

"What did you expect?"

"Well, you know, I'm a planner. But I sat the first day, and the second, and I didn't come up with a plan. So I had to just start. I have no idea where it's going. Actually it's kind of exhilarating."

"How many words are you up to now?"

"It's hard to say. I counted a page and it was 340 words. 12 pages, so around 4,000. I'll need to pick up the pace, it's day five."

"Have you written a novel before?"

"No. A lifelong dream."

This was new for me, as well. I wasn't sure of the etiquette. "Do you want people to read it, or not? Would you let me read it?"

I watched her closely to gauge her response, but it was clear: she beamed. "Would you?" She handed me the book.

I turned to the first page. It was like being transported into her life, her past; as I stepped into the story of courtship I guessed I was reading a real experience, not fiction. It was the late 1960s, the heroine was a teenage girl; the boy was awkward, soft, and she loved him. I had noticed the ring still on her finger, but she had come here alone – had her husband died? Was this boy on the page him, or someone earlier? I felt my mind work on two levels as I turned the pages, coming too quickly to the hanging end. Her eyes were on my face as I finished.

"It's lovely. Is it . . . autobiographical?"

She nodded. "Unoriginal, huh?"

"Not at all. Every person's experience is different." I wanted to ask about her current situation, but feared intruding. "I'd like to read more, as it comes."

She smiled, and the smile widened. "Thank you."

"How does it work, actually, the challenge? How do they assess whether you've got there or not?"

"If you have it in a word processor you can send it to them and they do a count. I wasn't going to bother, I can't type, I'm slow enough at writing."

"But someone else could type it for you."

"Who?"

"Do you want me to find you someone? A typist?"

"Well sure."

It turned out there were a lot of takers for the typing service. At $20 an hour it worked out just a couple of hundred dollars or so to get a whole 50,000 word novel typed. They numbered and titled the pages and used the fax machine each night to send that day's pages away. By the next night they had a word count and a printed copy. This also made sharing their manuscripts easy, and the mood of mutual encouragement increased. There were those who still kept their work to themselves, but I saw some of these looking over at the laughing, hugging groups with longing.

One night the core large group were heading to Theo's for dinner. The deal was they could pick their night, just booking by 10 a.m. on the day – with partners this group was nearly 30 people. I called Theo to make sure he could handle this number and heard myself offering to help.

"There'll be hardly anyone here, anyway, Cathy can handle things."

I called a bus company and herded them out onto the street at the right time. There were a couple of habitual stragglers, but I had told them we were meeting fifteen minutes earlier and they were there with the rest.

Arthur Hollis had taken a liking to Brian, asking him about his plans and aspirations, offering advice. Brian seemed to like him, too, and they were still deep in conversation in the bookshop when nearly everyone else was on board.

Celia stood impatient at the door. "Arthur, are you coming?" Brian gave him a friendly wave goodbye.

We arrived at my old front door, standing wide open with an umbrella stand propping it against the light Nor' west wind. The back door must be open, I could feel the breeze flowing through. Theo had placed some tables on the lawn and offered aperitifs outside while they looked at menus. There was a call for champagne and the already jovial mood rose further.

When I could get them to focus I took their orders and went into the kitchen. Theo looked over my shoulder to see if anyone was watching and wrapped his arms around me. "You are a god-send. Why didn't I see it before?" He kissed me on the lips and I sank into it, having to force myself to come up for air, let go before he did.

"Careful." I said, lightly. "You'll turn my head."

"Well, what if I want to?" His voice was slightly strained. I narrowed my eyes, trying to judge his mood, wanting him to mean it so much I didn't trust my senses.

"Well, then, I . . ." I stared into his eyes. The moment lengthened. His face was smiling, then serious. "I . . ."

"Hey, what's happening?" Theo was facing the window. His eyes shifted to look past my shoulder; he frowned, then moved suddenly towards the door.

I turned to see a table tipping over and one of my writers reeling backwards across the lawn. A brawl had broken out.

36

It was hard to see at first what was happening. The round wooden table was on its side and several glasses were scattered on the grass. Four or five people hid the scrambling couple of fighters from view; I had to push them aside to get in and help Theo, who must have run around them.

The fighters were tumbling over and over, rolling from one side to the other, the woman tearing at the man's hair, he snarling and pulling at her shoulders, trying to loosen her grip.

Theo kicked a glass out of the way just a moment before they would have rolled on it. He seemed at a loss as to how to intervene. I would have to do it. It would help if I could call out their names, but with their faces hidden by each other I hadn't yet worked out who they were.

"Stop!" I called, in the voice that had saved my children from traffic on several occasions over the years. The action slowed for a moment, then accelerated again. "I said STOP!" I waded in, stepping between the tangled legs and grabbing at the two uppermost elbows. A split second later I was sprawled on top of them. Someone gasped. I felt fingernails rake my bare right arm and screamed. That did it, and the fused pair broke open, leaving me lying between them, nursing my bloody limb. "What the hell was that about?"

Theo seized the man and pulled him up; he was thin and wiry, dressed in shades of leprechaun green. One of the other women gripped my sharp-finger nailed assailant – Lillian – and helped her to her feet. Her top was torn from the shoulder, barely decent. Mr Hollis leaned down towards me, his hand held out. "Are you all right?"

"No," I sobbed. "I'm bleeding."

"Come on, Celia, bring your bag. We'll take care of you."

I found myself sitting in the bathroom I still technically owned half of, my arm on a towel, disinfectant being dabbed into my wound.

"Does it need stitches? There's a lot of blood." Arthur's voice was shaking.

"No, I don't think so. It's running from the dew on the grass. It'll clean up fine." Celia seemed so pale and thin next to her husband but she was definitely cooler in a crisis

"What happened?"

"They were arguing, then they were fighting. It took us all by surprise."

"What were they arguing about?"

"Word counts."

"Word counts!"

"Julian was bragging about his 25,000 words. Lillian told him to shut up, she couldn't stand it. She's only at 6,000, you know. He said it wasn't his fault if she wasn't up to it, and she called him a one-dimensional faggot. I'm not sure who moved first."

This was something I hadn't expected. "I knew tensions were high, but . . ."

They both nodded. "Also I think she likes him," said Celia. "There may be more to it than was said."

"What do I do now?" I thought through the hotel layout. "They're just down the corridor from each other.

Celia shrugged. It was Arthur who answered. "Well, I don't know about women, but he's a man, he's probably over it now the fight's over. He'll be all right."

Celia and I looked at each other. A woman scorned might just stoop to poison in the breakfast-tray orange juice. I would need to have a word with her. Maybe applying a little guilt about my arm would help.

We went out to the restaurant where the rest of the group were now seated. Julian was holding an ice pack to his cheek; Lillian was wearing a top I recognised as one of Rachel's. They had their backs to each other but the mood in the room was still wary. Fortunately the first entrees were on their way. Hunger and alcohol had probably fuelled the situation. I gestured to two empty chairs for Celia and Arthur. "Thank you so much," then stepped through to the kitchen where Theo was leaning against the oven, shaking with laughter.

"You think it's funny?"

"It's partly the shock. But yes, I think we'll be telling this story for a while to come. 'Writers in restaurant brawl' I might even leak it myself, it would be good for business."

"How?"

"Human interest, restaurant mentioned. All publicity is good publicity." He raised an eyebrow and surprised me by grabbing me around the waist. "Now what was I saying when we were interrupted?" And he kissed me, like we were kids.

I thought I should have been happy, but I moved through the evening with a sense of unreality. I served the food, chatted to my writers and their partners, answered questions about my link to the restaurant, dimly observing fascination when they realised the connection between Theo and me. My answers to their questions set up a buzz of gossip; I smiled but I was not at ease, not content, not satisfied. Something needed to be said.

I bundled the last group into a taxi and gave the direction to the driver, then turned and looked back at the house. I always loved this place. Through my own restlessness and even dissatisfaction, through my declared wish to own less, travel light through life, this house has always pulled me. It was a home for my family. My ambivalence towards it was perfectly consistent with my ambivalence to my relationships. I love being loved and I love being alone and I've never found the balance point, always been on one side of happiness or the other.

That's why I created failure, of course. Half of me wanted Theo to reject me so I could be alone. In either situation, half of me was unsatisfied.

As I looked up at the house, I knew I didn't need Theo, I just wanted him. Half the time. It seemed an impossible contradiction, but I would be true to myself and ask for it.

He was waiting when I opened the front door and went back inside.

"Can you stay?"

"Maybe." I looked straight at him, the illusions of need and fear of rejection pushed aside. I really do love him, at least for now. "I'd like to stay."

"But?"

"But I'd like to get some things said. I don't like this confusion, this ambiguity."

"Well?" he said, when the pause got too much for him.

I took his hand. "Come and sit down."

The romance was gone now, the moment for action in the heat of passion was past. He looked slightly annoyed.

I gazed around me, taking my time. "It's great what you've done here."

"Thank you."

"It's such a relief for me to see you do something for yourself."

"Relief?"

"I felt so guilty, through our whole marriage – well, at least after Rachel was born."

"Rachel? Why?"

"Don't you remember? You weren't sure about having children. I persuaded you. I promised it wouldn't change our lives too much. But it did."

"But you know the way I felt about it changed as soon as I saw her! You were right. I wouldn't have not had her, or Brian, for the world. You know that!" He was emphatic, but also pleading.

"That doesn't change the fact that I broke my promise. Our lives did change."

"For the better!"

"It was still a promise."

"I don't know what you're getting at."

"I always got what I wanted, and sometimes at the expense of you getting what you wanted. I think that's what went wrong."

"Do we need to go into this now? It's in the past."

"Is it?"

"Yes. What do you mean?"

"I mean, here we are. On the brink of spending another night together. Our relationship isn't over, but if it's going to stay in this half-way, moment-to-moment state, I don't want it."

Theo rolled his eyes. "Here we go. It's always about what you want!"

"That's just it! I know what I want, I'll stand up for it. I want you to stand up for what you want, I can't keep feeling guilty about it."

"You? Feel guilty?"

"Of course I do. Did. I won't any more. Here's what I want, laid out in the open. I want you to have your life, and me to have mine. I want you to be responsible for your happiness, and me to be responsible for mine."

Theo's face was shadowed, angry.

I sighed. "I'm not saying . . . oh, I don't know! I love you, but I can't make you happy. Only you can do that. I'll do anything I can to support you, but you need to tell me what. I'm exhausted trying to read your mind."

He leaned onto the arm of a chair, half sitting, and looked at the ground. His mouth twitched sideways. I watched him, fascinated. "So what are you asking for, how would it work? You'd move back here, what?"

"No. I have the hotel. That's where I live, that's where I spend my time. And it's full time. We may not have much time together, I don't know even how many nights we'll spend together. But I want our relationship formal, absolute. I only want you."

He looked up, with an expression I remembered from our first night together, our first moment of commitment. I reached out for him, put my hand on his cheek. My eyes closed and I swallowed. My body moved closer to his, I felt my breast brush his arm. Hold on. I told myself. We need to resolve this.

"Can we do that? I live my life and you live your life and we have this wonderful thing between us. Can we?" The hairs on my arms were standing on end, I imagined sparks coming off them. I felt Theo's breath on my face, rapid. I didn't know how long I could keep my hands off him. "Please, Theo, what do you want?"

"Right now? To go to bed."

"I mean . . ."

"I know. I think so. Can we talk about it in the morning?"

I felt my logical mind go at that moment, just let go, give up. There was peace and vibrant tension in my heart. "Yeah. We'll talk about it . . . in the morning."

I opened my eyes to sun streaming in the window, the smell of toast under my nose. A wide smile broke across my face. "Good morning." I took a piece, buttered it, picked up a coffee cup and sipped.

"Okay," Theo said, "so let me get this straight. We both have our lives, our jobs, you at the hotel, me here."

"Or wherever you want to be."

"Okay. And we keep money separate?"

"Probably."

"But we're together, a couple, sleeping together, committed, just . . ?"

"I don't know exactly how the logistics will work out. If we want to be together, we'll work it out. And I really want us to be together. So it's up to you." Despite the vulnerability of the question, I felt strong, knowing what I wanted and stating it clearly.

He dropped his lashes, spread butter on a piece of toast. "And would it be like it was last night?" His voice was coy, teasing.

"Maybe. If you're good."

"Oh I'm always good. When I want to be."

I kicked him through the duvet. "So that would be a 'yes'?"

"I guess so."

"Bastard. That's not good enough. I want a clear yes or a clear no. Offer expires in 60 seconds."

He looked at his watch. I saw his lips move as he counted down. I knew he was messing with me but my heart sped up anyway.

I looked round his arm. "Come on! Five, four, running out . . !"

"Okay. Yes."

That infuriating smile. I so loved it. I threw my arms around his neck, bit my lip and squeezed my eyes tightly shut. "I love you so much. I've missed you so much."

His arms tightened around me.

37

Okay, I could handle anything. Theo was coming over that night after the restaurant closed, to stay here with me until he needed to be back there tomorrow. I closed my eyes and shuddered like he was here with me now.

Julian and Lillian had made up – and also both apologised profusely to me – and there was a cool truce between them; they were part of the same small group, the single writers who had come on their own. There were seven of them sitting together this morning. I wondered who was missing: ah, Helena. Was she at dinner last night? She was a quiet, nervous woman. Conflict probably wouldn't be her favourite thing. I made a mental note to check up on her later.

The next thing was to see off a group of partners who were going sightseeing this morning. They varied in their ability to occupy themselves while their other halves were writing, so Brian had offered this extra day. They would go to Sumner, walk on the beach, have lunch in a café then take in the Lyttelton shops before returning.

Brian was holding Matt while their loose congregation came to order. Someone went back for a sunhat. Someone asked about sunscreen and Brian told them there was a dispenser in the front of the minivan – his idea, after a couple of cases of sunburn. Finally he raised an eyebrow at me and we began a pincer herding movement towards the doors. There was scuffle or two over the best seats; I took Matt and Brian got in next to the driver.

"Are we ready? Then let's go!"

I hugged Matt to me as they drove away. He patted my face. "Granddad's coming later," I whispered. We both beamed.

I found Liberty, who was working on the next major event. We were nine days into November and the wedding was rapidly approaching. I had asked Liberty to talk to Sharon about the details – Sharon and I were fine talking about day-to-day matters of the hotel but the Roger subject was still a little delicate.

Liberty pointed around the room as she described the use of space. "We'll move the sofas out, set up chairs facing the Goddess Diana statue – it makes a logical focal point on this axis."

"How many guests?"

"They've sent out 150 invitations. Sharon's got her eye on promotion for the hotel as well as the celebration. I'm calculating around 100-110. We'll have ten rows of 12 chairs, 6 on either side of the aisle. It will work. Then we've ordered larger round table tops for the café tables, and we'll spread them out into the whole area once the seating for the service has been broken up."

I nodded. "Fine. That should work."

"What about the guests, though? The hotel guests. What can we say to them?"

"I've explained, the public areas won't be available that day, at least on the ground floor. There's still the second floor lounge and the soundproof rooms. I'm a little nervous, though. The wedding is only three days from their deadline. Tension is already building. I'm worried . . ."

"You're worried there'll be a scene, what?"

"Nothing. It doesn't matter. I'm sure it'll be fine." No point trying to anticipate it. Whatever happened would happen. I rubbed the slowly healing scars on my arm.

"There's one more thing I wanted to ask you." Liberty's nose was wrinkled.

"What is it?"

"You know Sharon wants someone to go with her to choose a dress."

"Yes, I thought you went on Friday."

"We did. It didn't go well. I'm not sure . . . she kept saying things like 'you could wear this, you're young, I'd just look silly.' We're supposed to go again today, but I don't think it will be any different. I think it would be better if someone, you know, nearer her age went with her."

I bridled. Nearer her age. I was nearer Liberty's age than Sharon's. But she had a point, I was also nearer 70 than Liberty was. "Oh, God."

"I know you don't want to, but please? I'll take Matt and go buy the white ribbon for the chairs."

I hesitated, then through the awkwardness came the memory of my night with Theo, our resolution. It was time I put this behind me. My face cracked into a sudden smile. I could do anything today.

"Okay. Take Matt while I go find my jacket. What time is Sharon arriving? You don't think she'll mind."

"Eleven o'clock. You're meeting her at Ballantynes, so she won't be able to complain."

I wasn't convinced, but I was sure I could work it out. Maybe I'd even tell her about Theo and me. We could bond over our happy loves.

We met at the glove counter. Liberty suggested starting here, tentatively selecting these, with the decision to be finalised once the outfit was chosen.

I'm not great with clothes. I like to dress simply, my happiest clothing times being when I have been slim and looked good in anything. I like simple lines – but of course, these only work when the body cooperates with a streamlined silhouette. I gazed into space as I waited for Sharon. What would she look good in? Her everyday look was classic pleated trousers and twin sets. And what colours were suitable for a 70 year old's second wedding? I laughed. Anything she damn well likes.

"Lisa!"

I turned towards the sound of Sharon's voice. "I asked Liberty if I could come instead of her. It's a long time since I've had a day in the shops." The white lie came easily. When did I learn to do that? I'd heard of the hotelier's curse. 'Sorry, the previous occupants were late checking out, your room will be ready as soon as possible.' 'As soon as one of the front rooms becomes available, we'll let you know, have you moved.' 'Yes, luggage left here is watched at all times.' Little fibs to smooth things over. I felt a twinge of unease.

"Well, this will be fun." She tried to smile but her face was grim.

I linked my arm through hers. "I think it will. And I've got some news."

She turned in my grip, responding to my warmth. "What?"

"Theo and I have made up. It's all okay!"

She didn't respond as I expected, pulling further away. "Are you telling me you'll be leaving the hotel?"

I was aghast. "No! No, that's not what I meant at all!"

She stretched her forehead sceptically.

"We'll work it out. For now he'll come to me, to stay. If that's all right. You know I love my job."

"Well, let's discuss it later. We're looking at gloves."

I nodded, sighed quietly. Perhaps this was not such a good idea after all.

She pulled on the second of a pair of wrist gloves, short, white, with a flared detail at the back. She held out both hands, palm down. They were fine, but I preferred the elegance of the much longer gloves. It was a few moments before I realised she was not looking at her hands any more. Her eyes were on the floor, and they were glistening.

"Sharon?"

"I'm sorry. That was horrible. Of course I'm happy things have worked out with Theo. I know you wanted it very much. Congratulations. I'm sorry I was such a cow."

"Sharon? What . . ?"

"I just wish someone would be happy for me." She tore off the gloves and flung them on the counter, turning away quickly and heading for the exit. I followed, catching her as the slow automatic door caused her to pause.

"Sharon?"

She held a hand out and shook her head. We walked at a rapid pace towards the river. Cashel Street seemed long and crowded, we had to push through a bustle outside the Irish Pub before breaking into clear space as we crossed the road. The Bridge of Remembrance was empty; Sharon veered suddenly to the left and leaned out over the river, watching her pallid reflection in the geometric-patterned water.

"I wish someone would be happy for me."

"You have friends, your business partners, surely they . . ."

"They think I'm making a fool of myself, marrying someone so many years younger."

"Maybe they're just jealous."

"Just jealous! Don't you know how poisonous jealousy is? Those friendships may not recover; at my age new friends don't come along that easily, and I'm not naïve enough to think Roger is going to meet all my emotional needs. I can't do without them now. And I so wanted to be happy."

Her shoulders shook. I patted her awkwardly, then was overwhelmed by her grief; I pulled her to me in a full hug. "It's okay. You'll be okay."

She clung to me and sobbed for 30 seconds, a minute, then I felt the shaking subside. A moment later she pulled away, hid her face in the activity of searching her bag for a tissue.

"I'm sorry I haven't been more supportive."

"You thought I was an old crone who had bewitched Roger from you – I understand that. Can't accept it, like I don't really think of the face in the mirror as mine, but at one level I understand."

I shrugged apologetically.

"But now you're happy again with Theo, could you be happy for me?" Her eyes lifted hopefully. She twisted her handkerchief into a thin line.

"Yes, I could. I was jealous when Roger dumped me for you, but it was only pride, I was only playing while I waited for Theo. Anyway, that's history now, so yeah! I'll be happy for you and you be happy for me."

We shook hands. She smiled. "And maybe my friends will come around in the end."

"Sure. Let's find you something stunning to wear."

We wandered back towards Ballantynes. "You've no idea how beautiful he was when I met him." Her voice was slow and dreamy, remembering.

"Tell me."

"He was twenty five, idealistic, with this glowing love for historic architecture. We had a project we were doing – Somerset House, you know. It was run down, derelict, we got it for next to nothing in that property slump in the late '80s. I knew it was going to be a huge job to renovate, but I fell in love with it. Everybody said I was mad, and then there he was, this miracle! Standing beside me and seeing the same vision I did. At first I thought this must be what it would be like to have a son, but pretty soon I realised that wasn't what it was. I was embarrassed to be having the thoughts I was having. I didn't want anyone to know. So I started avoiding him, and that's when he told me. He got more and more upset over a period of a few weeks then there was this, wow! spectacular display of emotion: despair, agony. He told me he loved me. God, look at me, I'm almost crying now! It was like everything fell into place."

"But you didn't marry then."

"I wish we had. He begged me. I refused. I made him keep it a secret. It was a huge mistake – the secrecy, I mean. It poisoned it. He accused me of being ashamed of him, but I wasn't, I was ashamed of myself."

"And now your friends . . ."

"Exactly. This reaction is exactly what I feared 17 years ago. There's no point wishing I'd faced it then, but I do wish I had. True friends would have accepted it. And if I'd lost some then, I could have made more. It's not so easy at 70."

"You say that, but are you sure?" I squeezed her arm and she smiled.

"Well, maybe it is possible."

We looked through the first rack of dresses together, discussing each possibility. Once I thought I was on her wavelength we separated, holding up the occasional outfit for a nod or a shake of the head. She took five into the changing room. I stood outside.

"I'm so pleased you're having the wedding at the hotel."

"But you weren't initially."

"That's true. But that's before I understood it. It's an honour, that you think it's special enough to celebrate your marriage there."

"Well, you know Roger loves it too. And it's not just the architecture, it's the atmosphere. It's unique."

"You really think so?"

"Sure. You've found your metier, your purpose."

"I'm just a hotel manager."

Sharon opened the door, wearing a raw silk apricot pencil skirt and short jacket. "You're not 'just a hotel manager'. You put your soul into it. And a hotel with a soul is a rare thing." She held out her arms and looked down at the suit. "What do you think? It's a little big, but we might be onto something."

I found her a size 8 and it was perfect. "Shoes?"

"I've got some, those white heels."

"Then just the gloves." The short pair which had seemed arbitrary and a bit pointless earlier in the morning now were the natural completion of the outfit. "I think you're ready to go."

She sighed happily. Her face was glowing. "I think I am."

38

My purpose. My metier. I walked back into the hotel feeling very grounded, very sure of myself. I stood near the entrance and looked around. There was a feeling of calm. Liberty was playing with Matt at the reception desk, holding out toys for him to reach for and grab, then let go of again as the next one presented. Occasionally his laughter chirped through the room, followed by Liberty's low chuckle.

Three women were sitting together in the café and at the library/bookshop end of the room Sarah was holding a creative writing session. I noticed Lillian amongst the group, relaxed and smiling. Sarah had obviously helped her unblock and she was scribbling fast into her notebook.

It was hard to say what Sarah did. I'd sat in on one of her sessions once. I'm no writer, but I wanted to know what happened, why the guests were raving. It was very subtle. She spoke for only a few minutes, pulled out of her leather satchel an odd assortment of items: images from a Salvador Dali calendar, a box of magnetic words, a candle which she lit at the beginning of the session with discreet ceremony, and softly blew out at the end, the signal for the group to look up, thank her and drift away.

She pulled books from the shelf behind her, apparently at random, opening one to a page near the end and handing it to one of the group as she passed, no eye contact, no words. The recipient looked at the page, then up at her, amazed, taking a few seconds before closing his mouth and beginning to type at double speed. She just seemed to allow creativity, or more actively, to expect it. And it came, for everyone.

I paused at the back of the group and she glided over to me.

"How are you?" I whispered.

"It's going well. We're having fun."

There was an extreme stillness over the group.

I squeezed her arm. "Thank you. So much."

"It's you. All you."

I shook my head.

"A team effort, then."

It seemed there was nothing for me to do. I closed my eyes and felt the hotel around me, rooms and guests in rooms, cleaners with their muted bustle. I decided to take a tour through, open my eyes and see what needed doing. The courtyard was in serene order. I glanced into the kitchen; everything under control. Liberty smiled as I passed and I swung the door into the main building. The guest rooms were all occupied so I only looked into the ones where the maids were working, dropping a few words of thanks. All was well. The upstairs lounge hadn't been attended to yet. I straightened the magazines on the table and stepped out onto the veranda, bringing the scattered cane chairs back into their sets of four to each low table. I took the bird's eye view over the courtyard, feeling the low hum of life rise up to me.

Julian was reading in a corner.

"Not writing today?"

"I've already done my 3,000 words, I'm just mulling, letting tomorrow's scenes shape themselves in my head." His face was smug. I could see why Lillian went for him.

"You're making friends amongst the group?"

His eyebrows raised. "It takes a while for me to really get to know someone. It's only a month, I don't really expect to . . ." His face became curious. "Do you think I could?"

"Don't ask me. I just assume people are already my friends. Maybe it's a New Zealand thing, but unless we've actually come to . . ." Oops. Come to blows, I was going to say, but that wouldn't be tactful. "Unless there's a very clear reason why not, everyone's my friend."

"I don't find it so easy to talk to people. But you seem to. How do you do it?"

"I don't know, I just . . ." His face was eager. I thought for a moment before answering. What did I do? I just liked people. "I'm interested. If in doubt, I let them talk, ask them questions – not too many questions," I amended, hurriedly, as I saw him begin to take notes. "Just opening questions, and let them talk."

He sighed. "You make it sound so simple."

I shrugged and smiled.

"Can I practice on you?"

"Sure, sounds like fun."

"Hello, I'm Julian."

"I'm Lisa."

"And why are you here, Lisa?" Unconventional, a bit blunt, but I could make something of it. I was thinking how to answer, just about ready to speak when he went on. "I'm here for the Novel Writing Challenge. It's going really well, at this rate I'll be finished 10 days ahead of the deadline. I don't think the others are finding it so . . ."

I put up my hand. "What happened to letting me talk?"

"You didn't answer me. I don't like silence."

"Well, maybe stretch your tolerance of it. Count to yourself, if that helps – not out loud. Try counting to fifty and see if people start talking by then. Being okay with silence can be very powerful."

He looked unconvinced. "Well, I'll try it."

"Shall we go again?"

"And why are you here, Lisa?"

"I'm the manager of the hotel, in fact, it was my idea, to have a hotel for writers." A pause. No response. "That's great, Julian. You can talk now, ask me another question if you like."

"Like what?"

"Well, I just said I had the idea to have a hotel for writers. Ask me a question about that."

"Well, Lisa, how did you get the idea to have a hotel for writers?"

I was a little distracted seeing his lips form the numbers as he counted silently to himself, but then I considered the question and smiled. This brought back the happy side of the project. If the hotel was my purpose, the idea itself was inspiration. "I just knew it was something I wanted to do. I was sitting with my journal after a completed project and wondered what I wanted to do next. Immediately I knew I wanted to renovate a hotel, a beautiful old building. I don't know when I knew it would be for writers, but once I realised it, it seemed like that had been the idea all along."

Julian frowned, I could almost hear him thinking what to ask next. "And what did you do then?"

"Good question! Leading, wide open. Great work!"

He blushed. I suspected he was counting again, but it was less obvious this time. Again I considered the question. I liked having someone to talk to, most of my conversations these days were fast, efficient, an exchange of detail. I relaxed back into my chair. "You know, you're great company."

The blush turned into a beam.

It was eleven when I finally made it upstairs that night. I had been hanging around doing paperwork to fill in the nervous hours 'till I could expect Theo. I started the water running for a bath and poured in some lavender oil. I felt nervously bridal. Our first night after our recommitment. I was glad Sharon was in the loop now, and happy about it. It was bad enough feeling like I had to sneak Theo past Brian and Liberty.

If things went well tonight I'd tell them tomorrow; until I was sure I didn't want to risk any yo-yo revelations in the event it didn't work out. I wouldn't even think that. We were properly on, I was sure.

I heard Matt crying and Brian shushing him. I would have to bite my tongue tonight. Oh, for sound-proofing! Now that was an idea. There was a little sofa in each of the writing rooms, and they had locks . . . No, too weird. I'd bring Theo to my room . . . as I sank into the hot water I disappeared into a full shag-fantasy. My eyes sprang open. Okay, breathe, relax. He'll be here soon.

Life slipped into an easy rhythm. I had a sense of moving slower, gliding through my days. Theo spent every night at the hotel, slipping into my bed any time after 11 and murmuring in his dreams as I got up and dressed for my day around 6. I wasn't getting enough sleep but I was very happy. I sang as I helped out in the kitchen or worked as a waitress for breakfast in the café. I loved the smiles of the guests as they commented how blissful I seemed. Once breakfast was over I checked on the maids, straightened the shelves in the bookshop, chatted to the increasing number of local patrons who came in to browse.

A week before I had had the idea to put my old sandwich board outside "Lisa's Bookshop" and email out to my list of regulars – there were lots who had been disappointed when I had closed down. It felt great reconnecting with some of them as they sought me out here. In the shame of failure I had forgotten how I loved the shop, the books, the customers, the whole way of life. There had been time to read then, as people browsed. I never had time to read any more. Well, that was something I could change.

As I moved amongst the writing guests now I gently asked them if they would let me look at what they had written. Some eagerly pushed a sheaf of pages into my hand; others were shyer, giving me just one page at first and watching for my reaction. It took a while to get used to the unpolished aspect of first draft work, but after a day or two I found I could enter the flow of the story, suspending my critic, and feel my way into the hearts of the guests, the writers. I always found something positive to say, something which genuinely touched me or made me laugh. I watched their faces blossom into smiles and found myself sought after, pages left on my desk, turning around at any moment to find a hopeful face close to mine, a new chapter flapping against my busy hands.

"I just need to finish this, Julian, then I'd love to read what you've written. Where can I find you?"

At first there was lots of nervous interjection and disclaiming as I read, the author would watch me, apologise for errors, imagined and real. I learned to look up, straight into their eyes with a reassuring expression, perhaps hold out my hand to stop them speaking. "It's fine, it's all fine. I know it's not finished yet, not polished. I'm enjoying it."

And I found I did. No matter how clichéd or light or superficial, I found the heart of the writer in their writing. Just sometimes you had to dig a little deeper. I had compassion for them. They were looking for themselves among their words.

Several of the guests were blogging their experiences as well, of writing, and of being at the hotel. They created links back to the hotel web-site and over the days the number of hits snowballed, with comments coming in from other NaNoWriMo bloggers around the world. Julian told me about Google alerts and I set them up for myself, finding many other relevant blogs and adding comments. It was so easy, so much fun to feel myself part of this community; and a divine side-effect was the number of hits to the hotel web-site were ballooning, with bookings into next year and emails from fascinating people who loved the idea of a hotel where they could write. By the 24th we were already booked out for next November. Sharon was delighted, and I was wildly proud.

39

It was the 26th; the wedding was tomorrow. Theo would close his restaurant for lunch so he could take Matt for most of the day; Liberty was managing the event, wound up and nervous, and Brian would be wonderful running unexpected errands and keeping a cool head.

Tonight we had a pre-wedding party for the guests, all of whom had got to know Sharon, at least by sight, over the last 26 days. Tomorrow they would be farmed out around the city, so we wanted them to have tonight to feel involved.

There was champagne and finger food. Brian had found a band which played slow jazz and moody torch music, with a wonderful, soulful singer. They set up in a corner of the bookshop and the haunting notes filled the space. Roger and Sharon stood together surrounded by a knot of well-wishers. Sharon smiled over at me, radiant. I felt proud that I had helped her to this point.

I moved through the room with trays of food, being drawn into conversation wherever I went; I had learned to gracefully slide through most of them, smiling a warm acknowledgement and moving on. Occasionally I would find myself with a follower, someone determined to get my attention. Then I handed my tray to Brian or to Liberty and gave them five minutes of full absorption, finishing with a hand on their arm, another smile, an apology, and went back to my rounds.

The party was winding down. Pretty soon the band would pack up and I could go to bed. I was tired from lots of short nights, lots of conversation and very little time to myself over the last few weeks. I was stretching, yawning when Sharon appeared at my side. "Hi. Had a good time?" I was confident, I knew she had.

"Yes." She sounded distracted. "Can I talk to you? I need to discuss something with you, but I don't want to spoil tomorrow."

"Spoil it?"

"That's not what I mean, I just . . ." She was impatient. "Roger and I have made a decision, and it's going . . . well, mostly it will impact on you."

I sat down on the arm of a leather sofa. Sharon wasn't meeting my eye and there was a sick, guilty expression on her face. She looked around to make sure no-one was listening.

"Sharon, for goodness' sake, what is it? You're scaring me."

Still she hesitated.

"Do we need to do this in the office?" I noticed my breathing was shallower, my voice tight like something was wound around my chest, squeezing.

"Possibly." But instead she just pulled me off into the corner a little more and stood uncomfortably close to me as she talked low. "The last thing I want is to hurt you. You've been a God-send these last months, and I've loved watching you blossom – you've become such a good friend."

"Sharon, say it!"

"Roger and I have decided to take a year off, go travelling. It's been a dream of his for a long time, and I have always had the hotels, I've done short trips, but only a few weeks. He's never even been to Italy, for goodness sake! He's an architect, a brilliant architect and he's never been to Italy."

I felt theoretical sympathy for Roger, but was more interested in what was coming next. "And?"

"You know I leveraged very highly to buy the hotel – I used all the equity I have to buy it, to do it up."

Another band tightened around my chest. "We're doing well. Better than projected."

"And we knew that things would be a stretch for the first few years."

"That was all built into the plan. Things are going really well, we're ahead of schedule."

"But that was all decided before Roger and I got engaged. Before we thought about this year of freedom. I bought it mostly as a project for Roger, because he loved it so much, but now that part is over."

"All right, Sharon. What are you saying?"

"I'm saying we're going to sell it. I'm sorry." She met my gaze now, eyes pleading.

"Sell the hotel? But what . . ." I felt like I had been hit by a truck.

"I had meant to support it for much longer, I'm sorry. But things change."

"But . . . what will happen? Will the new owner . . ?" What was I asking? Will the new owner keep me on? Will it be the same?

"I can't answer your questions. I don't know. It depends what offers we get."

"But you said! You said this was my purpose. You can't just let it go."

"I know what this means for you, the effect on you. I wish that part of it could be different. I had to tell you before the wedding, it has been weighing on my conscience since we decided. Please, can't we enjoy tomorrow, and talk again when Roger and I get back from honeymoon. Please?"

I turned away from her to find Brian watching me. His expression told me what my own was like; I faked a smile, gave him a wave and found my bed.

40

Usually I fall asleep as my head hits the pillow, but not tonight. It was only ten minutes later that Theo joined me; I was tossing in frustration. He lay down, sturdy and solid. I slid across the bed to cling to him.

"What is it?"

"Sharon's going to sell the hotel!"

His arms tightened around me. I squeezed my eyes tight. "So what's going to happen?"

"I don't know! I can't lose this place now. It's who I am."

Many years of training paid off now as Theo bit back his instinctive solution-finding and waited for me to speak again.

"I don't know if a new owner would want me as manager. Maybe they would, I've made it a huge success in a very short space of time. But I don't think Sharon will be picky, and there can't be many people out there who would want it. They might have their own manager. They might want to manage it themselves. They might not even want to stay with the theme, it might become a generic, soulless . . ." My voice disappeared into sobs of frustration.

Theo squeezed me gently again. "You could always come home."

"But this is who I am now. I'm nothing without this place."

I felt his silent disagreement.

"And all those bookings for next year. All the guests I've got to know this last month. I'm even appearing in blogs, becoming a minor celebrity. I didn't expect that but I . . . like it." My voice grew small. I wasn't sure what Theo would think of this, I felt silly admitting it.

He laughed quietly. "Did you think that would be a surprise? I know you've put a lot into this place, but even if you couldn't continue here, you could do it again. Would you want to?"

Do it again. "You mean, if they sell here and I lose my job, would I start again?"

"Yeah. Could you do it again? Or has this been a fluke, a one-off?"

"No. I'm sure I could do it again. I might even enjoy it more – doing it the first time was a bit scary, and I didn't have . . . you, I was worried I'd never have you again." I burrowed my face into his chest. He kissed the top of my head.

"So whatever happens, it won't be the end of the world?"

I felt a little smile whisper at the corners of my mouth. "No. I think I'll be able to go on, somehow, whatever. Thanks, Theo. I love you."

Matt slept late in the morning so Theo helped with breakfast. A bus was taking all the guests who wanted to go through the mountains for the day, a quick stop at Arthur's Pass and lunch in the Café de Paris in Hokitika. Then they would come back for dinner at Theo's. The wedding was at eleven with lunch afterwards. Sharon and Roger were leaving for the airport at four and I expected the wedding guests to clear soon after. With luck it would be a quiet evening.

Sharon was using my room to dress and make up. She arrived at 8:30, charged with nerves. I waved as she crossed the courtyard and once the bus left I went up to check on her. I found Liberty coming out of my room. "She's in the bath," she whispered. "I thought she needed to calm down. Can you wait here in case she comes out? I need to show the quartet where to set up."

I sat on the edge of my bed, made up with hotel crispness. I had cleared my dressing table; Sharon's make-up bag sat on it. To give myself something to do I opened it and arranged the contents in front of the mirror. It was a long time since I had lingered in front of my reflection. I looked young and healthy; my smile was relaxed and I had a glow about me. The threat of last night, of losing the hotel, had burned through, leaving me stronger. I sat on the low stool and took my hairbrush from the drawer.

The door opened and I stood to greet Sharon.

"I was sick, I'm so nervous. My toothbrush is in my suitcase downstairs."

"You sit down. I'll get it for you. Do you want the whole bag?"

"No, just open it. The toilet bag is near the top."

"Let me get you a glass of water." I put it in her hand. "You're shaking."

"I'll . . . I'll be okay. I'm just nervous."

I was torn. She didn't look good at all, but maybe she was right, she just needed to freshen up and she'd be fine.

"Go, please. I think there's some Rescue Remedy in my sponge bag as well. That will help."

"I'll be back as fast as I can."

She nodded, a tiny movement. Her knuckles formed sharp corners as she gripped the bed.

Liberty caught up with me as I bounded back up the stairs. "How is she?"

"Not great. I think maybe we should call a doctor."

"Not really!"

"I don't know."

We opened the door. "Call 111." Sharon had collapsed onto the floor.

She came round before the ambulance arrived. "Don't tell Roger," were the first words out of her mouth even before her eyes were fully open.

I helped her up onto the bed. She was pale and her pulse was weak and fluttering.

"Don't tell him."

"I'll have to tell him. The wedding . . ."

"I'm still getting married today." Her lips locked together after she said it. I didn't want to upset her by arguing. Liberty met the ambulance staff at the door and brought them upstairs. "What are they doing here?"

"You collapsed."

"Nonsense! What a fuss."

"Let them look at you."

They did a series of tests and asked her a lot of questions. Finally she shooed them out. "I was nervous, I didn't eat breakfast, I fainted. I'm fine now. Lisa will bring me something to eat. Now go."

I lingered inside the door before going down to the kitchen. "You're sure?"

"Of course I'm sure. What a melodrama!"

"You stay here with her?"

Liberty nodded, almost as pale as Sharon.

"She can start doing my hair."

I watched Sharon closely through the day. She was shaken, but nobody who wasn't paying such close attention would have noticed. Roger certainly didn't. He face was shining. His elation now that the day was finally here removed the last trace of my resentment. He had only ever toyed with me because he thought he couldn't have Sharon. His eyes followed her around the room, brightening as she came closer or caught his eye. He must have seen something I didn't, however; to me she seemed frail, smaller than before.

An elbow touched mine. Charmaine, one of Sharon's original business partners.

I gestured towards Sharon. "She looks beautiful, doesn't she?"

I expected polite agreement but instead there was a snort. "She's losing her freedom. She looks like a caged bird."

"You don't think at seventy she would know what she wants."

"Seventy! Is she behaving like seventy? She thinks she's eighteen."

I looked back at Sharon, smiling up into Roger's face. There was something girlish about her. "Well, is there anything wrong with that? He loves her."

Charmaine's face fell. "Yes, I suppose he does."

"Let me find you a drink. Come and sit down. It's almost over."

I took a glass of sparkling wine from a tray Liberty was carrying and carried it to one of the tables. "Come on, sit down. Let's talk."

She hesitated then pulled out a chair. "I know you think I'm being spiteful."

"Well, I'm happy for her . . ."

"And you think I'm jealous."

"Are you?"

"I don't think that's it. I really want the best for her." She took a sip from her glass then pushed it away from her across the table. "I really shouldn't drink when I'm in this frame of mind."

"What frame of mind is that?"

"Looking back. Regretful. Wishing I'd said something years ago, when it could have made a difference."

"Said what?"

She stared straight at me, brown eyes large. Lines of tension fanned from the sides of her mouth. "Told her how I felt. I always sort of hoped that she felt the same about me. That it was an undeclared but mutually recognised thing. Now it's too late."

"But you knew she was seeing Roger. She's been seeing him for 20 years."

"She never told us. She never told us. That's why we all feel betrayed now. But of course it's worst for me. Because I love her. And I convinced myself she loved me."

I looked into the well of despair, felt the anguished abandon of confession. Her eyes dared me to condemn her, but I didn't. As I continued to gaze her expression softened. I thought she was close to tears. "You've never told anyone this?"

She shook her head. "I'm seventy three, and I'm only now realising I have wasted my life in silence."

We sat on at the table looking out at the crowd; I felt our two hearts beating in time with this awful truth.

41

I woke with a headache and lethargy which had nothing to do with the half glass of champagne I had tried to drink to toast the happy couple. I recognised the shift in mood, the ebb in confidence and resisted it. Why couldn't I always be strong and clear and confident.

Usually my body wakes me at six or before but when I rolled over to look at the time it was nearly seven. I should get up. There was lots to do.

But what was the point? The hotel was being sold. This might be the end of my dream. I could already feel it crumbling around me. I wriggled over and put my arms around Theo. He was so warm. Maybe I should just give up now and go home.

The thought caused me to fling my arm back away from him. I couldn't do that. Sometimes the acknowledgement of purpose feels like a cage. It's wonderful knowing what I need to do next, but sometimes that thing I know I need to do seems impossible. Sometimes I just want to crawl away, claim cowardice as an excuse and deny my truth. But it never works, and it's always far scarier than taking the next necessary action.

I groaned over the familiar "Oh no, not that!" sensation. Delaying asking myself what the next step might be, because I knew I already knew what it was, and I knew I wouldn't like it.

Maybe if I just kept myself busy. But no, that didn't work. Serving at breakfast I made mistakes, delivering the wrong meals, calling people by the wrong names. When I dropped a tray of used plates Cathy finally sent me to my room. "Whatever it is, work it out."

I stood with my back against the door. Theo had pulled the blankets vaguely straight before he left, but it wasn't hotel perfect. I kept my eyes off my journal while I smoothed it out, picking up his pillow and inhaling him to give me another few seconds of security. I couldn't avoid it forever.

There is a little desk built in under the window of my room, with a view out over the trees of Latimer Square – if you look in the right direction. The alternative is the dull façade of the language building across the road, tinted windows giving only hints of hermetically-sealed life within.

There was a light easterly breeze blowing and the bright new leaves played with each other, flickering silver and white in the sunshine.

I opened my journal. I had had the same one for a long time. I flicked back through the pages. Since opening the hotel there hadn't been much space for contemplation. I had taken a smaller book to England, so those thoughts weren't here. There were short paragraphs of misery from the cold times, which quickly descended into wordless tears. These pages took me back to before the failure, before the split, another time.

Curious, and also delaying, I scanned through looking for that pivotal moment, the second when I knew I wanted to renovate a hotel. That was the decision which broke Theo's back. That was the moment which lead me here. A moment of devastating and terrifying truth. But my truth. I always know my truth.

So what was it now?

I looked at the page.

"What do I want to do next?"

"Renovate a hotel."

So simple. So clear. In retrospect such a personal bombshell.

I turned forward to the next blank sheet and hesitated, superstitious. My pen hovered over the page. I wouldn't ask the same question. It was no longer as simple as knowing what I wanted. There was an imperative now, a finality, a sense of the loss of choice, like I had left it back there somewhere, in the childhood of my marriage. My pen was moving before I knew it, forming the words. "What do I need to do next?"

And the answer. "Find someone to buy the hotel."

I breathed in loudly and blew out. My arms were heavy. The pen wouldn't move any more. There it was, like a judge's sentence. I felt my courage pace restlessly across my chest. It would be called for, but I did not yet know for what. I had to find someone to help me continue. This hotel had to go on, with me as the beating heart; whatever it cost me, that was what I had to do.

It was up to me to find them, to convince them. There was no question, except of how. Where would I find them? How would I convince them? How would I conceal the ice-fire of zeal in my soul? I mustn't frighten them off.

My eyes closed. I felt leaden. I curled up on my bed and cried.

The wave past, my eyes opened again. Two words were echoing in my head, two names: Julian and Frank. It was crazy to think I could go to see Frank now, when the novel writing challenge had only two days to go. Tension was palpable for several of the writers who were pushed up against the November 30th deadline. Lillian still had 10,000 words to go, and hissed every time Julian passed her.

He had finished his first draft days before; he was tactfully keeping his head down but I had insisted on a celebration. More had followed, about ten had reached the 50,000 word target and rounded their stories off. That meant 24 needed to finish in the next two days if they were going to make it – actually 22 if you removed the two who had cheerfully given up after a week or so and just enjoyed the holiday, wandering from group to group reading others' stories.

I took Julian aside in the quiet half hour before lunch.

"Can I tell you something? Something I shouldn't?"

One eyebrow flexed. "I suppose that's up to you. You can, for sure."

"I shouldn't. But something tells me to do it anyway. Can I have your confidence, that it won't go any further?"

"Certainly you can, unless something tells me to break it."

"Don't tease! Listen."

He pulled a mock serious face. I walked over to the door of the lounge and closed it, then pulled him to the window. Echoes rose up and filtered around the gaps in the veranda doors.

"The hotel is being sold."

"Sold! But why?"

"The wedding. You know. Sharon wants to travel."

"But you seem to be doing so well."

"We are. We are. She's just changed her mind, wants her money out."

"I see." He stared at the floor. I counted to ten to hold back my impatience.

"My gut tells me you might be able to help."

He shrugged, tilted his head and looked up at me. "I don't see how."

"You don't?" The feeling had been so strong, that this was the right thing to do.

"Not right away. You're disappointed. What did you expect?"

"I don't know . . ." I turned away. "I'm sorry I bothered you. You won't tell anyone?"

I felt my hand lifted and turned to see him holding it. "I'm sorry to disappoint you, please don't . . ."

"Don't what?"

"I'm grateful you confided in me. Really. Stay and talk a little longer. Tell me your plans."

I shook back my head and blinked, looking upwards. I wanted to get away before I started to cry. "Thanks, Julian, maybe later. At the moment I don't think I have any plans."

He squeezed my hand, trying to prevent me from leaving. "Look, wait, maybe Arthur, he has more contacts than me. Can I talk to him for you?"

I shrugged. "Okay, okay, whatever. Just keep it quiet." I pulled away, taking a gulping breath as soon as I was through the door. I ran up the stairs to the sanctuary of my room, beating my fists on the bed.

"I am such a fool!"

"Mum?" I hadn't heard the door open again. Brian stood there, his mouth open. "What is it?"

"I'm okay, really. Give me Matt for a while?"

He moved towards me and Matt held out his arms for me to take him. I swear he understands everything we say. "Do you want me to do anything?"

"I think I'll just stay up here for a bit. Call me if anything happens downstairs?"

"Okay." He was turning to go; I felt a strong impulse, like a kick in the stomach. I had to see Frank, today.

"Hold on." I couldn't go. We had a full house, I had promised to read for some of the writers, give them feedback, bounce ideas. I could call him, just talk, that would be so much more practical. But I needed to get away, get perspective; the voice in my head was clear. 'Go!' Brian was waiting, confused. "Sorry, take Matt again. I need to go to Dunedin. I need to see Frank. Can you manage things here? I'll ask Cathy to stay. And tell Dad I'll be back in the morning."

Matt went just as happily back to his father as he had come to me. Being passed back and forth was one of his favourite games, reaching for whomever was passing. He chuckled as he gripped Brian's neck again.

"Is Liberty in tonight? Maybe she'll help."

A lost expression crossed my son's face. "She's got a date."

"Oh." I had forgotten that potential complication.

"It's okay. Go. We'll be fine."

I took my wallet from my bedside drawer. "Call me if you need anything. Leave a message if I'm out of coverage. I'll see you tomorrow."

42

I shook my head as I pulled out into the midday traffic, but a cool calm in my stomach told me I was doing the right thing.

After getting Frank's voicemail the third time I didn't leave any more messages. What was I doing? What if he wasn't there? When the text beeps came just south of Oamaru I pulled over immediately to read the message. "In meetings 'till five. Meet you outside the café."

Yay! I pulled back onto the road and pressed hard on the accelerator.

Frank took me to his apartment, in a new complex overlooking a crashing ocean. We sat out on the balcony, each with a glass of whisky. He had wrapped me in a blanket. "It's too cold out here, but let's sit here anyway." His face was grave. "Tell me what's wrong."

"What makes you think there's something wrong?"

He just looked at me.

"How do you know everything?" No answer. "All right. Sharon is going to sell the hotel."

"Okay. And what else?"

"What do you mean? Nothing. Nothing else."

He tilted his head, sceptically, then realised I meant it. I saw a look of confusion cross his face, a split second of panic, then concern. "Tell me what happened."

I went through the whole story, passing quickly over my part with Roger, the awkwardness, the reconciliation with Sharon, the wedding. For some reason I also told him about Sharon fainting. "So I didn't know if she was dead, just for that moment. It was like a shadow passed over, a shadow of death. And I suppose if she died, it would probably be sold anyway."

"A shadow of death," Frank repeated. He stood up quickly and turned towards the door.

"Frank? Tell me what you see. Everything you have seen has happened – you saw the hotel, the success, and it happened. Tell me what will happen now. It would help me so much, to know it will work out."

"I need another drink." He returned in half a minute with the bottle, offering it to me. I showed him my untouched glass and he nodded, sitting again, putting the bottle on the floor next to his chair. He avoided my gaze, looking out to sea. It was getting dark. "But things are going well. You've got bookings into next year, full for next November. You'll find a buyer easily." His voice was unconvincing, he spoke as if he was arguing against someone unseen.

"How do you know all this? About the bookings?"

He rolled his eyes. "I read Liberty's hotel blog."

"Oh."

"So if it's just that . . ."

"But it can't be just anyone. What if they want to run it themselves? What if they fire me? They can't! This is my life. I have to be the heart of it."

Frank looked at me with an expression I didn't understand.

"What?!"

"You are already the heart of it. You have created it. You will live there forever, whatever happens."

I snorted. "That doesn't help! I want to be there, in person. How can you say I'll always be the heart if the hotel continues without me? Even assuming it does continue."

"It will continue, I . . ."

"I know! Your foresee it! And you're never wrong. But what about me!"

Frank took my hand, leaned forward in his chair and pulled my chin up so my face was square to his. His eyes were deep, deep black, and so full of sympathy and love.

"What . . ?"

"Lisa . . ."

"What?!" I was almost screaming. Something was desperately wrong.

"You don't have much time. I . . . I see it . . . I don't want to see it." He sank back into his chair, elbows on his knees and pulled at the back of his hair with his fists.

"What do you see? Frank! Tell me?"

It was a long time before he spoke. "You said it yourself. The 'shadow of death'."

I'm not normally superstitious but I grabbed my bag and ran out of his apartment. I drove as fast as I could into the approaching night to get away from him and his vision. I couldn't be going to die. Why? How? He couldn't know this, why should I believe it? Except he never had been wrong, whenever he had told me what he foresaw. It had always come true.

I was home by midnight. Theo would be in our room by now, I needed to go somewhere else. I needed to get a grip on myself before I saw him.

I sat in the lounge, my thoughts tumbling. Herman came to sit on my knee, warm and comforting. I stroked him absently.

Finally at 2 came the idea that turned the tide of my self-pity. "I can't die yet. I haven't finished my paperwork." Then I began to laugh, and the blackness was over. If I die, I die. I knew I was going to anyway, sometime. But maybe I'd get the paperwork done, just in case.

43

The calm of perspective settled over me. The panicked chaos of writers against deadline would happen, would come and go over the next two days; it meant little to me. I took Brian aside the next morning, feeling his arm through his sleeve in the grip of my hand, noticing the contours of his face.

"Once everyone has gone, I'd like you to help me get the office in order. Would you do that?"

"Sure. Why now?"

"Things have just got a little out of hand over the past few weeks, and there is still stuff I need to file since way back, from the renovation."

"Okay, just let me know when." He leaned back against the wall and watched me with dispassionate eyes. "You okay?"

"I'm fine." I didn't want to talk about me, I wanted to get inside his head, to know what was happening in there. "Are you happy?"

"Yeah, I guess."

"Are you proud of yourself.'

A tiny little smile. "Yes. I am."

"You know you're unique?"

"I know, Mum." He was beginning to get impatient. "What do you need?"

"I just need to know you're okay."

"I am okay, Mum. You know kids don't want to worry about their parents."

"Meaning?"

"Meaning I don't want to worry that you're worried about me."

"I'm not. I trust you to make your own choices." I chewed my lip. "Not all mothers do that, you know, trust their kids."

"I do know that. You're doing well. Can I go now?" His grin was cheeky. He knows just how to wind me up.

"You worry about Matt, too, right?"

"No, actually. I don't worry about him. I just look after him, give him what he needs."

"Can love really be like that?"

"Real love is always like that."

"How do you know? How would you know that?"

"Same way I know everything. I think. I work it out."

I took Matt out in his pushchair that afternoon, to see if I could make Brian's theory true for me. Finally I admitted I couldn't. I would always fear for those I loved. I would always think they need protecting, feel the dread of loss along with the intensity of love. I couldn't even imagine the serenity of a love which didn't hold that. What would it be like? Surely it couldn't be real.

For me, every moment holds the next and the next, every possible permutation of the future. The next moment might be joyful, it might be sad, it might be dull. So whatever the present is, it is never pure, it always holds the potential opposite. With fear comes hope, with hope comes boredom, with boredom comes a new plan. When I think about it like this, life is a bit monotonous, like the brown you get when you mix all the colours together.

I had a sense that Brian lived each moment for itself, and that made it more varied. Maybe I could practice doing it myself. I stopped walking and came around to the front of the stroller to look into Matt's face. His attention was immediately all mine. He held out the toy he was holding. I grabbed it and he pulled it back to himself. I reached in beside him and held up another. They were all pinned to the stroller on bits of ribbon, so that when he discarded one it stayed attached. He dropped the squeaky rabbit and took the stripped worm, holding it out to look at it then putting it to his mouth to feel the texture. His eyes fixed again on mine.

"You are so beautiful." And mixed with the joy of love I felt the unbearability of parting. If it were up to me I would never relinquish this moment for the next. But then I did, smiling and squeezing his hand and walking around to the back of the stroller again, shaking back tears. I couldn't be going to die.

Cathy brought me my mobile phone as soon as I returned.

"It's been ringing and ringing."

"Who?"

"Frank."

"Did you answer it?"

"No. Should I have?"

"No."

"Are you going to call him?"

"Maybe. I don't know."

"It must be important."

"It is, and it isn't. I'll think about it."

I could feel Cathy's eyes follow me as I strolled over into the café, sitting down at a table where a group were laughing. The phone rang again. I switched it off.

"Who's celebrating?"

"Me," said Lillian. "I can't believe it. After all the drama, it was so easy. It just came together. A whole day to go." She handed me a thick wad of paper. Would you read it?"

"Sure. I can't wait to see what happens, I was riveted at the end of the last chapter I read." I flicked from page to page looking for the point I remembered, finding it about three quarters of the way through.

"I got so stuck, trying to see a way through. I wanted a big finish, so I set up a seemingly unconquerable challenge. And then I couldn't see how to resolve it. I stared at it for hours."

"So what did you do? How did it work out?"

"I used that self-hypnosis technique you taught me."

Several heads round the table nodded. I had mentioned it in lots of contexts.

"And?"

"For a start it wasn't easy to relax, but I closed my eyes and asked for a simple solution, with minimum effort. And just like you said, I asked for my eyes to open as soon as my unconscious mind had done the processing it needed to do to find it. But they opened right away. So I closed them again. And they opened again."

Laughter bounced around the group as Lillian overacted the repeated slow blink.

"So what then?"

"So I figured, it must be okay. And I got this intuition to start writing. I took my notebook out into the Square. I was up to 49,000 words, so I knew it could come fast. And it was like the pen moved itself. Straight out of the previous sentence, so unexpected, so exciting. An hour later I was done. When I counted it up, it was exactly, I mean exactly, the number of words I needed. And the story finished itself, rounded off, nothing more to say. 50,014 words. It couldn't have been more perfect!"

I smiled, feeling her elation, but as if it were behind glass. I felt myself pulled away from the group, I wanted to be alone.

Arthur was at the table. I sensed he was trying to get my attention. Our eyes met, and he gave a small jerk of the head to the side. I nodded and stood up. "I'm so happy," I said to Lillian. "Congratulations."

She sprang out of her chair and threw her arms around me. "I couldn't have done it without you! Thank you, thank you, thank you."

I nodded, squeezed her for a moment then stepped away. I was turning from the table, heading for the door, when something made me turn back, take her manuscript from the table. "Let me read this now?"

She nodded, eyes bright.

"Lisa?" Arthur's voice was a hoarse whisper, but still audible. I drew him further away, into a corner of the bookshop. "Julian talked to me. Celia would be heartbroken if we couldn't come back next year. Me, too, especially when we got in quick to nab the best room."

I forced a smile.

"I'm making some calls. I can't promise anything."

I put a hand on his arm, nodding my thanks. I just needed to be on my own.

Herman was on my bed. I closed the door behind me and lay curled around him, stroking his circular back. He lifted his head then stretched out a front paw and lay his chin on it. I didn't want to move, ever. I could feel Lillian's manuscript against the back of my leg as I lay there. The soft sheet against my cheek was so wonderful, so much more friendly than the idea of sitting up and taking myself into the inside of someone else's mind. Especially Lillian: a complex and expressive woman, with ideas which didn't always sit well with mine. Her love story had become a ghost story, and although some of the situations were intriguing it wasn't what I would choose to read. I was surprised it called so strongly to me. Sit up. Read. Now.

I found my place, a spirit frustrated in her attempts to communicate. The story had three main characters and as the narrative moved between them without warning, I often felt dislocated. I had gently broached this subject with Lillian, and she said it was intentional, a continuation of the metaphor, the feeling of being lost, out of body, out of control.

The scene began ambiguously, someone lamenting a lost love. It could have been any of the three characters: both men had been lovers of the woman; she had fallen out of love with one and into love with the other.

There was a fight between the rivals; the scorned lover and the woman were killed. I don't like violence but the death scene was strung through with love and beauty, the beauty of love, the beauty of anger and the anger of love. It was painted in slow motion, each blow a ballet of flight and embrace, each moment outlined in complex, shifting, intense feeling, each microsecond explored and explained and deep with imperative emotional logic. Then the deaths. Then after the deaths, silence. A pregnant silence. Then a whisper of movement.

One ghost, the beloved, emerged from the blankness, grieving, reaching out for the still living lover. She cries out in disbelief, and her cry awakes the other. 'It's all right, Love, I am here, we can be together.' 'No! You have done this. You have stolen from me my love.'

I was drawn deeper than before into the after-world. Up 'till now I have turned from any reference to death. Now it fascinated me, it held me frozen captive, I desperately needed Lillian to show me a way out. This half-world would be mine now, until I could find a way free. 'Make the transition possible.' I begged her. 'Show me a way through.'

Herman moved beside me. His warm, living body seemed a long way away.

44

Everywhere I looked, any tiny thing out of place annoyed me. There was so much incomplete, so much to be done. Okay, take a moment, breathe, prioritise. I felt disconnected from everyone around me. Only getting things done mattered, only getting things tidy. A little voice at the back of my head told me I had things the wrong way around, that these things didn't matter at all.

"What is going on with you?" Liberty swung me around and peered forward into my eyes.

"What do you mean?"

"I've asked you four times where Matt is. Brian said you had him, you took him out for a walk again this morning."

"He fell asleep. I took him up to bed. The monitor's here." I picked it up from the floor beside me where it was all but buried under a pile of papers.

"What are you doing?"

"Sorting things. Stuff I should have done months ago."

"Some of the guests were asking where you were. Are you coming out?"

"In a bit. I've got lots to do." She looked around. I had made a bit of a mess. "It always looks worse before it gets better."

"How long will it take?"

"A few hours." I was lying. There was at least a couple of days work.

"Do you need to do it now? Couldn't it wait? The party's tonight, we need to get organised."

"I've been putting it off." I picked up another sheet of paper, looking at it without registering what it was. I wondered how many times I had looked at it already.

"Lisa . . ." I was hardly aware of Liberty's presence any more. It was like the world was growing bigger, pulling everyone away. I vaguely heard a whimper from the monitor. When I looked up a few minutes later I realised I was alone. I listened to my heart for a beat or two. Something felt familiar. Ah, this was like that other time, the break down. I stopped noticing other people then, too. I frowned. I didn't want what happened then to happen again. My mouth fell open, forehead creased in concentration. What should I do? Go back out and be with people. Remember who I am.

I noticed my face felt numb as I picked up the haphazard piles and dropped them without order into a large box in the corner. Liberty was right, they could wait. I plucked my jacket from the hook on the back of the door. Stepping out into the atrium was like unwrapping cotton wool from around my head; sound and colour were vivid once more. I blinked. I had a sense of danger averted. I shivered. How could I stop it from happening again?

"What did you think?" Lillian was eager. I thought back to the dramatic climax of her book, the desperate lover driven to suicide, the lovers reunited. It seemed a dangerous myth to perpetuate, but the effect was eerily satisfying.

Looking into her smiling face my moral judgement slipped away. "Scary. But wonderful."

She jumped in the air, clapping. "Thank you! Thank you! Oh, I can't believe I did it! I thought I never would. But those last 10,000 words came so quickly, it was a miracle. All thanks to the hotel. I never would have made it without you."

Cathy came up to us with the hotel phone. "Call for you, Lisa."

I took it from her, nodding to Lillian. "I'll catch up with you later, at the party."

"I think I'll go find Julian, mend our old wounds."

"Great." I stepped away a little as she turned. "Hello, Lisa speaking."

"Thank God! Finally. You haven't returned my calls."

"It's all right, Frank, I'm all right."

"I've never done that before. I only tell people my positive visions, my positive feelings of the future. I know the power of the fortune teller, I know most often the things I say come true simply because I have said them. It's mostly in the power of suggestion. I'm terrified I have pointed the bone at you and it will do dreadful harm."

I tried to laugh. It didn't work. "Relax, Frank. I'm not so susceptible."

"Really?"

"Really. Listen, you're a scientist, you don't really believe this stuff!" I tried again to generate a laugh, to lighten the mood, but it came out hollow.

"So you don't think you're going to die."

The words formed to reassure but they wouldn't come out loud.

"Lisa?"

"Look . . ."

"I've made a terrible mistake."

"You haven't."

"Tell me you know you're not going to die."

"Frank . . ."

"I'm coming. I'll be there in five hours. I have to convince you."

"There's no need . . ." But it was too late, he was gone.

I couldn't get one thought to follow another, everything pressed in on me, unfamiliar. I closed my eyes in a slow blink. Maybe I was just hungry. Actually I couldn't remember when I last ate. There was the dinner I didn't eat at Frank's. Did I have anything yesterday? Maybe not. No wonder I was losing my grip. I'd eat something, and I'd be fine. That's all it was, surely . . .

45

I love people one-on-one, but entering a crowd is overwhelming for me. Until I can get one person alone, create a cocooned conversation, simulate a private moment, I am outside of myself, not really there. The alternative is to speak, to address the crowd as a whole, to control the flow of information back to me to a manageable level.

"Do you think I should say something?"

"Yes. It's eight o'clock. It's time." Liberty forged a path for me through the press of bodies to the stage which would later hold the band. She brought the microphone to where I stood looking out at the sea of very familiar faces. I took a minute to look from one to the next to the next, one-by-one remembering our individual contact, the deep relationships which had been built over the last intense month, people under pressure, not always at their best, human. They stood expectant.

I closed my eyes and felt a wave of emotion. Here was my dream come true. This was what I imagined over a year ago – not this crowd in one place, but this feeling, this space where creativity happened, the flow of synthesized life.

"A year and a half ago I had a vision of renovating a hotel. It was so clear, it was like I was seeing something already real. It was a surprise, a crazy scheme which almost cost me my marriage. Most of you have met Theo – he's a patient man, beautiful. But this nearly pushed him over the edge." There was laughter. I had never made a crowd laugh before. "You all know what it's like to have a dream that drives you, that takes hold and pulls you forward. It took a while to get started, but once we were on our way it was like it created itself. A hotel is a hotel, but this was to be a space of inspiration, a timeless place where the magic of writing could happen. We all know writing is not a linear thing, the moment of fluidity needs to be captured, maximised. I hope this is a place which allows that." Heads nodded. I stood up straighter. "You all know I'm not a writer myself, but I love stories, I love books. It has been such a privilege to read your stories as they grew, organic, miraculous; I have loved moving through the hotel hearing discussions, encouragement, frustration – you have all lived through the moments when nothing was coming with a grain of faith, that everything is temporary. Every state feels like the way things will always be, but each moment is unique, precious, the blocks as well as the flow. Each moment grows out of every other moment, but is separate also, to be experienced on its own. This is what writing tells us.

"The Old Occidental Writers' Hotel started with a few bald words in my journal. I had no idea what to do next. Then I met Sharon, our owner. She has been so generous, teaching me, supporting me, ultimately providing the finance to make this happen. Then Roger, her new husband, our inspired architect. The previous owners of this building, who saw our vision and stood behind it enough to give us the time we needed to find the investment. Cathy, with her years of experience and stabilising calm. Igor, our chef, our cleaners and waiters.

"My wonderful son, Brian, and Liberty, the mother of my grandson. Both have held me together and helped me make it work. Theo, who came back to me and returned to me the other half of my soul.

"And you, with the richness of your life, the experience of knowing you, the layer of history your creativity, your presence has left permanently in this place. You are part of this place forever; we will never forget you. Congratulations, and thank you. Thank you."

The room erupted, feet stamping, hooting cheers. I realised I was crying. I stepped down off the stage into many, many arms.

I looked around for someone to talk to. They all wanted me, but I needed one person on their own, not a group. I felt a tug on my arm. Julian. Perfect.

"You didn't tell them."

"What?"

"About the hotel being sold."

"I can't do that! You know I can't. We have bookings, people need to be assured we'll still be here in a year's time. And please keep your voice down," I added, petulantly, although he had spoken softly.

"But there is money here, and commitment. You could have asked for investment." His expression was teasing. I didn't understand.

"We'll find investment. I don't want to start a panic."

He rolled his eyes, then broke out into a smile. "This is pretty special, huh?"

I felt my calm return as I looked around. Faces were shining, lit up. "It feels different. I don't know exactly what is happening, do you?"

"Yeah, I do. This is celebration. It's a rare thing in the world, a true moment of celebration. I think that is the miracle you have created: the space for creativity, expectation, inspiration, that's all true, but here is the magic of it, the permission to really celebrate. This group will keep in touch, some of us, at least, for the rest of our lives."

I looked into his face, revelling in his glowing expression. "Thank you."

"You're welcome." He looked up. "Hang on a minute." He waved over at Arthur. "Anyway, on the subject of finance, we have some news for you."

My head swivelled between them. Arthur was beaming. "Can you come to the States the week after next, and talk to a group of people who might be interested?"

"Yeah, sure. Not really? Wow! Fantastic."

"No promises, but it looks good."

After that I floated through the crowd, proud and happy. I had forgotten about Frank.

I felt the chill as the outside door opened and closed, turning to see Frank's white face fixed on me. He rushed up to me, pulling me aside from the knot of people around me.

"Really, Frank! I'm okay. You needn't have come." But in the sight of his face I remembered again my mortality: after this success, in the midst of the celebration, I had lost my acceptance of death. The possibility hit me again, hard. I felt my face whiten.

Sensing something unusual, the crowd opened a space around us. A hush spread slowly and more and more people turned to stare.

Frank's terrified face scared me. "You shouldn't take any notice. It was just a momentary thing. It's never happened before. Usually I see good things for people, things they want to come true. Maybe it's not foretelling the future, maybe it's creating it. Lisa, really, you're not going to die, I'm sure."

Die! The whisper ran around the room, irretrievable. I felt a surge of annoyance. "For God's sake, Frank. Shut up!" The whisper intensified, my anger feeding it.

"Tell me you didn't believe me."

I stared into his stricken face and the deep resonance returned.

"Oh my God!" He put his hands to his face. "What have I done? You're already gone."

"I am not!" I tried to stare him down but my gaze faltered. I counted the beats of my heart, slowing.

"I can see it in your eyes. They're . . . blank."

"Stop being melodramatic!" I turned to appeal to the person next to me. It was Lillian. "There's nothing wrong with my eyes, is there?" She shied away, horrified. "Brian?" His expression was shocked.

"What is he talking about, Mum?"

Theo came up behind him. "What is it? What's going on?"

"This man said Mum is going to die."

46

"It's okay, Brian, Theo. We can't do this here. Take Frank to my office, would you, Bri? Frank, I'll come and see you soon. I need to settle the party."

Theo stayed close as I moved through the room. It didn't help. "Really, I'm fine. Please, relax." He allowed me more rope, but I knew he was still watching me.

There was concern all around me. I needed to be alone, to get myself back together. First I had to deal with Frank. With a huge effort of will I turned conversation after conversation back to the celebration of the night, reminding the guests of their success, pulling their spouses into the triumph. I felt like a hot air balloon, releasing the ropes which held it down, one by one. Finally there was only Theo. I walked over to where he was helping at the bar. "Where's Brian?"

"He went to check on Matt."

"Okay. I'm going to talk to Frank now . . . no, I'll go alone, really, I don't want you to worry. I'll only be a few minutes."

"Who is he, Lisa? Where did he come from?"

"He's an old friend. He's been sort of a mentor for me, when I was starting the hotel."

"And what's his . . ?"

"I can't explain any more. We'll talk after the party. Please?"

He nodded, reluctantly. "I'll be right here."

I closed the office door behind me with relief. Frank turned towards me. "Lisa, what are you doing?" He gestured at the piles of papers.

"I was just sorting through things, getting things in order . . . I know, it looks like chaos . . . oh, Frank, why did you come? Tonight of all nights?"

"I'm lost. So out of my depth. I've never done anything like this before."

"Like what?"

"Predicted anything bad."

"Is dying bad?"

"We don't know you're dying. And you tell me? Is it bad?"

I sank into the swivel chair. Frank took a spare café chair from the corner and pulled it up near me. He reached for my hand but I pulled it out of his way. "Of course I don't want to die. I've just found my thing, this hotel, being a mother and grandmother. Theo."

Frank did a slow blink. "You've worked things out with Theo?"

"Yes." I frowned and shook my head. "I didn't tell you?"

"No." His voice was quiet. The disappointment on his face disturbed me.

"Oh." There was a long silence. The buzz of the party filtered through the door. "How does it work, what you do?"

He shrugged and his shoulders turned so one arm was hanging over the back of his chair. "It started out as a bit of a joke, a little game I played with myself. I like listening to people. I'm a good listener."

I nodded. "I know. Go on."

"People say things they don't hear themselves. They give themselves away. It might just be their choice of words, or the way their faces light up when they talk about one subject as opposed to another. Once people relax they tell you everything about themselves, if you know how to listen. I started to see people's dreams. I tested it out by telling them back to them. You'd have thought I was a clairvoyant, the way they responded. 'That's exactly right! How did you know?' That was the catch phrase: 'How did you know?' I liked the mystery of it, so I didn't explain. Then all I did was feed those desires back to them, and tell them they were going to come true. It was what they wanted, anyway. I felt good about it. Then people started coming back with their success stories: achievements, life following a bright path. They told me about series' of coincidences, asking me how I could possibly have known. I began to get a bit arrogant. I began to believe myself that I had some special power. But really, I was just taking what they told me and feeding it back to them. There was no mystery, no unearthly skill."

"Then why this thing, why now? Why were you so scared, and why did you scare me?"

"I don't know. I don't know! It was just such a strong feeling. Maybe it was about my feelings for you."

"What feelings? You've never said anything."

"I'm so used to staying detached from life, observing. I felt close to you, we've been friends for a long time, and hearing your plans, seeing you, talking to you, imagining you walking through these rooms . . . I didn't realise it was something more, until I saw you this last time. I don't know. It's all so new. Maybe what I saw was the death of my hopes, that you were back with Theo and happy."

"I'm not convinced. Everything you ever said about the hotel came true. You can't deny that."

"Because you wanted it! That's always been how it worked. You wanted it, I told you you would make it happen and you made it happen. Simple."

"There were too many coincidences. Your words always gave me confidence."

"Exactly!"

I took a big chest breath, tilting my head back. I rubbed my forehead with one hand, then both. "I don't know what to think."

"I didn't foretell your death. And there is danger in your believing I did."

"You mean if I believed you did I could make it come true?" I snorted.

"That's exactly what I mean. I need to know you have no shred of belief left in it."

"Oh . . . just relax, would you! You're making me nervous."

"I had already made you nervous. Now I want to give you peace."

"Everlasting peace?"

"Bad joke, Lisa. Very bad joke."

The corners of my mouth turned up momentarily in a tired fake smile. "I think the only thing for it is alcohol. Get drunk with me?"

"You know you're not going to do that."

"Come on, just one glass of champagne."

47

The atrium echoed with silence. The last guest was gone. We had bookings, the next lot of guests would arrive later in the day but for now it was eerie. I sent most of the staff home; I hated having them standing around, staring at me as the only point of interest. I couldn't settle to anything. There was nothing to do at reception. I spent ten minutes filing but that only made me nervous. Brian was moping because Liberty hadn't come home the night before, the day after the party. We both knew she was with this new boy. I had tried to ask him how he felt about her now, but he didn't want to answer, it was as close as he ever got to angry, telling me to lay off and leave him alone.

They say when parents worry, it's never about the child, always about the parent. Concern for our plan for genetic immortality: the children have to survive, and the children of the children.

"Don't I have some excuse for guarding my immortality?"

"Fuck off, Mum, I'm immune to guilt. And it's not funny, either," he added as I laughed, slightly hysterically. "The hotel is your legacy. Leave me and Matt alone."

"You don't think Liberty . . ?"

"I said lay off, Mum. How would I know what Liberty will do?"

"Sorry. I'm really sorry, I . . ."

"Time to shut up now, Mum. Why don't you go for a walk. Or go see Dad. He can always use help at this time of day."

I arrived at my old house feeling small and scared. Theo welcomed me distractedly then twisted around as I hugged him tight. "Can I help out?"

"Sure, pick me some rosemary from the garden. Hey, are you okay?"

Tears were in the corners of my eyes and rolling down my cheeks. I sniffed and wiped the back of my forearm across my eyes. This was not the time. "I'm fine, I just want to be home for a while. What next?"

"Setting tables. And some of the silver needs polishing, would you sort it as you go?"

I knew I was moving at half speed; still, it was satisfying placing cutlery and napkins, arranging small bouquets from the garden in the cut glass vases, just like my grandmother used to do when she came for Sunday lunch. When Tanya, the waitress, arrived she took over and Theo lead me aside. "Come on, you can't mope around here. Don't you need to be at the hotel, anyway?"

I shook my head, staring at the ground. We stood in the hall with its polished floor; the grain was lovely. I traced it with my eyes.

"What do you want to do, Love? I need to be back in the kitchen, we've got bookings from 12."

I shrugged. I wanted to put my arms around him again but I was wearing out his patience.

"Look, we've got no-one staying tonight. What if you made up our old room, then you can sit up there and watch a DVD? I'll come and find you when we get a lull, bring you something to eat."

I sniffed and nodded.

"Okay." There was relief in his voice. "You know where everything is, sheets and everything?" He gave me a little shove towards the stairs. "I'll be up later."

I ran my hand along the new polished wood banister, so much richer and smoother than the cheap timber one which had been here. I watched my reflection in the hall mirrors like I was staring at myself through a window. The sheets were in the mini-hall cupboard. The corners of my mouth twitched as I recalled Brian's name for the little entrance to the bathroom, the room which was his and Rachel's bedroom when we moved in, when they were too little to sleep on a separate floor to us.

It was a lovely bathroom, bright and spacious, but it had been a small bedroom. They slept in bunks and had a playroom downstairs where we kept most of their toys. What did Theo do with the toys? I wondered. I hope he didn't just throw them out. There were so many memories in the many old favourites. I couldn't bear it if they were simply gone. But I couldn't think where they were if he had kept them, there were so many, and every room was in use now.

I stripped the bed, conscious again of my slow movements. I had this down to an ergonomic art, could do it in two and a half minutes on a normal day.

It isn't possible to flip a duvet cover over a duvet without a strong, confident twitch; I made a couple of failed efforts, catching the cover on the knob at the end of the bed, pulling a muscle in my shoulder. I wanted to cry but I couldn't fail at this or life as I knew it would end. I did it the fool's way, pulling the cover over, turning it and matching the bottom corners of duvet and cover, buttoning it and shaking it again, leaving the ugly folded edges which always resulted if you tried to do it this way. I pulled at them and gave up, dragging it into place on the bed. I propped up the pillows and climbed up, leaning against them. My thumb went into my mouth, startling me. I haven't sucked my thumb since I was eight. It felt bizarrely, primevally comforting, the taste startlingly familiar.

The remote control for the television was on the bedside table. I hadn't brought anything up with me, maybe I could make do with what the guests had been watching. I pressed play. The Matrix. Hardly the best for my mood. Neo was just being drained from his battery cell fluid, dramatic and disgusting and overwhelming as the full scope of the lie being lived by the whole human race became apparent. The futility of human existence. Definitely not the best thing to watch. My eyes stayed fixed on the screen. The story unfolded and as the familiarity of it took over I experienced a double focus. My legs were weak. I had every excuse to be exhausted, but something about it troubled me. My muscles seemed less under my control than I was used to. I felt like lying down, sleeping. I thought about it over and over, imagining myself turning off the movie, crawling under the covers, pulling my knees up to my chest; instead I stayed frozen in my propped position, flicking a finger on the volume button only as necessary to avoid disturbing the lunch guests downstairs. This film had a lot of sudden loud music and sound effects.

I always love the scenes where Neo learns to bend his mind to the new unreality, achieve amazing feats of strength and speed and agility. I almost believed that I could do it, too. That I could learn to live forever, instead of dying, too soon. What was that? Not part of the story. Who said anything about dying?

"You're weak, you know you are." The voice in my head spoke out clear.

"I'm tired. This last month has been frantic."

"That shouldn't affect your legs. You can hardly walk, you stumble."

"It's nothing," I argued, against myself.

"Better get it checked out, especially if you're going to The States to see Julian's investors. Better call the doctor, make an appointment."

"I don't want to see a doctor, I don't want . . ."

"Don't want what?"

"I don't want to find out there's something wrong."

I shook my head to stop the internal conversation, returned my attention to the screen. Where was Theo? The movie was nearly over. I didn't want to face the silence alone.

Another hour later he found me asleep, finally having mustered the will to pull the blanket over myself. It was warm, but I had stretched my hand out to turn on the electric blanket anyway. My electric blanket, from a lifetime ago.

"Hey."

I rolled towards him, my face hot where it had pressed the pillow. "Have the guests gone?"

"Yeah."

"And Tanya?" Tanya, a statuesque Russian beauty, was Igor's wife. He had eagerly recommended her when one of Theo's waiters resigned; she was hard working and efficient, a little scary.

"She's setting up for dinner, she'll be a few minutes more."

I reached around him and lay my head in his lap. He was warm and safe as long as he didn't start asking questions.

"Lisa . . ."

"It's okay, really. I'm strong. I will be strong again. Just give me today, okay?"

"Sure, if that's what you need. Can you eat something? I made you an omelette."

I lifted my head and became aware of a glorious smell. I knew I still wasn't eating properly, I so often just didn't remember. Theo knows just how I like my omelette, liquid gruyere, and the egg still soft. I put my hands behind me and pushed myself upwards. "Wow." I picked up the fork and began my return to life.

48

Another plane, another adventure. I was nervous – about the flight, about connecting in Los Angeles, about the meeting which was the point of my journey.

Julian reassured me on the phone before I left. "They just need to meet you. You talk about what you do. They hear your passion and they're sold." He hesitated. "You are okay, aren't you?"

"I'm fine," I lied. "I'll be fine."

"I've printed out the financials you sent me, rearranged them a bit, pepped them up with graphs etc. Your projections are great."

"I know."

"You haven't thought about buying a share yourself?"

"How would I? I don't have any capital."

"I thought your husband owned a restaurant."

"That's his livelihood!"

"Well, I don't know, wouldn't it make sense to pool your resources, work together. It seems weird having you split like this, one in one part of town and the other in another. Have you asked him?"

It was too much to explain the history; it probably did look weird. I didn't have an answer.

"Even if he doesn't want to, you could borrow the money, against your share."

I was glad he couldn't see my face. I so wished I could do what he suggested, but Theo was more important; it had taken so much to prove myself financially stable, I wouldn't risk losing him again. "Theo's not a risk taker. I want him to be happy, to feel secure."

"And what about you? What about your security? You could lose your job any time while you're just the manager. Doesn't he care about that?"

"I honestly don't think he's thought about it. What was that snort for?"

"Hasn't thought about it. Selfish son-of-a-bitch!"

"You don't know him," I said, quietly. "There's a lot of history there. I haven't been the most responsible wife."

"I don't see you as the sort to run around."

"Not that. Money. I'm no good with money." I could barely whisper it.

"What do you mean? Yes you are! These are the best returns I've seen for a business of this size, in a notoriously flat market! This hotel is a work of genius. Your genius."

"I won't risk my marriage again."

"There are no guarantees in life, Lisa. Make sure that protecting it one way you're not risking it another. How would you feel if you lost the hotel while you are saving your relationship?"

"It would be worth it!"

"How much would you resent it?"

"I . . . A bit, I suppose. I'd get over it."

"Are you really sure?"

In the end I broached the question with Theo the day before I left. I saw the old fear in his eyes, a slight withdrawal.

I back-pedalled. "We don't need to decide anything yet."

"Okay."

"Just forget about it. We'll talk when I get back."

"Sure."

I realised Julian was right, if I lost the hotel for the sake of this missed opportunity now, I would resent it. I felt like Eve in the garden of Eden, with Adam staring at the apple in my hand.

Julian met me off the plane in Boston. Los Angeles airport had been overwhelming and foreign, a place to rush through, but even in the airport here I felt at home. There was snow on the ground outside. I pulled my coat around me and shivered, fresh from the New Zealand summer.

"Don't you have gloves?"

"Yes." They had been a last minute purchase, a gift from Sharon who took me to Ballantynes and had them open a secret drawer.

They were Italian, soft black leather lined with silk. Julian nodded. "We'll get you something thicker for snowballs."

Sometimes it's hard to tell when he is joking. We found his Mercedes in the car park. His remote blipped and the lights flashed. It wasn't a big car, but it was streamlined and so clean it was almost invisible, metallic grey reflecting me and everything else around us.

"Is this really all?" Julian asked as he lifted my small bag into the trunk. "We didn't forget to collect your luggage from the carousel?"

I was tired and nervous. I tried to summon a polite laugh but it sputtered to a halt. I walked around to the left side of the car and waited. "You going to drive?"

Left hand drive car. I almost cried with embarrassment. "I've been flying for 20 hours!" I wailed.

"It's okay, I'll take you home, you can get some sleep, you'll feel better."

I leaned back against the grey leather, watching the airline-quality display of lights on the dash. Julian pulled into the early morning traffic, the cocooned quiet of the parking building replaced with the shushing of the snow on the roads around the airport and then the swish of the freeway. The sun was up, somewhere, but the clouds were thick grey.

Julian peered upwards. "There's going to be more snow." I was disoriented by the reverse turns, the traffic coming from the wrong side; once we got into the fast flow I allowed the rhythmic flash of the street lights to calm me. As the futuristic display of Downtown wound into view, exhilaration rose in my chest. I was really here. It felt like the centre of the world.

"Do you live in the city?"

"No, in the Berkshires, about two hours once we get out of Boston."

I looked at my watch. 8.10. "What time did you have to get up?"

"Four. But don't sweat it, I'd have been up then writing anyway. Can't seem to kick this new habit." He grinned.

I blinked gratefully. "You are a prince and a gentleman."

"Yeah, I know."

Sometime later I opened my eyes and stretched. "Did I fall asleep? Where are we?"

"On the 190. We'll pass by Springfield soon. Stockbridge is about another forty miles. We'll get some breakfast then head out to the house. It's a mile or so out of town."

Breakfast. I realised I was very hungry. I rubbed my eyes and pulled myself up in my seat. The road was lined with trees with glimpses of hills and towns in between. I watched the view pass around me, a good feeling in my chest. I liked this place.

Something about the Stockbridge streetscape was familiar. "Why do I feel like I've been here before?"

"Probably from the Rockwell Christmas card." Julian paused in front of a shop window and pointed to a postcard display.

"That's it! That's here? Amazing!"

He guided me into a classic diner, easily finding a table in the mid-morning lull. The food was fabulous, French toast and eggs and hash browns and strange, thin coffee which warmed me but didn't really wake me up. I couldn't make the waitress understand me; Julian translated my order. She hovered, pad in hand.

"Get it over with, Doris. Say what you have to say." His inflection was strained and he was blushing.

"Where'd you pick up Miss Exotica? You never brought a girl in here before."

"She's from New Zealand. And she's a business associate. She's married, Doris, don't go talking."

Doris turned away, nodding and smirking. "Business associate. Right."

He looked over at me, wary.

"She knows you," I remarked.

"Yeah. It's a small town."

I wanted to ask about our meeting, when and where it would take place, but beyond the barest details – two days' time, Maine – I couldn't take it in. "I think I need to sleep now.'

"Are you sure? You'll adjust better if you can stay awake."

"I really have to." My flight had left at 11 p.m. the day before yesterday, I'd missed two nights, only managing to doze for minutes at a time on the flights, distracted by the proximity of so many people and the individual movie screens. I saw other people cover themselves with blankets and sleep for hours at a time. I didn't know how they did it.

He put my bag down in a room which took me back to Stella's house, floral print duvet, a sense of well padded luxury. Only the view was different, wide, snow-covered hills dotted with winter-bare trees, distant, solitary houses emanating a faint glow. I felt like I could stare at it forever.

"I'll get some work done. When shall I wake you?"

"Maybe three? This room is gorgeous, thank you." I turned to see the nervous smile on his face.

"I don't often have house guests. It was like this when I moved in. I bought the house, furniture and all. It seemed easier. But don't worry," he added, quickly, "the housekeeper put fresh sheets on."

I laughed. "I can tell. Thanks, Julian, it's perfect." I kissed him on the cheek again. "You've been so kind. Now go so I can cry without embarrassing you."

He scurried out again. I sat down on the bed; tears welled in my chest but they came to nothing. I remembered my phone, still off from the flight. I thought about calling Theo but I couldn't work out the time difference. My eyes stretched wide to keep from closing. Shower, pyjamas and bed. I sank down into the pillows and felt like nothing could ever go wrong again.

The next day we visited Norman Rockwell's house. The paintings filled me with a relaxed joy, easy and inspiring and absorbing. Then at my request we went back to the diner for lunch. Doris raised her eyebrows again but said nothing.

"I think she likes you," I teased.

"You don't know what you're talking about. What do you want for dinner?"

"You're the chef. I could eat what we had last night again, it was delicious. And actually I don't need to eat at all after that lunch."

"Pah! We'll go to the market, you can pick something out."

I strolled through the aisles, fascinated by the different products, different packaging, different ways of selling familiar things. I ignored Julian's request that I chose something, keeping my hands behind my back, absorbing.

"I like this place."

"The store, Stockbridge, The Berkshires, what?"

I waved my hand broadly. "The whole thing. I feel at home."

49

I sat at the bar while Julian cooked. He reminded me of Theo, confident, flowing movements, unhurried.

There was a background nervousness in the pit of my stomach. "Tell me again about tomorrow."

"We'll fly up to Maine in the morning. Arthur's friend, Bob, has a house near Wiscasset, Arthur is meeting us there, and a couple of others. Bob's on vacation, he doesn't want to come back to the city, so he's sending his helicopter for us."

"He doesn't mind breaking his vacation for this?"

"Well, not to offend you, but this doesn't really register on his radar. It's too small to really be a business venture. We approached him from his human interest side, told him it would be fun to own a little writers' hotel down in New Zealand."

"So why are we meeting others as well?"

"That's the part I didn't tell you. This is not just about your hotel. I have a bigger idea."

"Bigger how?"

"I think we should expand it to a chain . . . now don't react like that, just listen. Not a chain like, all the same, but a set of unique places, all for writers. Not everyone wants to fly all the way to Christchurch for a week of creativity. You won't believe it, but some Americans think that's a long way."

I pulled a face.

"I know, shocking! But it really works, and it would work in other places as well. Bob doesn't have the time, I don't have the knowhow, you have both, you could do it without blinking an eye."

I considered. It was an idea which had occurred to me before. I had dismissed it as unnecessary. One hotel was enough for me. But why not dream bigger? It was a surprise but even with that it felt right, it sat comfortably in my mind. "So what do I need to say?"

"Don't even think about it. I'll lead you through. When it's your turn to talk I'll ask you questions, you just answer, you know it all, and you're . . ."

"What?"

"Well, you're kind of mesmerising when you get excited. Your passion takes people's breath away."

My eyes met his for a moment. There was a spark and a jump in my chest. Oops. Keep my mind on the job, it's nothing, just flattery, just gratitude. I needed to find out what time to call Theo. I thought maybe now would be okay, mid morning. I opened my mouth to ask.

"There's just one thing," Julian went on.

"What?"

"That thing that happened at the party, the guy who turned up. Was there anything in that? You seem so healthy. I feel stupid even asking the question, but, you're not really going to die, are you?"

A gust of nervous laughter escaped me. "I don't really know how to explain it. It was a weird moment. You're right, I'm perfectly healthy . . ." What else was there to say? It was nothing, and it was something. "I guess you can just put it out of your mind. I'm trying to put it out of mine."

Julian didn't look convinced, but he nodded.

"I have a question for you."

"Yeah?" His face was wary.

"Why are you doing all this? Picking me up, having me here, holding my hand through the whole thing? What's in it for you?"

He blushed and looked at the floor. "I like you. No-one's ever taken time for me like you did. And I want to come back to the hotel next year, do the whole thing again. It was the best month of my life."

I slid off my bar stool and hugged him. "Thank you. Thank you so much." I pulled back and our eyes met. I felt the thumping in my chest again and let go of him, turned away. This sort of thing didn't happen to me. I was happily married, faithful. I felt a flicker of frustration. Julian believed in me; Theo still thought I was going to steal his money. Stop it. Don't think like that. Get a grip.

"What time is it in New Zealand now? I said I'd call home."

Julian looked at his watch and counted forward. "11 a.m."

"Great. Now would be a great time." My enthusiasm was overdone. It felt fake even to me.

Julian picked up a phone from the wall and handed it to me.

"It's okay, I'll call on my mobile."

"Don't be silly, that will cost a fortune. Here."

Our eyes met again as I took the phone from him. My 'thank you' sounded like 'Sorry.'

I called Theo at the restaurant. We talked for a couple of minutes, he was distracted. "Listen, I have to go, we have a big group coming in." I kept my back to the kitchen as I dialled the hotel to talk to Brian.

"How are you, Honey, everything okay there?"

His voice was dull as he gave me a rundown of routine.

"Brian, is there something wrong."

There was a pause. "Liberty. She's moving out."

"When? Is she . . ." I couldn't even frame the question.

"She's taking Matt."

I suddenly felt a very long way from home.

50

"Listen, no, listen! Wait!"

I was pacing, frantic, shook off Julian's arm as he tried to restrain me.

"Look, you're here now, just wait another day. What are you going to do when you get there anyway?"

"I'll talk to her, I don't know, make her change her mind. Brian has stood by that child when she would have given him up. She wouldn't even have him if Brian hadn't done what he did."

"You don't know that. You can't. Slow down."

"Don't tell me what to do!" I was shouting. "You have no idea."

"Yes! I do! Behave yourself." His voice was like a slap. I stopped pacing and stared at him.

"How? How do you know?"

"I have a child, too."

"You said you'd never been married." The puritanical accusation surprised me even as it came out of my mouth.

He stared at me and I felt chastened. "It was my parents' maid. I was eighteen. Mom didn't treat her well, she was ashamed of me, of her grandchild, of even being old enough to have a grandchild. So Maria left, she took him away."

"I . . ." Automatic questions arose. Did he see him, or her, what had happened? But I had more pressing concerns.

"He's grown up now, I've seen him a couple of times, he's married himself, I'm a grandfather, too. But I just meant to say, I understand. I understand. I know how you feel. You want to move the world to stop it. But just take a moment. Think. What are you going to do?"

"Talk to her."

"Fine. Talk to her. Call her. But don't throw away your own life, do what you came to do. It's only a day, then you can go home the day after, if that's still what you want to do." He handed me the phone. "Call her. What are you going to say?"

"I don't know. Don't do it? But that's not going to work." I was talking to myself now.

"Why don't you just ask her what's happening, and take it from there?"

I nodded. Pressed redial. Cathy answered the phone. "Hi, it's me again. Yeah. Is Liberty there, can I talk to Liberty?"

It took a supreme effort of will to feel anything for her, to think about what she was going through, but when I managed to ask her, to listen, I heard what was going on.

"This new guy . . ."

"Shay."

"Shay. How does he feel about you having a baby?"

"He's sort of okay with it. He loves me. He's fine." She sounded younger, less sure of herself than normal.

"Has he lived with a baby before?"

"No. But I'm not leaving him, I'm not giving him up."

"That's great, Liberty. Matt needs you. But maybe there's a way this can work for everyone. You take week about. Matt keeps both his parents. Brian and I get to spend time with him, too. And you and Shay have time to develop your relationship, just the two of you."

"I hadn't thought of that. That might work." She sounded relieved. Most importantly she agreed to wait a few days, 'till I got home.

"I'll be back on Monday, we'll talk then, help you sort it all out."

Okay, breathe, focus, do what I came to do.

I'd never met anyone really rich before. Julian is very comfortable, with a beautiful home and independence, but still at a level I could understand. Bob showed me around the 8,000 square foot house which was just his holiday home, lined with antique timber and built on a cliff overlooking the sea.

He wore an open necked shirt and argyle cashmere sweater and looked like something out of a magazine, glowing with a huge flow of life and health. Every movement was graceful and effortless, like he was subject to less gravity than the rest of us.

"The others will be here soon, they're just a few minutes away by chopper. Let's have a drink on the porch."

Arthur was already here. We hugged, close and warm. He felt like an old, old friend. "Celia says hello. She would have come but she's busy editing, wants to get her novel off to a publisher as soon as she can."

We sat in cane chairs surrounded by double glazed floor-to-ceiling bi-fold doors which would open out fully in summer. The Maine coast was wild and exhilarating, another jewel in the treasure chest of New England. If it weren't for the dramatic pull of home I would be thinking of settling here, asking for a job as a servant in this opulent home. I wasn't proud, I would clean or wait tables. I bit my tongue. That wasn't why I was here.

Bob had invited two more colleagues to meet me, friends, too, as it turned out: their greeting was warm with laughter and questions about family, about life. We moved into Bob's study, a vast replica of a Frank Lloyd Wright interior, built-in wooden furniture and a room-sized desk. Sofas sat around a low coffee table.

"Let's sit here, it's not so formal."

I glanced at Julian, who smiled encouragingly.

"Now, tell us your idea, Julian. Arthur says you've both been in New Zealand."

"At a novel-writing retreat, no less."

"Well, good for you. How'd it go?"

"Something I've always wanted to do and it had never happened. That's why we're here, to talk about the hotel that made it happen, and how we can replicate that around the world."

I smiled at Julian's enthusiasm as he raved about the hotel, the atmosphere, the service, the décor. He described the clientele, and their experience. Arthur nodded, confirming what Julian said. Then Julian turned to me.

Just like he had promised, it was easy to speak once he asked me the questions. I did know everything I needed to know to talk to these guys, although I never would have been able to communicate it without Julian's guidance. Soon all five men were nodding, glancing at each other, eyes lighting with the spark of imagination.

After less than an hour Bob stood up. "I think that's all we need to know, the rest we can work out between us. Would you give us a moment to talk a little more?"

I sat in Bob's library, surrounded by shelf after shelf of books on art and architecture from every country in the world. Part of me ached to eavesdrop on their deliberation but the walls were completely soundproof, and maybe I didn't want to hear anyway. The books both calmed and intimidated me. How much would it cost to buy this many beautiful photographic books? These would be $100-$200 each and there were hundreds. Could he have read them all, or even looked through them? My gut told me he had, he knew them well. They didn't have any air of neglect, and if they were for show they wouldn't be shut away here, separate from the public rooms.

I looked at my watch. 1 p.m. If I was going to catch tonight's flight out I would need to leave soon. Slow down. One thing at a time. Don't rush this.

The door opened and Julian put his head around it. "Come on. They've got a proposal for you."

"Okay, we'd like to buy this hotel of yours, and then we'd like you to develop two more on the same lines. To start. Do you think you can do that? Can you set the existing one up to run by itself while you oversee the next?"

"Yes. Where would they be?"

"One here in New England, one in Northern California. Just to start, you understand. We're thinking England, Europe, maybe somewhere in the South, one of those grand plantation houses . . . but these two first. What do you think? It would mean travel, time away from home. Can you do that?"

"I think so. I would need time to think."

"Of course. And then, if you want to do it, we would like you to have a financial stake in this as well, a personal investment. My experience is, that motivates people, the stick and the carrot."

I turned to Julian. Hadn't he told them I had nothing? "Bob, I would love that, but it's not possible. I don't have any capital. If I did I would have bought the hotel myself."

"We understand that. We can lend you the money, to be repaid out of your profit share."

"And if it didn't work?"

"You'd still owe the money, you would need to pay it back. Like I said, stick and carrot."

"Excuse me." I stood up, turned away from them, walking towards the window, bringing the view closer, wishing I could hear the sound of the crashing waves. Another financial risk. I felt nauseated. I had had a fantasy that this would be easy, an effortless unfolding of a dream beyond my dreams, and now this hidden barb. But I had tasted the bait and I was caught, they just had to reel me in. "And if I said no to doing the other places, would you still buy the Occidental?"

"No, it's too small an investment for us, too much overhead for too little return. The chain is more exciting."

"And how much would you want me to . . . be responsible for; how much would you expect me to borrow?"

"What's a number that scares you?"

"$800,000." It was the value of my home, outright. It terrified me.

"So that's about half a million U.S? Or a little more."

I looked from one face to another. They were politely holding back smiles. "I know that's nothing to you . . ."

"Don't be offended. We admire you, we admire what you've done. Of course, if you take a bigger risk, there would be a bigger potential gain for you."

I shuddered. If I even lost this much it would be the end of my financial future forever. And probably my marriage, too. Even this much would freak Theo out. I felt a surge of resentment. It always came back to Theo. Left to myself, I'd just go for it.

"Think it over. Get back to us in a couple of days. Now, if you get in the chopper now, we can get you on that plane back home. Julian said you had a family crisis, so we appreciate your taking the time to stay and meet with us." Bob nodded to Julian, who took my arm as I stood rooted to the spot.

"I don't know how to thank you for giving me this opportunity. I wish I could give you an answer now."

Bob waved his hand, and Julian pulled me to the door. I had already been dismissed.

51

I stared out the window as Boston dropped away below me. The sun had set on the ground but it rose again out of the west as we climbed into the sky. We would chase it across the country but it would gradually slip out of reach.

This would be the perfect time for thinking but I felt numb. I couldn't think about Brian and what he must be going through, I couldn't reduce the uncertainty of what Liberty would choose to do. I wanted to strangle her, to fight, but I knew Brian would never agree to a court case, probably wouldn't win anyway, and that ultimately it would hurt everyone, including Matt. It would be the Caucasian Chalk Circle. Brian was the only one who was behaving well.

Then, somewhere deep inside me, I was profoundly angry at this timing. When I had this huge opportunity for myself, other people's chaos was intruding. A big part of me wanted to throw all these people away, but my son and my grandson pulled at my heart. They had done nothing wrong and I loved them. I had grown to love Liberty, also, a daughter in Rachel's empty place, so loyal when I had my breakdown, a creative godsend for my hotel. She had made this one mistake . . . well, I knew it wasn't a mistake. She was finding love, and it was inconvenient for me.

I was thinking in circles. I set myself off into a dream, a theoretical reality where I could make one decision separate from all others. What if I did this, took a share of the hotel and began creating two more? My heart sang at the prospect. I saw beautiful buildings transforming to fit my vision. I saw guests and staff inspired, and myself moving dreamlike among them. I wanted to do this. I relaxed into it like a hot, lavender-scented bath, submerging all other thoughts and washing myself clean.

I woke five hours later sensing a change in height. We were banking over Los Angeles and there were close lights out my window. I hastily put away my iPod and journal, panicking slightly in my sleep-confused rush.

"What time is it?"

My neighbour looked at his watch. "8:20 local. We'll be on the ground in about ten minutes."

"Thanks." I brushed an eyelash off my face and yawned. I wanted coffee but I knew it wasn't a good idea before my long second flight.

Something was happening in the airport. It had felt busy last time I was here, foreign and overwhelming, but this was different, there was a sense of urgency and tension. I wandered through in a daze, dragging my little wheeled bag behind me. Several people bumped into me, one tripping on my suitcase and sprawling on the floor. "I'm so sorry. Are you all right?" But he waved away my help and scurried on. People were staring up at the television screens. "What's happening?"

"Hijack!" The man's voice was thin and high.

I stared at the reporter's moving lips, trying to read what she was saying. Unrelated headlines flickered across the bottom of the screen, distracting.

The man spoke again, a continuous high-pitched note. "Nobody knows what's happening, they threatened to crash. Now they're circling."

"Where?"

"Up there."

There was a scream and someone pointed out the window. A hundred people ran towards it. I joined in the back of the crowd.

"That's it!"

It was low, too low for safety, surely. There was a roar as it passed overhead. More screams. People threw themselves onto the ground, but it was higher than it seemed. It was huge through the window, I saw the wheels clearly, looming large, but it must still be hundreds of feet in the air. It was surreal, but at this point I lost interest, deathly fatalism kicking in. I found a seat in the deserted café, wondering idly why they weren't evacuating us. Maybe nowhere was safe. They didn't know where it might hit. Maybe this was what Frank saw. In that case, I wouldn't run, I would face it. I had got things sorted, pretty much. For the rest, the others, my family, they would just have to work things out themselves. And in that moment, I found freedom. They could do it. They could work things out themselves.

A couple of hours later I felt a tug, pulled out my phone. I had forgotten to turn it back on. There were six frantic messages from Theo, a text from Brian asking if I was okay. I dialled home, it was the middle of the night but it looked like they were up. No coverage. Network overload. I sent a text which went on the third try. Ten minutes later came Theo's answer. "I love you. Please come home."

At the same moment, in the distance, I heard a cheer. It spread through the airport, voice to voice, until it reached me. A surge of feeling made me join in, even though I didn't know what had happened. The crisis must be over, with a happy end. I laughed quietly to myself, then grasped the handle of my bag and went in search of news.

I landed in Christchurch 35 hours after leaving Boston. Nothing had taken off from Los Angeles for nearly six hours, and world flight schedules were in chaos. Ours had been one of the last flights to land, already in LAX airspace when the crisis unfolded.

Theo squeezed the breath out of me, I felt his tears on my neck. I was calm, patted him gently. "I thought you were never coming home. I thought the bastard was right."

"Who? Frank?"

He didn't answer, just hugged me tight again. People were watching us, intrigued by the drama. I smiled weakly.

"It's okay. I'm here now."

"You're not going out of my sight again."

"Okay."

"Don't tease me. I'm serious."

"Of course." I nodded sagely but ruined the effect by laughing. Theo's face was thunderous for a moment, then he smiled, too.

"Am I over-reacting?"

"It's okay, I like it. Let's go home, I want to tell you my news."

52

Brian was at reception, holding Matt on the counter showing him his toes. I turned to Theo. "Give me a minute with him, will you?"

"Sure. There's something I need to talk to Igor about, I'll be in the kitchen."

Brian grinned when he saw me and hugged me tight. Our hugs were smoother ever since my breakdown, but this was something more again. "So you made it out alive."

"Yeah. It rattled the ghosts a bit, but now they're gone."

"So that's the end of Frank's premonition."

"I think so . . . Where's Liberty?"

Brian's eyes turned wary. "She's packing, she's leaving today."

"And Matt?"

"She's agreed to week about, he'll stay here while she gets settled in her new place and then she'll pick him up next Sunday."

"That's great."

Brian gave me a long, thoughtful look. "Thanks, Mum. I didn't want him to go."

I felt a twang in my chest. He would never have admitted it if Matt had gone, but I knew. I knew how he must feel.

"And . . . what about . . . Liberty? Are you okay with that?"

His lips pulled together in a pug expression. "I knew it would happen sooner or later." He pulled Matt towards him, protecting him with his arms.

"But are you . . ?"

"Mum! Don't worry about me. It doesn't help."

I swallowed. I knew he was right. The best thing I could do for him was trust him to work things out on his own. So why was it so hard?

"Anyway, tell me what happened? In America. Are you going to be an international hotel tycoon?"

"Maybe. I need to talk to Dad."

Brian pointed. Theo was coming back out of the kitchen.

"Hey there." I handed my bag to Brian. "Keep this for me?" and to Theo. "Want to go for a walk?"

"Mum, wait! First you need to call Rachel."

"You told her?"

He rolled his eyes. "Of course we told her! What do you think? Call her. She's waiting."

"It's the middle of the night."

"Wake her up. She wants to hear your voice."

I was doubtful, but I took the phone from him, and he was right, she sounded relieved.

"Just a week, Mum, and I'll be home for Christmas."

She sounded like a child again. I didn't know if I wanted to laugh or cry.

Theo and I took a stroll across the central city, finishing up on a park bench in Latimer Square with a good view of the hotel. "So that's what they're offering me."

"It sounds like a dream come true."

"It is. And there's this risk attached. So I don't know."

He nodded, thoughtful. I hated the fact that I couldn't read his mind. "You must be ready for a bath."

"I smell that bad?" The humour was weak and he didn't get it.

"I just mean you must be tired. Let me take you upstairs, start the water running for you."

"Yeah. Thanks."

Brian woke me at 5 with a cup of tea. I shook myself out of an angry dream, I was handcuffed to a penguin and it made even the simplest activity awkward. At the same time I had an indignant sense that the penguin resented being handcuffed to me. I was sweating in the December afternoon heat, the sheets trapping me.

"Dad said to tell you he's making you dinner at home. He wants me to drive you over when you're ready."

"Home?"

"You know, home. Our old house."

"Oh."

"The restaurant's closed tonight. He's cooking you dinner." He spoke slowly, like he thought I wouldn't understand.

"I need a shower." I sipped at the tea. The caffeine spread through my body, allowing my limbs to move again. "This is great, thanks."

"I'll find you a towel. We were getting low this morning."

"There are some in the cupboard." I watched him open the doors and pull four towels off the pile. He put them to one side and straightened the ones that were left. There was something in this attention to detail which told me he had grown up. His fifteen year old self would have left the pile askew without a thought.

"I'll be downstairs when you're ready. Um . . . Dad said to wear something nice."

I took my time, still working out the residual anger in my veins. Something nice. Why? Why should I? I found a black floor length dress I'd hardly ever worn, sleeveless and split to the hip. He'd asked for it, he'd get it. Let's see if he could handle it.

The front door was unlocked. Brian waved as I stood on the doorstep then backed out of the drive. I hesitated, door ajar, my foot hovering over the threshold. I wasn't sure I was ready to see him, my thoughts were still confused, and I felt reluctant to examine them more closely.

"Lisa? Is that you?"

"Yeah."

He met me with two glasses of champagne, leaning sideways for me to kiss him on the cheek. "You look superb."

"What are we celebrating?"

"Life. And opportunity."

My nose twitched with annoyance. "Opportunity is not success."

"It's the first step."

"Only if I take it."

"That's what I want to talk to you about. Come and sit down."

The centre table was set for two, a bowl of white roses in the middle. There were white candles, lit too early. My favourite Diana Krall CD was playing. He was trying to make me happy, and that was the last thing I wanted.

I sat down but didn't relax. He reappeared from the kitchen with Caprese salads, rich red tomato layered with almost liquid mozzarella, sparkling sprigs of basil completing the multi-faceted Italian flag. He sat down opposite me and raised his glass again.

"Here's to opportunity."

"For God's sake!" I crashed my champagne glass onto the table, breaking off the base. I caught it awkwardly. "Will you stop saying that! I won't take it. I can't take it. I'm telling them no."

Theo's mouth sagged open. "Why?"

"I won't risk our marriage again, that's why! It's taken too much to get it back together this time."

"But this is your dream."

"It's a financial risk."

He shook his head. "You can't walk away from a dream."

"I haven't before, and look where it got me. Penniless and alone. All those risks: the bookshop, the renovation; those were dreams, too. I lost you."

"But this is different."

"How? How is it?"

"Isn't it?" His voice was small and he was staring down at the table. Finally he lifted his eyes to mine. "Isn't it?"

"No!"

Another pause. "Then I'm sorry. I didn't get it. I didn't understand what you were doing, what you needed. And now it's different, because this time I do."

I waited, impatient to know what he meant, unwilling to prompt him.

"Listen. I have a plan how this can work out. Igor wants to buy the restaurant, the house. He and Tanya have been saving madly since they arrived in this country, and they can get a loan on the building. We sell it to him and you use that money to buy into the hotels. You don't have to borrow the money at all."

"That doesn't make sense – in so many ways."

His eager expression fell. "Why not?"

"Well, I'm short a chef, to start."

"I'll do it, I'll be your chef. You need to travel to do this, I can oversee the hotel while you're away. We'll be a team."

"Well, but, but . . . how does that work? What about the mortgage, we don't own all of the house."

"There's the goodwill, the value of the business."

"Well, and . . ." I was confused now. What was the argument? "Wait . . . You really think I should do this? You'd come into it with me? You'd help me?" It was too fast, I couldn't reorient my reaction, there was too much anger pulsing through my heart.

Theo didn't answer. His movements had frozen and his eyes were locked onto my face. This bloody champagne glass, I couldn't put it down without its base and I felt like a fool waving it around. "I'm so angry and I don't know why." I stood up and paced back and forwards, tears of frustration brimming.

Theo stood too, tried to put his arms around me. I shook him off.

"I'm angry that I had to feel guilty for having dreams, for trying to make them real. I hated failing, and I couldn't grieve because of the guilt. The bookshop. The renovation. Every stupid project I started and couldn't finish. Not being able to travel, not being able to do what I wanted to this house. It was so devastating to me and I could only think about you. I felt your accusing eyes on me, and now you do this, you even take away my right to be angry." Words of hate were on my tongue; I didn't say them but I knew he could see them in my eyes. I had scared him. He stepped back. "Oh, for God's sake, don't be such a coward. This is me! Do you want me or not?" I spun on my heel. This was goddess anger, powerful and strong. Did I really want to be married to a mortal? I flung the broken glass through the serving hatch into the sink where it shattered. Champagne splashed across the kitchen floor.

Theo's hands clenched into fists.

"Come on! Stand up to me! Fight back!" His eyes narrowed. I wanted to get at his anger, too. "I will go after my dreams, but not because you say. And I will defend my dreams, even when they fail, and not feel guilty. I live up to my responsibilities, I pay my way. Whatever happens, I will live my truth. It's up to you to live yours."

His head jerked backwards. "Are you saying I haven't?"

My mouth twitched into a momentary sneer.

"Well, I have."

"Prove it!" My eyes and my voice challenged him. "Prove to me you have any courage at all."

"There's this restaurant."

"Okay. Granted."

"And there's the fact that I lived with you for over 20 years."

"And then left me. Threw me out."

The defiance left his eyes. "That took courage, too. You know it did." His head tilted and his eyes were pleading. I felt my anger start to fade. He held his arms out and I stepped into them, laying my cheek against his shoulder, beginning to relax. I closed my eyes.

"Can we really do this? I expected you to stop me, to try and stop me, to say I was mad. Can we really do it together?"

I felt him nod. "At least we can try." His voice rasped. It echoed through his chest into mine.

"What if we fail?"

"Then we fail together. We live through it. And we start again."

~ ~ ~ ~ ~ ~ ~ ~ ~ ~ ~ ~ ~ ~ ~ ~ ~

If you have enjoyed

The Old Occidental
Writers' Hotel

Please email jennifer@jennifermanson.co.nz
to join my mailing list and receive information
about further publications, or see
www.jennifermanson.co.nz.

I welcome your feedback.

Please post your review on Facebook.
Search for "Jennifer Manson Author"

With my very great thanks,

Jennifer.